Rough Neck

The Gang Buster

Rough-Neck

The Gang Buster

By

E.S. Bennett

Megaverse City L.L.C.

Rough Neck: The Gang Buster

First Edition
ISBN: 979-8-9993452-1-9
LCCN: 2025919191
Cover Design: Exlus Bennett & Megaverse City Design Team
Interior Layout: Megaverse City Design Team
Printed in the United States of America

For information, permissions, or bulk orders, contact:

Megaverse City L.L.C.

www.TheMegaverseCity.com

Dedication

For the children who resisted the call of the streets and chose another way.

For those who once walked in darkness but found the strength to step into the light.

For those who still struggle each day to keep their distance from the pull of gangs.

And for the men and women in law enforcement who bear the burden of standing against the tide.

This work is dedicated to your courage, your endurance, and your unyielding spirit.

"They call me a Rough Neck like it's an insult. But I'd rather be a Rough Neck than a coward broken on these streets." — **Henry Clarence Mann**

Table of Contents

Chapter 1

The bus lurched as it pulled away from the stop, the hiss of the brakes followed by the collective sway of tired bodies pressed shoulder to shoulder. Henry Clarence Mann gripped the overhead bar with one hand, his knuckles pale against the metal. At six-foot-five, his head brushed close to the roof, forcing him into a half-slouch that never seemed comfortable. Around him, commuters shifted and avoided his gaze, their eyes sliding past as though his very size took up too much of the air. The conversations were low, hurried—Boston on a weekday evening, filled with people trying not to notice one another.

The bus jolted again, and Henry realized too late that the packed aisle had kept him from stepping off. His stop slid by in a blur through smudged windows. He sighed, pulling the cord, but it would be another block before the driver grunted the vehicle to the curb. The doors snapped open, and Henry stepped down into the city's damp evening air.

He adjusted his work jacket, the smell of sawdust and grease still clinging to him from the construction site, and set off on foot. The neighborhood was a patchwork—some brownstones kept with care, others sagging with neglect. He moved with quiet purpose until the familiar glow of O'Malley's Grocery came into view.

Inside, the bell over the door chimed, sharp against the hum of fluorescent lights. Henry ducked his head, careful not to brush the doorframe. The shop was small, narrow aisles lined with canned goods and produce crates. Behind the counter, O'Malley himself looked up, his lips tightening in a reflex Henry knew too well. The man's eyes flicked over Henry's size, then lingered on the darkness of his skin before snapping back to the register.

Henry kept his face neutral, breathing steady. He'd learned long ago how to measure moments like this—how a single look or tone could carry an entire history of assumptions.

"Evening," Henry said, low and calm, his voice carrying the weight of politeness.

O'Malley gave a curt nod. "Need somethin'?" The words had an edge, not quite hostile but heavy with suspicion. Henry crouched to pick up a carton of milk and a loaf of bread, the simple staples of his family's table. His hands were deliberate, movements clear, as though performing for an unseen audience. At the counter he placed the items down softly, sliding a few bills across without comment. O'Malley rang them up quickly, his eyes never meeting Henry's.

"Have a good night," Henry offered.

O'Malley hesitated, then muttered, "Yeah."

The air felt lighter when Henry stepped back into the street. He exhaled, long and controlled, and continued toward home.

By the time he reached his brownstone, the tension had melted from his shoulders. Through the window he caught sight of Dani moving in the kitchen, her figure graceful in the soft light. The sound of Kalee's laughter carried faintly, bright and unguarded. Henry climbed the stairs to the front door, unlocked it and stepped inside. The city's weight slipped from him. In this space, with his wife's smile and his daughter's arms flung around his legs, he was no giant, no threat—just a man, loved and whole.

The door had barely shut behind him when Kalee's small feet pounded across the hardwood floor. Her arms flung wide as she barreled into Henry's legs, her face tilted up with a grin that could have lit the whole street.

"Daddy! Daddy! What did you get me today?"

Henry crouched low, setting down the grocery bag, and reached into the pocket of his work jacket. From it he pulled a small figure he'd carved during a break at the site—nothing more than a scrap of wood shaped into a little bird, but Kalee's eyes widened as though it were treasure.

"A sparrow," he said, placing it into her waiting hands. "Strong wings, quick feet. Just like you."

Kalee gasped in delight, turning it over in her fingers.

"It's perfect! Thank you, Daddy!" She squeezed him around the neck, her laughter bubbling in his ear.

From the kitchen doorway, Dani crossed her arms, smiling despite the mock scold in her voice. "You're spoiling her, Henry. Every day it's something."

Henry rose, sweeping his daughter up into one arm before reaching with the other to pull Dani close. "If I don't spoil her, who will? Besides," he teased, pressing a kiss to Dani's cheek, "I've got enough love for both of you."

Dani swatted at his chest, though her eyes gleamed with affection. "Charmer."

"Truth teller," he countered, wrapping both his girls against him in a moment that felt untouchable by the world outside.

Dinner was a simple affair, the kind Henry preferred after long shifts: roasted chicken, a pot of beans, and bread still warm from the oven. The three of them sat at the table, Kalee perched between her parents, swinging her legs that couldn't yet reach the floor. Henry asked. "How was everyone's day?"

"My turn first!" she declared, raising her hand like she was in school. She recounted her day with breathless energy—her teacher's new shoes, a funny song her friend had made up, how she'd painted a picture of the family and put it on the classroom wall. Henry listened intently, nodding and asking questions, as though each detail was of vital importance.

When she finally ran out of steam, Dani leaned forward, resting her chin on her palm. "Work was chaos today. Two clients in the same hour, both convinced they were the center of the universe." She laughed softly, shaking her head. "People don't realize how exhausting it is trying to keep them calm."

Henry reached across the table, brushing her fingers with his. "Yes, but you always make it look easy."

She smiled, though a shadow touched her expression as she glanced toward the muted TV in the living room. The scrolling news ticker carried grim headlines: *Gang violence escalates in South End; robbery at Copley Square store leaves two injured; Council gridlocked on policing reforms.*

"This city feels like it's coming apart at the seams," Dani murmured. "Every day, more shootings, more robberies... It's not safe anymore."

Henry exhaled through his nose, steady, thoughtful. "Boston's always been rough. But it's our home. We make it safe—here, for her." He gestured to Kalee, who was humming softly to her new wooden sparrow, oblivious to the weight of adult fears.

Dani gave a small nod, the warmth of her smile returning as she squeezed his hand. For now, within these walls, they were unshaken.

After dinner, Henry carried the dishes to the sink, rolling up his sleeves. Dani followed, shaking her head. "You worked a twelve-hour shift and now you're going to do the dishes? You trying to make the rest of us look lazy?"

Henry grinned over his shoulder. "What can I say? I've got energy to spare."

"Uh-huh. Big strong soldier, saving the world one dirty plate at a time."

Her voice carried a teasing lilt, but when she stepped close, brushing against him as she reached for the towel, her smile softened into something more private. Henry slid an arm around her waist, pulling her flush against him. She whispered, "Save some of that energy for me later tonight".

"You know," he murmured, lowering his voice so Kalee wouldn't hear from the living room, "spoiling you is even better than spoiling her."

Dani swatted at his chest again, though less forceful this time. "You're incorrigible."

"And you love it."

She tilted her chin up, eyes gleaming with challenge. "Do I now?"

Henry bent low and kissed her—gentle at first, then deeper, the kind of kiss born not just of passion but of years of trust and familiarity. She melted against him, the warmth of her body a reminder of everything worth holding onto.

When he pulled back, he whispered, "I'd marry you all over again if I could."

Dani's laugh was soft, almost embarrassed, but her arms tightened around his shoulders. "Five years and you still talk like it's the first date."

"Five years isn't long enough," he said. "Not for you."

They stood there for a moment in the narrow kitchen, the hum of the refrigerator the only sound besides their breathing. The outside world—sirens in the distance, the restless city pressing at the edges of their neighborhood—felt miles away.

From the couch, Kalee's voice cut through, sing-song and impatient. "Eww, you two are kissing again!"

Dani pulled back, laughing, her forehead resting against Henry's chest. "See? Already she's judging us."

Henry scooped his daughter up with one arm as he returned to the living room. "Jealous, huh? Don't worry, Daddy's always got time for you." He dropped her onto the couch with a playful growl, tickling until she squealed with laughter. Dani watched from the kitchen doorway, shaking her head but smiling so wide it reached her eyes. This—this was the life they'd built together. Not perfect, not without worries, but strong. Solid. A family anchored in love, even while the city outside threatened to crack apart.

As the evening wound down, Henry leaned back in his chair, Dani curled against his side, Kalee snuggled under a blanket with her wooden sparrow clutched tight. The TV flickered with more news of robberies, gang clashes, and political turmoil, but Henry muted it. For this moment, he didn't care. The world could rage all it wanted—inside these walls, he had everything he needed. Later that night, the house had settled into its quiet rhythm. The dinner dishes were washed and stacked, Kalee's school bag packed for the morning. Henry leaned in the doorway of her small bedroom, watching as Dani tucked their daughter beneath the blanket patterned with cartoon stars.

"Don't forget Mr. Sparrow," Dani said, placing the wooden bird onto the nightstand with a flourish.

Kalee hugged it close before setting it down, her eyelids already heavy. "Daddy makes the best presents," she murmured, drifting into a yawn.

Henry stepped forward, smoothing a curl from her forehead. "And Daddy's gonna keep making them. Now get some sleep, princess."

"'Kay," she whispered, already half gone, her breathing soft and even.

Together, Henry and Dani lingered a moment longer, the light from the hallway spilling across their daughter's peaceful face. Closing the door gently, they moved down the hallway, their footsteps falling into an easy rhythm.

In the living room, Henry dropped onto the couch with a sigh, stretching his long frame across the cushions.

Dani joined him, curling her legs beneath her. She handed him a mug of tea, steam rising between them.

"You ever think about how lucky we are?" Henry asked after a quiet sip.

Dani raised a brow. "Lucky? You mean with the hours you work and this city going to hell?"

He chuckled, low and deep. "Yeah. Even with all that. I come home, and I've got you, and her. That's more than a lot of men ever get."

Dani's expression softened, her hand sliding over his. "You know... sometimes I think you try too hard to carry all of it. The world, the family, even my worries. But you don't have to do it alone, Henry. You've got me. Always." Her words sank into him, and for a moment he simply looked at her, memorizing the curve of her smile, the warmth in her eyes. He pulled her closer, pressing his forehead to hers. "I know. I just don't ever want to lose this. Either of you."

Dani's laugh came light, meant to chase away the heaviness. "Then don't screw it up. Simple as that." They sat in silence for a while, the muted city noise seeping through the windows—distant sirens, a car horn, the thrum of restless streets. But inside the brownstone, it was calm. Their calm.

Henry wrapped an arm around her shoulders, holding her against his chest. "You realize," he said, voice teasing now, "if I keep making those little toys, one day she's gonna have enough to build a whole army."

Dani smiled against him. "Then she'll be ready to conquer the world. Just like her father."

Henry kissed the top of her head, letting out a contented sigh. For tonight, at least, the world could wait. The living room light was dim, the only real glow coming from the television. Henry sat stretched out across the couch, Dani tucked firmly under his arm, her head resting against his chest. The muted sounds of the city filtered through the windows, but the real pulse of Boston seemed to flicker on the screen before them.

The anchor's voice carried no warmth, only weary cadence. *"Another shooting in Roxbury tonight leaves three wounded. Police say it was likely gang-related, though no suspects are in custody."*

The image shifted to shaky cellphone footage—sirens washing blue over a crowd of onlookers, yellow tape stretching across a street Henry knew too well. Dani's fingers tightened slightly on his arm.

He kissed her temple, murmuring, "Don't look so hard at it. It's always the same story."

"I know," she said, though her voice trembled with frustration. "But it's not just background noise anymore, Henry. Every week it feels closer. Roxbury, Dorchester, South End. What happens when it's here? When it's us?"

Henry pulled her tighter, his arm firm around her shoulders. "Then it won't be us. Not while I'm here. You know that."

She gave a soft, humorless laugh. "You can't fight the whole city."

"I don't need to fight the city. Just need to keep you and her safe."

They fell into silence as the news droned on—stories of robberies downtown, a city council bickering over policing budgets, and a bleak forecast of rising unemployment. Dani sighed against him, her breath warm through his shirt.

"Sometimes I think about the suburbs," she admitted quietly. "Somewhere with quiet streets, maybe a yard.

Where she could ride her bike without me worrying about stray bullets."

Henry stroked her arm slowly, thoughtful. "Yeah. I think about it too. But then I think... this is our home. Our friends, our family, our lives—they're here. I don't want to run from it."

Dani shifted slightly, looking up at him. "I don't call it running. I call it living smart."

He smiled faintly, leaning down to kiss her. "And I call it giving up. Guess we'll just have to argue about it for the next fifty years."

That drew a genuine laugh from her, the kind that chased shadows away. She nestled back against him, letting the rhythm of his heartbeat steady her. Together they watched the rest of the broadcast, not because they wanted to, but because it was what people did— bear witness to the world unraveling, then try to sleep anyway.

When the program ended, Henry clicked off the television, plunging the room into quiet. He rose, pulling Dani up with him, and together they moved through the familiar steps of shutting down the house—lights off, doors checked, one last glance at Kalee asleep in her room.

In their bedroom, Henry wrapped his arms around Dani as they settled beneath the covers. For a while they lay in the dark, the city's noise a distant echo. His last words before sleep were simple but steady. "Whatever tomorrow brings, we face it together."

The morning sun slanted through the blinds, painting the kitchen in pale stripes. The smell of coffee lingered, mingling with the faint warmth of toast cooling on a plate. Henry stood by the counter in his work jacket, slipping his lunch into a battered cooler. His boots were laced, the day already calling him back to steel and dust.

The knock at the door came just as he reached for his thermos. Dani's voice rang out from the hall. "Mom! Come in!"

Yvonne Barros entered with the confident grace of a woman who had seen life from every angle and refused to be diminished by any of it. At sixty-two, her hair carried silver streaks that only sharpened her striking features. Her figure tells everyone she works out and her beauty seems God blessed. She set down a bag of fruit she'd carried, eyes brightening as she spotted Henry.

"Off to break more rocks, Henry?" she teased, her accent still carrying the faint lilt of Cape Verdean roots.

Henry chuckled, straightening. "Somebody's gotta build this city, Ms. Barros. Might as well be me."

Yvonne gave him a pointed look, her lips twitching. "How many times have I told you? It's Yvonne, not Ms. Barros. You're family, boy."

"Yes, ma'am," Henry said with a grin, raising his hands in surrender. "Just showing respect."

"Respect is good. But don't make me sound old."

Dani rolled her eyes affectionately as she took her mother's coat. "You two are going to spar all morning if I let you."

Henry bent to kiss Dani's cheek, then leaned down so Yvonne could swat at his arm. "You behave now," she said, though the smile in her eyes betrayed her fondness.

"I always behave," Henry answered, already moving toward the door. "It's everyone else in this city you gotta watch out for."

The line hung for a moment, heavier than he meant it to, before he gave them both a wave and stepped outside. The rumble of the city greeted him at once—the distant siren, the grind of a bus pulling away at the corner. He adjusted his jacket and started down the sidewalk toward his stop.

Inside, Yvonne turned to Dani, her expression softening. "That man is a rock," she said, shaking her head. "But even rocks can crack, you know. This city... it's not the place I wanted for you, filha."

Dani busied herself at the counter, pouring her mother coffee, but her shoulders tightened. "We've talked about it, Mom. Moving. He doesn't want to leave."

Yvonne sighed, settling at the table. "He's stubborn, that one. But he loves you both more than anything. That's why I worry. Love makes a man blind sometimes. Makes him think he can hold back the tide with his bare hands."

Dani slid the mug to her mother and sat across from her, the morning sun falling across both their faces. "Maybe he can," she said softly, though even as the words left her lips, doubt clung to the edges of her smile.

Yvonne cradled the coffee mug between her palms, letting the steam warm her fingers. Her eyes wandered the kitchen—framed school drawings on the wall, the stack of bills tucked beneath a ceramic fruit bowl, the photo of Dani and Henry from their wedding day. Her mouth curved into a faint smile, but the lines around her eyes held worry.

"You've built a good home here," she said, her voice thoughtful. "Solid walls, warm light. But home is more than wood and brick, filha. It has to be safe. And I look around this city... I don't see safety anymore."

Dani wrapped her hands around her own mug, staring into the dark swirl of coffee. "Henry thinks it's still worth it. He says we can make it safe—at least in here. He doesn't want to give up on the place we started."

Yvonne's laugh was short, without humor. "That's the soldier in him talking. Always thinking he can outlast the danger. But the danger doesn't sleep, Dani. It doesn't care how strong a man is. It'll come knocking whether you're ready or not."

Dani frowned, chewing lightly on her bottom lip. "You think I don't see it? I watch the news too. I walk these streets with Kalee. I see the gangs on corners, the looks they give. But if we leave... doesn't that mean they win? Doesn't that mean we're running?"

Yvonne reached across the table, taking her daughter's hand firmly in her own. "Sometimes running is the bravest thing you can do. You take your child, your husband, and you put them where the bullets don't fly past windows. Where the sidewalks don't bleed at night. That's not running—it's surviving."

The conviction in her mother's voice cracked Dani's composure. She blinked, tears stinging her eyes. "I just... I don't know how to ask him. He loves it here, Mom. This house, this city. It's like... leaving would be betrayal."

"Listen to me," Yvonne said, squeezing her hand tighter. "Love is not about the ground beneath your feet. It's about the people you hold. If Henry really loves this family the way I know he does, then one day he'll see that. He'll see that leaving isn't betrayal—it's salvation."

Dani leaned into her mother's hand, taking a shaky breath. "Do you ever regret staying? After Papa passed? After everything?"

Yvonne's gaze drifted to the window, the city beyond it. "Every day. But regret doesn't change the past. It only teaches you to fight harder for the future. And that's what I want for you. A future. For you. For Kalee."

For a long moment they sat in silence, the hum of the refrigerator filling the space. Outside, a siren wailed faintly before fading into the distance. Dani's grip on her mother's hand tightened, as though clinging to something solid in a world already beginning to tremble.

Dani sat back, her hand still tangled with her mother's, her gaze drifting toward the hallway where Kalee's laughter had echoed the night before. The memory brought both warmth and unease. "She's five, Mom. Five. And already I catch myself warning her about things kids shouldn't even have to think about. Don't talk to strangers. Stay close to the door when we're outside. Don't pick up anything off the ground. It feels like I'm raising her to be afraid instead of free."

Yvonne's eyes softened, but her voice carried steel. "Fear isn't weakness, filha. Fear keeps you alive. I told you the same things when you were little. Back then it was different gangs, different dangers—but the lessons were the same. The world outside is not gentle, not for women, not for our people. You have to teach her that, or the world will teach her in harder ways."

Dani looked down, her thumb tracing the rim of her mug. "But when I see her face, so bright, so... untouched, I just want her to have a childhood. I don't want her carrying the same weight we did. She's supposed to laugh, play, dream. Not wonder why police sirens keep her up at night."

Yvonne leaned back, studying her daughter. "Every mother wants to shield her child from the ugliness. But sometimes the best we can do is give them strength, not shelter. The world isn't going to change just because you wish it so. But if you give her strength, she'll know how to stand when the ground shakes."

Dani's voice dropped low, almost a whisper. "What if I'm not strong enough to give her that? What if something happens when Henry's not here?"

Yvonne's expression softened, the sternness giving way to compassion. "Then you lean on the people who love you. Me. Your cousins. And yes, Henry too. He may be stubborn, but that man would tear the sky down for you and that child. Don't ever doubt that."

Tears welled at the corners of Dani's eyes, but she blinked them back. "Sometimes I look at him and I think—he's holding so much inside. Like he's just waiting for something to snap. And I don't know what happens when it does."

Yvonne reached across the table again, cupping her daughter's cheek. "Then you remind him of this—of home, of love, of her. You remind him he doesn't have to carry it all alone. That's what marriage is, filha. Not perfection. Not peace. But holding each other up when the world tries to crush you."

Dani let out a shaky breath, leaning into her mother's hand. For a moment she allowed herself to believe it— to believe that between Henry's strength, her mother's wisdom, and her own resolve, they could keep the darkness at bay. But outside, the city hummed and growled, never sleeping, never satisfied, reminding them both that safety was fragile, and peace was always borrowed time.

The sound of small footsteps pattering against the hardwood broke the weight of the conversation. Dani and Yvonne looked up just as Kalee appeared in the doorway, her hair a tangle from sleep, clutching the wooden sparrow Henry had given her the night before. "Morning, Nana!" she chirped, rushing forward with arms wide.

Yvonne's face transformed instantly, the lines of worry smoothing as she gathered her granddaughter into her lap. "Ah, meu anjo, my little angel. You're getting taller every time I see you. Soon you'll be as big as your daddy."

Kalee giggled, shaking her head. "No one's as big as Daddy. He's like a giant." She stretched her arms as wide as they could go to prove her point.

Dani laughed softly, brushing a curl from her daughter's forehead. "A gentle giant, though. Don't forget that part."

"I didn't!" Kalee protested, then turned her attention back to the bird in her hand. "Daddy said this sparrow is me. Because I'm fast and strong."

Yvonne raised a brow, impressed. "He's right. But do you know what else sparrows are? Survivors. They may be small, but they're clever. They always find a way, even when bigger birds chase them."

Kalee's eyes widened with delight. "So I'm clever too?"

"The cleverest," Yvonne said, kissing the top of her head.

For a moment, the kitchen filled with laughter and chatter, the heaviness of earlier words pushed back by the brightness of a child's world. Kalee clambered off her grandmother's lap and danced around the kitchen, humming to herself as she made the sparrow "fly" through the air.

"She doesn't hear it yet," Dani whispered, watching her daughter spin with a mixture of pride and sadness. "The sirens, the shouting, the gunfire at night. She's still... untouched."

Yvonne laid a hand over her daughter's. "Let her be untouched as long as she can. That's the gift you and Henry are giving her. Childhood, even in a place that tries to steal it."

Kalee stopped her dance and looked at them with sudden seriousness, the kind only children could conjure. "Are you talking about me?"

Both women smiled, startled by the directness. Dani quickly pulled her onto her lap. "Always, baby girl. Always about you."

Kalee seemed satisfied with that answer. She tucked the sparrow into her pocket and leaned her head against her mother's chest. The warmth of the embrace wrapped around all three of them, for a moment pushing back the world outside.

Yvonne looked at her daughter over Kalee's head and spoke softly. "Hold on to this, Dani. Hold on tight. Because one day, she'll remember the love more than the fear. And that's what will carry her through."

The clang of steel and the hum of machinery filled the air, the construction site alive with the grind of another long day. Dust hung like a haze, catching in the throat with every breath. Henry tightened his gloves, the familiar ache in his shoulders reminding him that the day had barely begun.

"Hey, Mann!" The supervisor's voice cut through the noise, sharp and impatient. A stocky man in a hard hat, clipboard tucked under his arm, strode across the gravel. "We've got a delivery of rebar that needs unloading and stacked by the south wall. Get it done before lunch."

Henry glanced past him to the other workers—most assigned to framing on the upper levels or running machines. The rebar job was backbreaking, dirty work, the kind no one volunteered for. He nodded anyway, keeping his voice even. "Got it."

The supervisor clapped the clipboard against his thigh, already turning away. "And take Wilson with you. Make sure it's done right."

Wilson, a broad-shouldered man a few years older than Henry, gave him a look as they fell in step toward the delivery truck. "You notice how it's always us?"

Henry didn't answer right away, bending to grip the steel bars, the weight biting instantly into his palms. He set the first one down on the growing stack before finally speaking. "Yeah. I notice."

Wilson snorted, wiping sweat from his brow. "They think we don't. But I see the pattern. We're the only brothers out here, and somehow it's always us knee-deep in the filth while everyone else gets the easier cuts."

Henry hefted another length of steel, muscles straining. "Maybe it's because we get it done."

Wilson gave him a sideways glance, half amused, half bitter. "That's what they count on. You take it without complaint, and they pat themselves on the back for being fair."

Henry stayed quiet, methodical in his movements, his silence less agreement than restraint. Years of service had taught him discipline, the art of swallowing frustration when the mission demanded focus. But Wilson's words lingered, gnawing.

As the sun climbed higher, sweat plastered Henry's shirt to his back, his body working through the load with mechanical precision. Around them, laughter rose from the men working the upper floors. It wasn't malicious, just careless—the sound of those who never had to wonder why the dirtiest jobs fell their way.

Wilson leaned against the stack for a moment, catching his breath. "You're a big man, Henry. They see that and figure you're built for the heavy lifting. But we both know it's not just size they see."

Henry looked out across the site, past the scaffolding and steel, his jaw tight. "I've carried worse," he said finally. "This isn't what breaks me."

Wilson studied him for a long moment before shaking his head with a low chuckle. "Yeah. I believe that. Still don't mean we gotta like it."

The foreman's whistle blew from across the lot, barking out orders. Henry bent again, gripping another bar, the strain in his arms mirrored by the quiet weight pressing against his chest. The lunch whistle cut across the site, sharp and metallic, and men began to gather in the patch of shade by the equipment trailers. Henry lowered the last steel bar into place and rolled his shoulders, the muscles in his back burning from repetition. Wilson sank down onto an overturned bucket nearby, tearing into a sandwich wrapped in wax paper.

"Man," Wilson said between bites, "this city's gonna kill us one way or another. If it ain't the work, it's the streets."

Henry unscrewed his thermos, taking a long drink before answering. "It's not that bad."

Wilson gave him a look, skeptical. "Not that bad? You don't hear it? Every night—sirens, gunshots, somebody screaming. My cousin lives near Dorchester. Says they found a body in the alley last week, execution-style. That's not just noise, brother. That's warning bells."

Henry stayed quiet, eyes tracking the horizon of half-built walls and scaffolding. He heard it too—the city's pulse, a rhythm of unrest that crept closer each day. But saying it aloud felt like giving it more power than it deserved.

Wilson leaned closer, lowering his voice. "Word is, the African Lords and the Hell's Gentlemen are circling each other again. Fighting over the South End. And when they clash? Doesn't matter where you live, the bullets don't check addresses."

Henry's jaw tightened. He'd spent enough time in places where stray bullets weren't stray at all—they were messages, carved into flesh and concrete. He forced his shoulders to relax, focusing instead on unwrapping the sandwich Dani had packed for him.

"You always know too much," Henry muttered.

Wilson shrugged. "I listen. Better to know trouble's coming than pretend it isn't." He pointed with his sandwich toward the far side of the lot. "And speaking of trouble—there's your buddy."

Henry followed the gesture and spotted a lean figure in glasses making his way across the site, a hard hat slightly askew. Steven Fitzgerald didn't belong among the grit and sweat—his steps careful, his clothes too clean, his tablet clutched like a shield. Yet the man carried himself with a kind of quiet confidence, unbothered by the looks some of the crew threw his way.

"Steven," Henry said with the faintest smile, watching him weave awkwardly between stacks of lumber.

Wilson snorted. "That man's got no business out here. Looks like he'd break a sweat just carrying his laptop."

"Don't underestimate him," Henry said, his tone edged with loyalty. "Brains count just as much as muscle. Sometimes more."

Wilson raised his brows but didn't argue. He stuffed the last of his sandwich into his mouth, muttering, "All the brains in the world won't save you when the streets go bad."

Henry leaned back against the stack of rebar, letting the words hang. The sun beat down, the air thick with dust, and beneath it all, Boston's heartbeat thudded—louder than ever, a warning waiting to be heard.

Steven reached the shade where Henry and Wilson sat, adjusting his hard hat like it had been borrowed for a costume. He gave Wilson a nod before pushing his glasses higher on his nose. "You two look like you're trying to break a world record for most sweat lost in one morning."

Wilson chuckled, shaking his head. "You wouldn't last ten minutes out here, Fitzgerald."

Steven smiled faintly. "That's why I stick to code and schematics. Less heavy lifting, more brain strain." He turned his attention to Henry. "Speaking of which—I finished looking over those designs you asked about. The contractors are cutting corners again. The supports won't hold the weight they're planning."

Henry's brow furrowed. "How bad?"

"Bad enough to be dangerous if no one says anything." Steven lowered his voice, glancing toward the supervisor barking orders at another crew. "You know how it is—cheaper is faster, faster is profit. Safety doesn't make the balance sheets look pretty."

Henry took a slow breath, chewing on the thought. He'd seen enough shortcuts in both warzones and construction sites to know they always came back to cost someone something. Sometimes a paycheck, sometimes a life.

Wilson leaned forward, frowning. "So what—you're just gonna keep quiet about it?"

Steven shrugged. "I'll file my report. Doesn't mean they'll listen. You think management cares what the 'nerd' has to say when the steel's already ordered?"

Henry gave him a firm look. "Then you let me handle it. They'll listen when I tell them."

Steven studied him a moment, then nodded. There was an ease between the two men that came from years of trust—different worlds, different skills, but a loyalty stitched tight.

Across the lot, the supervisor's whistle shrilled again, demanding movement. The crews rose, grumbling. Steven sighed, adjusting his tablet under his arm. "Another day in paradise."

Wilson stood, brushing dust from his hands. "Paradise is a long way from here."

Henry pushed to his feet, rolling his shoulders, his voice calm but edged. "Doesn't matter how they see us. We do the work, we watch each other's backs. That's how we get through."

Wilson gave a dry laugh. "Sounds more like a soldier than a construction worker."

Henry didn't answer. His gaze lingered on the city skyline visible beyond the rising skeleton of the building, the jagged mix of glass towers and sagging rooftops. Somewhere out there, gangs were already drawing lines, setting the stage for something bigger. He could feel it in his bones—the way a soldier feels the storm before it breaks.

The rest of the afternoon dragged beneath the weight of repetition. Henry pushed steel, hammered frames, carried loads heavier than most men dared attempt. Sweat burned his eyes, and the ache in his back settled into something dull and constant. By quitting time, the whistle sounded like salvation.

On the bus ride home, the city pressed against the windows. Storefronts with bars on the glass, graffiti curling across brick walls, clusters of young men at corners where deals were whispered and cash passed hand to hand. Henry stayed standing even when seats opened, his size a natural deterrent in the crowded aisle. He watched the streets roll by, a soldier's eyes scanning the world not for beauty but for threats.

When he finally stepped down onto his block, the day's exhaustion tugged at him. But before he even reached his door, he spotted them—four teenagers sprawled on the brownstone steps, hoodies up, smoke curling from cheap cigars. Their laughter was sharp, almost brittle, words flying too fast and too loud, daring the world to notice them.

Henry slowed, his jaw tightening. They weren't bothering anyone, not really, but this was his home. His sanctuary. And seeing them there felt like a crack in the foundation.

He approached with measured steps, his shadow falling over them before his voice did. "Evening, fellas."

One of the boys looked up, eyes narrowing as he took in Henry's size. He nudged his friend, who pulled the cigar from his lips with exaggerated slowness. "Evening," the teen said, mocking the tone, a smirk tugging at his mouth.

Henry kept his voice calm, level. "This is my house. I'm asking you to move along."

Another boy snorted, muttering under his breath, "Man thinks he owns the sidewalk now."

Henry's gaze swept across them, steady and unflinching. He didn't raise his voice, didn't need to. "You heard me."

For a moment the air thickened, the group shifting uneasily. They weren't cowards, not exactly, but standing this close to a man who looked like he could bend rebar with his bare hands gave them pause. One finally stood, brushing ash from his hoodie, the others following reluctantly.

As they stepped off the stoop, one tossed a glance back over his shoulder. "We were just chillin', old man. Don't gotta act like you run the block."

Henry let the words hang in the air, unacknowledged. He wasn't looking for a fight—not with kids. He simply waited until their voices drifted down the street, swallowed by the city's endless noise.

Only then did he climb the steps, his key slipping into the lock with practiced ease. As the door closed behind him, the sounds of laughter and smoke faded, replaced by the warmth of his home. Yet even inside, he carried the echo of it—youth already leaning toward a path that would pull them into the city's darker currents. And

Henry, despite all his strength, knew there was only so much he could push back against.

The smell hit him first as he stepped inside—garlic, onions, and the slow simmer of seasoned chicken filling the air. It wrapped around him like a blanket, easing the edge from his shoulders more effectively than any word could. Yvonne was at the stove, wooden spoon in hand, humming softly to herself. Dani was setting the table, and Kalee sat in her chair with a coloring book, her tongue poking out in concentration as she scribbled.

"Daddy!" Kalee squealed, leaping from her seat to crash into his legs once more.

Henry scooped her up, pressing a kiss to her cheek. "That's twice today you nearly knocked me over."

She grinned, showing off missing front teeth. "'Cause you're slow!"

He laughed, setting her back down. Dani's eyes met his across the room. She gave him a smile, but it faltered just slightly, her gaze lingering on the stiffness in his shoulders.

"You okay?" she asked quietly, once Kalee scampered back to her crayons.

Henry shrugged out of his jacket, hanging it by the door. "Just kids on the steps. Nothing serious."

Her brow lifted. "Nothing serious doesn't leave you standing like a storm cloud in the doorway."

He exhaled, long and steady, then moved toward her.

She reached out, brushing the back of his hand with her

fingers, her touch warm and grounding. "Let it go," she murmured. "You're home now. That's what matters."
Henry nodded, drawing her in for a quick squeeze before Yvonne clattered the spoon against the pot. "Don't you two start again with that mushy stuff when I've got food ready," she teased. "Sit, sit. You're not too tired to eat, Henry."
"I wouldn't dare," he said with a faint grin, sliding into his chair.
Dinner was hearty, Yvonne's cooking filling the room with comfort as much as flavor. The conversation flowed easily—Kalee proudly showed off her coloring, Dani rolled her eyes when her mother praised her cooking skills compared to hers, and Henry finally let his body relax, the day's weight slipping away piece by piece.
Halfway through, Yvonne stood, wiping her hands on a dish towel. "I should be heading out before it gets too late."
"Already?" Dani protested. "You don't have to rush."
"I know, filha," Yvonne said, leaning down to kiss her granddaughter's head. "But I've got things waiting at home. And you've got this one to keep you busy." She gave Henry a pointed look, half teasing, half serious.
Henry rose to walk her to the door, his voice warm. "Thanks for dinner, Yvonne. You take care getting home."
She gave his arm a squeeze before stepping out, her eyes meeting his for a heartbeat longer than usual. There was something in that look—concern, unspoken

but heavy. Then she was gone, her figure swallowed by the night.

When Henry turned back, Dani was waiting in the hall, her arms folded but her expression soft. She leaned in, pressing her forehead against his chest. "Whatever happened out there, don't carry it in here. Not tonight."

Henry closed his eyes, resting his chin atop her head. "I'm trying."

"Good," she whispered. "Because this—us—that's the part worth holding onto."

The clink of silverware and the hum of conversation filled the small dining room, the air rich with the smell of roasted chicken and spices. For a while, the talk was light—Kalee chattered about her sparrow carving and how she planned to paint it purple, which made Dani laugh and shake her head.

"Purple?" Henry asked, raising a brow. "Since when are sparrows purple?"

"Since now," Kalee said firmly, grinning as she stuffed a piece of bread into her mouth.

Dani smirked. "Careful, Henry. She gets that stubborn streak from you."

Henry gave a mock sigh, but his eyes softened. "Guilty as charged."

The laughter carried them a few minutes longer before the weight of the outside world pushed its way into the room. Dani glanced toward the muted TV, still showing the late evening broadcast. The scrolling ticker caught her eye: *Armed robbery at Copley Square jewelry store; suspects still at large.*

She leaned back in her chair, her tone thoughtful but edged. "Did you hear about the robbery? Big one, at that jewelry shop near the mall. Broad daylight, people everywhere. They didn't even care who saw them."

Henry stabbed a piece of chicken, his jaw tightening. "That's how it goes now. They don't fear nothing—not the police, not the cameras, not even each other."

Kalee, sensing the shift, looked from one parent to the other with wide eyes. Dani caught it and quickly softened her tone. "Don't worry, sweetheart. We're safe here."

Still, she looked back at Henry, lowering her voice so only he could hear. "The neighbors were talking this afternoon. Said a gang tagged the side of the laundromat again. Same crew that's been fighting with the others in Roxbury. They're creeping closer."

Henry's fork stilled. He'd noticed the graffiti too—colors and symbols marking territory like battle flags. It wasn't just art; it was warning.

"They won't bring it here," he said, though the certainty in his tone didn't quite match the doubt flickering in his eyes.

Dani reached across the table, touching his hand lightly. "You always say that. But it feels like it's only a matter of time. And when it does…" She trailed off, her gaze sliding to their daughter, who was now humming to herself, focused on her plate.

Henry gave her hand a squeeze, his voice low and steady. "When it does, I'll handle it. That's my job. To keep you both safe."

Dani studied him for a moment, then nodded, though unease lingered in her expression. She let go, turning her attention back to Kalee, whose cheeks were full as she announced proudly, "This is the best chicken ever!"

That broke the tension again, laughter spilling around the table. But beneath the warmth, the weight of the city pressed in, silent and unshakable, waiting just outside their door.

The plates were scraped clean, the laughter and stories giving way to that comfortable lull families fall into once the meal is done. Yvonne stood, brushing crumbs from her skirt, her eyes soft as she looked at her daughter and granddaughter.

"I should be going," she said, reaching for her coat. "It's late, and the buses don't wait for an old woman."

"You're not old, Mom," Dani said automatically, moving to help her.

Yvonne kissed her daughter's cheek, then stooped to hug Kalee, who clung to her neck. "Be good for your mama. And don't forget—sparrows fly together."

Kalee nodded solemnly, clutching her wooden carving as if it were a charm.

Henry walked Yvonne to the door, his voice steady. "Thank you for dinner. You saved me from an empty stomach after the day I had."

Yvonne gave him a look—half warning, half affection. "Don't carry the weight of the world on those shoulders, Henry. It'll break even a strong man."

He inclined his head, not trusting himself to answer. She kissed his cheek lightly, then stepped into the night. Her figure disappeared down the steps, the door closing softly behind her.

For a moment, the house felt too quiet. Dani leaned against the doorway, her arms folded. "She's right, you know. You carry too much."

Henry exhaled, running a hand over his head. "Somebody's got to."

Dani didn't argue. Instead, she gestured toward the couch. "Come sit. I need to tell you something."

He followed her into the living room, settling beside her. The TV glowed faintly, the sound turned down to a whisper. Dani tucked her legs beneath her, facing him fully.

"Today at work..." She hesitated, biting her lip. "A client came in, loud and angry. Accusing me of messing up his paperwork. He was red in the face, shouting so everyone could hear. Security had to step in."

Henry frowned. "Did he touch you?"

"No," she said quickly. "But the way he looked at me... it wasn't just frustration. It was hate. Like he needed someone to unload on, and I was standing there. I don't scare easy, Henry, but it rattled me. I kept thinking—if he'd had a gun, or if he'd lost control..."

Her voice faltered, the memory tightening her chest.

Henry reached for her hand, his grip firm. "You don't deserve that. None of it."

She squeezed back, her eyes searching his. "That's just it. This city feels like it's unraveling. People don't have patience anymore, don't have kindness. Everything's anger and desperation. And I'm scared that one day… it'll spill over into us."

Henry pulled her against him, her head settling on his shoulder. For a while they sat in silence, the faint city sounds seeping through the walls. His hand rubbed slow circles on her back, but his own mind churned. He thought of the teens on the stoop, the gangs Wilson had whispered about, the robbery Dani had mentioned, and now this—rage spilling even into her workplace.

The storm was coming. He could feel it in his bones.

The house had grown quiet by the time Dani led Kalee down the hall, her small hand tucked safely in her mother's. The little girl clutched the carved sparrow in her other fist, its smooth wood worn already by her constant touch.

In her bedroom, the soft glow of a night-light painted the walls in warm amber. Dani pulled back the blanket, smoothing the sheets before helping Kalee climb in. The girl wriggled beneath the covers, her eyes bright even as sleep tugged at them.

"Did you brush your teeth?" Dani asked, arching a brow.

Kalee nodded quickly, too quickly.

Dani leaned down, giving her a mock-serious look.

"Don't think I can't tell when you're fibbing."

With a sigh, Kalee pulled the blanket over her head, muffling a giggle. "Tomorrow, I promise."

"Tomorrow," Dani repeated, shaking her head with a smile. She bent low and kissed her daughter's forehead. "Goodnight, meu passarinho."

Kalee peeked out from under the blanket, clutching her sparrow. Her voice was small but certain. "Mommy… will Daddy kiss me too? I can't sleep without Daddy's kiss."

The words pressed at Dani's heart, the innocence of them cutting through all the heaviness of the day. "Of course, sweetheart," she whispered. She brushed a curl from Kalee's cheek. "Daddy wouldn't forget."

She slipped from the room, padding softly down the hall. Henry was still in the living room, leaning forward on the couch with his elbows on his knees, lost in thought. Dani touched his shoulder gently.

"She wants you," she said simply.

Henry looked up, the faintest weariness in his eyes melting at the sound of those words. He rose, his steps heavy but sure, and followed her into the small bedroom.

Kalee's eyes lit up when she saw him. "Daddy!" She stretched her arms out. "Kiss before sleep!"

Henry bent down, pressing a kiss to her forehead and then another to her tiny hand. "There. Double kiss. That way you sleep twice as well."

Kalee giggled, settling back against her pillow. "Goodnight, Daddy. Goodnight, Mommy."

Henry lingered a moment longer, watching her eyelids
flutter shut, the sparrow clutched tight against her
chest. The rise and fall of her breathing filled the room,
soft and steady, a rhythm he wanted to memorize.
When they stepped back into the hall, Dani slipped her
hand into his. No words passed between them. They
didn't need any.

The bedroom was dim, the only light a faint glow
slipping in from the streetlamp outside. Dani slipped
out of her robe and slid beneath the covers, the sheets
cool against her skin. Henry entered a moment later,
closing the door softly behind him, the day's weight still
clinging to his broad shoulders.

She watched him for a moment, her eyes tracing the
familiar lines of his frame. "You look like you're carrying
the whole city on your back again," she said softly.

Henry gave a quiet chuckle, pulling off his shirt and
setting it on the chair. "That obvious?"

"Always." She reached for him as he climbed into bed
beside her.

The mattress dipped under his weight, and she nestled
close, her hand sliding across the hard plane of his
chest. "You know what I think?" she whispered, her
breath warm against his skin. "I think the city can wait
until morning."

He turned toward her, his hand cupping her cheek. The
faint lines of worry around his eyes softened as she
leaned into his touch. Their lips met, slow at first, then
with a growing hunger that chased away the noise

outside. Dani's fingers curled into his shoulders, pulling him closer until there was no space left between them. For a long while, there was only the rhythm of their breathing, the heat of skin against skin, the shared tenderness that had carried them through five years of marriage. It wasn't rushed, wasn't just passion—it was the steady, familiar fire of two people who knew each other completely, who found solace in the touch they didn't have to ask for.

Dani laughed quietly when he kissed the hollow of her throat, the sound muffled by the pillow. "You'll wake her," she teased, though her arms tightened around him.

"She sleeps like a rock," Henry murmured, smiling against her skin. "Besides... she's used to hearing her parents happy."

Her laughter melted into a sigh as she arched against him, letting the world beyond their walls slip away. In that room, there was no gang graffiti, no prejudice at work, no robberies on the news. There was only the two of them—husband and wife, soldier and dreamer, man and woman bound by love.

When at last they lay tangled together, the night air cooling their damp skin, Dani rested her head on Henry's chest. His arm held her close, strong and certain, his thumb tracing slow circles against her shoulder.

"See?" she murmured sleepily. "The city can wait."

Henry kissed her hair, his voice low, almost a promise. "As long as I have you, it always can."

Morning came with the scent of coffee and the faint hiss of bacon in the skillet. Sunlight spilled through the kitchen blinds, cutting golden lines across the table where Kalee sat, swinging her legs and humming as she tried to balance her sparrow upright on the saltshaker. Henry entered still in his undershirt, hair damp from the shower, his steps quiet on the worn floorboards. Dani turned from the stove, spatula in hand, and gave him a smile that made the whole room brighter.

"Morning, sleepyhead," she teased.

He kissed her cheek before stealing a strip of bacon off the plate. "Not sleepy. Just slow to leave a warm bed when you're in it."

Dani rolled her eyes but her lips curved. "Charmer."

Kalee piped up from the table, "Daddy, watch this!" She let go of the sparrow, and it tipped over immediately, clattering to the table. She frowned. "It won't stand."

Henry pulled out a chair, sitting beside her. "That's because sparrows aren't meant to stand still. They're meant to fly." He scooped up the carving, held it aloft, and made a soft whistling sound like wings cutting the air. Kalee giggled, clapping her hands.

"Fly, sparrow, fly!" she cried.

Dani set a plate of eggs down, shaking her head. "You two are incorrigible."

Henry grinned. "And you love us for it."

They ate together, the small rituals of family life filling the room—the scrape of forks, the sound of Kalee telling half-finished stories about a dream she'd had, Dani rolling her eyes but laughing anyway, Henry listening like each word was gospel.

After breakfast, Dani slipped her arms around Henry's waist as he rinsed the plates in the sink. "See? Normal. Just us. This is all I need."

He dried his hands, turning to kiss her forehead. "And this is all I'll ever fight for."

From the living room came Kalee's voice, high and insistent. "Can we go to the park today? Please? Please, please, please?"

Dani laughed, looking up at Henry. "You up for chasing sparrows and swings?"

Henry's smile softened. "For her? Always."

The sound of their daughter's laughter echoed through the house, bright and unburdened. For one more morning, it drowned out the city's noise—the sirens, the anger, the darkness gathering just beyond their street. The day stretched easy and unhurried. After breakfast, Henry carried Kalee on his shoulders to the park down the street, her laughter ringing out as she bounced with each step. Dani walked at his side, her hand brushing his arm, their pace untroubled. For a few hours, life was simple—swings squeaked, sparrows darted across the grass, and the three of them sat beneath the shade of an old oak sharing ice cream cones.

It was the kind of day that seemed almost ordinary, yet Henry felt every detail sinking into him—the way Dani's hair glowed in the sunlight, the stickiness of ice cream on Kalee's cheeks, the sound of her voice as she sang a song she'd made up about birds and giants. He held it all close, as if some part of him already knew how fleeting such days could be.

By late afternoon they were home again, Kalee sprawled on the living room rug with her crayons, Dani stretched across the couch with a magazine, and Henry standing at the front window, watching the street. It was quiet, almost too quiet. Then he saw it—a police cruiser rolling slow down the block, its tires crawling as if measuring every face, every doorway.

The car passed without stopping, but Henry's eyes lingered, tracking the fading reflection of its lights in the glass. He'd seen enough patrols in enough cities to know what it meant: tension simmering just below the surface, waiting to boil over.

Behind him, Dani called softly, "What is it?"

Henry turned from the window, letting his expression soften. "Nothing. Just the city, doing what it does."

He crossed back to her, easing down onto the couch beside her. She leaned against him, her fingers finding his. From the rug, Kalee lifted her sparrow carving and made it "fly" in uneven circles, her laughter filling the room again. Henry wrapped his arm around Dani's shoulders and kissed the top of her head. He let the sound of his daughter's laughter and his wife's steady breathing sink into him, anchoring him against the unease lingering just outside their door.

If the world was going to turn against them, he thought, then let it. He would remember this day. He would hold it like a shield.

Chapter 2

The bus ride felt different that morning. Henry couldn't place it at first—it was the same route, the same stops, the same cracked pavement running beneath the wheels. But the air inside carried a different weight, thicker, pressing against him with every bump and lurch. The voices in the back weren't the harmless chatter of kids killing time; they were sharper, deliberate, the kind of laughter that had edges.

He sat midway down the aisle, one hand resting on the seat in front of him, steadying himself as the driver hit a pothole that rattled the windows. A group of teenagers occupied the rear seats, their sneakers propped against the torn vinyl, their eyes sliding over passengers like hunters tracking a herd. Their laughter rose and fell in waves, each burst of sound cutting across the silence of those who didn't dare respond.

Henry didn't look back, but he felt the heat of their attention. He had known that kind of energy before—restless, hungry, dangerous. He kept his posture calm, his broad shoulders squared but loose, his eyes fixed on the grimy glass of the window beside him. The city moved past in flashes: walls covered in fresh tags, a corner store's shutters painted with memorial names, wilted flowers stuffed into chain-link as if trying to hold grief in place.

At one stop, an older woman climbed aboard, clutching her bag close. Her eyes flicked nervously to the teenagers, then darted toward Henry as if measuring whether he was another threat. She chose the seat across the aisle but sat perched on the edge, her whole body taut with suspicion. Henry gave her a polite nod, but she turned away, staring out the opposite window. That sting was familiar, but it carried an extra bite today. In a city where gangs claimed corners like kingdoms, he was lumped in with them before he spoke a word. He thought of Dani, of Kalee's smile, of the small world they had built together inside their home. That cocoon was what kept him steady, what held his anger in check when moments like this scraped at him. He refused to give strangers his fire.

The bus jerked again, and one of the teens shouted something Henry couldn't quite catch—but he knew the tone. Provocation. The kind that searched for a spark. Another voice followed, louder, closer, as if meant for his ears. He breathed slow, steady, and adjusted his grip on the seatback, grounding himself.

Two more stops. That was all. He could last that long without letting his pride be baited. He reminded himself that he had work to get to, bills to pay, a daughter to raise. That was the fight worth showing up for, not the barking of kids who didn't yet know what the world would do to them.

Still, when the bus doors opened at his stop and he stepped down onto the cracked curb, he felt the sound of their laughter follow him into the street, trailing like a shadow that refused to let go. The plant was already alive with noise when Henry walked in. Metal clanged against metal, forklifts beeped in reverse, and the air carried that faint tang of oil and sweat that seemed baked into the walls. He swiped his badge at the clock, the scanner giving its reluctant green blink before recording his start time.

Some mornings, he could lose himself in the rhythm of the work—the heft of crates, the rumble of machines, the measured conversations with men who understood what it meant to grind out a living. But this morning, the rhythm faltered before it even began.

"Bout time you showed up," barked McCaffrey, the shift supervisor. He was a stocky man with thinning blond hair and a permanent scowl, his voice cutting across the floor loud enough for half the crew to hear. "Maybe try gettin' here early for once, huh?"

Henry glanced at the clock. He wasn't late—not even close. His jaw tightened, but he forced himself to nod. "Clocked in on time," he said, voice steady.

McCaffrey smirked, chewing on the words like they were a piece of gum he could spit out later. "Sure, sure. Don't let me stop you from takin' your sweet time." He turned and walked off, leaving a trail of mutters behind him.

Wilson appeared at Henry's side almost immediately, tall and lean with a grin that could cut through any gloom. "Man's got nothin' better to do than ride you, huh?" he said, lowering his voice.

Henry shrugged, lifting the first crate onto the dolly. "Let him bark. Ain't worth my breath."

Steven joined them a moment later, broad-shouldered and quick with his hands, already cracking open the next pallet. "He only barks 'cause you don't bite. Folks like him don't know what to do with silence."

Henry allowed himself the faintest smile. "Better to stay quiet and keep my job."

The three of them worked in rhythm, moving as if they had rehearsed it, the camaraderie softening the sting of McCaffrey's public jab. Wilson cracked jokes between lifts, Steven offered commentary on the Red Sox's losing streak, and Henry found himself relaxing into the flow despite the lingering burn of the morning.

Still, the edge of unease stayed with him. He caught snatches of conversation drifting from the other end of the warehouse: talk of a kid shot outside a corner store, whispers about crews fighting over new turf. Wilson leaned in at one point, his grin fading.

"Streets are heatin' up," he said quietly. "You hearin' the same?"

Henry kept his eyes on the crate in his hands. "I hear enough."

Wilson nodded. "Just sayin'—they're bolder now. Feels different, like they want people to notice 'em. Ain't just kids playin' anymore."

Henry's grip tightened around the crate. He had felt that same difference on the bus this morning. The air was shifting, and the city was changing around them in ways he couldn't yet name. Henry bent to lift another crate, the rough wood biting into his palms through the thin gloves. He welcomed the strain in his arms, the ache in his back—it was the kind of pain he could control, the kind that made sense. The other kind—the sideways comments, the suspicion, the way men like McCaffrey hovered over him with more scrutiny than anyone else—that pain had no outlet. It sat in his chest like coals. Across the warehouse, McCaffrey found another target. A younger worker had stacked his load unevenly, and the supervisor's voice rang out sharp, chewing him apart for everyone to hear. The man ducked his head, red-faced, while the rest of the crew stole glances and said nothing. Henry watched, jaw tight, until Wilson nudged him with an elbow.

"Don't let that fool get in your head," Wilson murmured. "Man screams 'cause he's scared somebody might see he don't do a lick of real work himself."

Steven chuckled under his breath. "Amen to that."

Henry gave a faint nod. It wasn't that Wilson or Steven didn't see the difference in how McCaffrey treated him—they did. They just knew Henry wouldn't air it out loud. He had learned long ago that answering disrespect too quick only gave men like McCaffrey more reason to twist the knife.

The whistle blew, signaling break, and the three men made their way to the corner of the floor where the vending machines hummed. Wilson dropped into a chair, stretching his long legs. Steven tore open a bag of chips, offering it across the table.

"You hear about the bust on Tremont last night?" Wilson asked, leaning in. His voice lowered, though the hum of machines masked their talk. "Two crews went at it—gunshots rang out for ten minutes straight. Cops rolled in late, like always."

Steven nodded grimly. "Cousin of mine lives two blocks from there. Windows shook like the devil was outside."

Henry leaned back, arms crossed over his chest. He remembered the laughter on the bus that morning, the sharpness of it, the way it seemed to chase him down the street even after he stepped off. "They're gettin' reckless," he said.

Wilson's grin vanished entirely. "Nah, brother. Reckless is when you don't care who sees. This here? This is on purpose. They want to be seen. They want the whole city to know it's theirs."

The thought sat heavy in Henry's mind. He thought of Dani walking Kalee to school, of neighbors stepping out for groceries, of families trying to live without fear. He had seen what happened when young men thought they owned the block. It never stayed at the corners; it spread, swallowing streets like fire.

The break whistle sounded again, and the men rose. Back to the crates, back to the rhythm. But Henry felt something different now. The weight he lifted wasn't just wood and steel—it was the burden of knowing the storm outside was gathering speed, and sooner or later, it would demand more of him than silence.

The afternoon light spilled across the kitchen table, warm and soft, but Dani couldn't shake the unease that clung to her. She had just returned from the corner market, her tote bag still resting on the counter, filled with bread, apples, and the small things that kept the household running. Yet her mind wasn't on groceries. It was on the two young men who had been standing outside the store, laughing too loud, their eyes following her all the way inside.

Yvonne sat across from her, sipping coffee like it was a shield. "You hear about what went down last night?" she asked, setting the cup down with a soft clink.

Dani shook her head, brushing a strand of hair from her face. "No... what happened?"

"Tremont. Shootout between crews. Folks say it sounded like firecrackers, but it went on too long for that. Ten minutes straight of gunfire." Yvonne's voice dropped low, as though the walls might be listening. "Cops didn't even show till it was damn near over."

Dani pressed her lips together, heart tightening. She thought of Kalee's school, of the walk they made every morning, her little girl's hand nestled in hers. "It feels like it's getting closer," she whispered.

Yvonne leaned back, crossing her arms. "Closer? Honey, it *is* closer. Those boys hangin' near the store? They ain't just passin' time. They're watchin'. Lookin' for who's weak, who they can lean on. They're settin' up shop right under our noses."

Dani stared at the mug in front of her, her fingers tracing the rim. "I don't want Kalee growin' up thinkin' this is normal."

Yvonne's eyes softened, but her tone stayed sharp. "Then you better talk to Henry. He's gotta see what's happenin'. He can't just keep walkin' past it like it don't touch him."

Dani bristled, though not at Yvonne. "You think he don't see it? Every time he steps outside, it's on him. Every bus ride, every store, every damn step. He carries it enough for all of us."

The room went quiet, the hum of the refrigerator filling the space. Yvonne sighed, her hard edges softening. "I know, girl. I know he does. But it ain't fair. He shouldn't have to carry it alone."

Dani looked toward the hallway, where Kalee's soft laughter drifted from her bedroom, the sound of dolls clattering together in play. That laughter was the thin thread holding everything together, fragile and precious. Dani wrapped her hands around her coffee mug, holding it tight as if she could keep that laughter safe by sheer force of will.

"Fair or not," she said finally, her voice steady, "we're in it now. And Henry... he'll do what he has to. He always does."

Yvonne nodded slowly, her gaze steady. "Let's just pray it don't take more than he's got to give."

Yvonne leaned forward, her elbows pressing into the table, the steam from her coffee rising between them like a veil. "You know Mrs. Alvarez down on Walnut?" she asked, her voice taking on that careful cadence people use when bad news is about to land.

Dani nodded. "Her boy goes to church with us sometimes. Why?"

Yvonne lowered her voice further. "He got jumped. Right outside their own building. Three of 'em, maybe four. Took his phone, his shoes. Left him in the gutter till neighbors dragged him back inside. He's only fifteen, Dani. Fifteen."

The words sank into the room like stones. Dani's throat tightened, a sickness curling in her stomach. "Lord have mercy…" she whispered. She thought of Kalee's small sneakers by the door, the way her daughter's feet still dangled when she sat at the table. Fifteen sounded too close, too possible.

Yvonne didn't stop. She never did—she believed the only way to survive was to face the truth head-on. "And it ain't just the kids. Mr. Talbot, you know him—the old man with the cane, always sweepin' his stoop? They broke into his place last week. Took his TV, smashed his liquor cabinet. Left the door wide open. He's too scared to sleep now."

Dani closed her eyes, picturing the frail old man sweeping dust off brick like it mattered, keeping dignity alive with every careful stroke of his broom. "This block used to look out for each other," she said quietly. "Now it's like we're all just waiting our turn."

Yvonne's jaw set hard. "That's what happens when nobody pushes back. The gangs don't just take space—they take the air, the light, the peace. Pretty soon, you forget what quiet even feels like." She reached across the table, laying a hand over Dani's. "But listen, girl. Don't you ever let them see fear in your face. Fear's the first door they walk through."

Dani's eyes lifted, locking with Yvonne's. She wanted to say she wasn't afraid—that she could be steel, that her family's love was stronger than the streets clawing at their windows. But she couldn't lie, not to Yvonne, not to herself. She was afraid. Afraid in a way that lived in her bones, that whispered every time Kalee walked out the front door with her backpack bouncing against her shoulders.

The sound of a siren wailed in the distance, sharp and fleeting, then faded into the hum of the city. Dani held onto Yvonne's hand a moment longer, gripping it like an anchor.

"I'm not scared for me," Dani said finally, her voice trembling but firm. "I'm scared for her."

Yvonne's gaze softened, lines of worry deepening on her face. She gave Dani's hand a squeeze. "Then we make sure she don't see it. We keep her laughter safe, no matter what it costs us."

The two women sat in silence after that, the weight of their words heavy, but underneath it all, the sound of

Kalee's laughter floated through the hallway—a fragile reminder of what was at stake.

The front door closed with a soft thud, leaving the apartment in a silence that felt larger than the space itself. Yvonne's absence lingered in the air, her words echoing like the tail of a storm. Dani stood by the table, her hand resting on the rim of her coffee mug, the liquid gone cold. She stared at it as though the answers might rise from the dark surface if she looked long enough.

The clock ticked in the kitchen, steady and indifferent. From down the hall came the faint sound of Kalee singing to her dolls, her voice light and unbroken, carrying none of the heaviness that gripped her mother's chest. Dani pressed her lips together, fighting back the swell in her throat. That sound—innocent, free—was everything she was trying to protect. And yet the world outside seemed determined to crush it.

She crossed to the window, pulling the curtain back just enough to peer at the street below. The late afternoon sun cast long shadows on the cracked pavement. Two boys leaned against a lamppost, their hoodies up despite the heat, passing something back and forth between them. Their laughter drifted upward, sharp and mean, cutting into the fragile quiet of her home.

Dani let the curtain fall, her hand trembling slightly as it brushed the fabric. She thought of Henry—broad, steady, always carrying the weight without letting it break him. He walked through suspicion every day, through stares, through voices that cut. And yet, when he came home, he left it at the door, stepping into their cocoon with a smile for Kalee, a soft touch for her.

But how long could one man hold that line? How long before the weight bent him, before the pressure outside leaked in and cracked the walls they had built together? Dani sat back down at the table, folding her arms on its surface and lowering her head onto them. She closed her eyes and let the fear wash over her, if only for a moment. Alone, she didn't have to hide it. Alone, she could admit the truth: she was terrified. Not of dying, not even of losing what little they had—but of what this world might do to Henry, to Kalee, to the love that bound them together.

The refrigerator hummed, the clock ticked, and from the hallway came another burst of childish laughter. Dani lifted her head, blinking against the sting in her eyes. She whispered into the empty room, her voice barely more than breath.

"God, just keep them safe."

Her fingers curled into fists, her resolve pulling tight around the fear. She would not let Kalee see her break. She would not let Henry carry it alone. And when the time came—because she knew it was coming—she would stand beside him, no matter the cost.

The front door rattled faintly with the wind, as though reminding her the outside world was never far. Dani straightened her back, wiped her eyes with the heel of her hand, and forced herself to breathe steady again. The storm might be building, but she would meet it head-on. Dani pushed herself up from the table, wiping the last trace of dampness from her eyes before walking down the hallway toward Kalee's room. The little girl's voice floated out in a singsong melody, her laughter punctuating the made-up story she was spinning for her dolls. Dani paused in the doorway, leaning against the frame, just watching for a moment.

Kalee sat cross-legged on the floor, her curls bouncing as she shifted her dolls around. She was mid-scene, her voice pitched high for one character, low for another, weaving them into some adventure only she could see. The innocence of it—so unguarded, so untouched by the heaviness outside—made Dani's chest ache.

"Whatcha got going on in here?" Dani asked softly, stepping into the room.

Kalee's head snapped up, her face lighting with a grin. "Mama! They're going to the castle! But the mean dragon's waitin' for them." She held up one of the dolls, its plastic hair frayed from too much love. "See? This one's gonna fight him."

Dani knelt down, folding her legs beside her daughter. "That's brave," she said, reaching to smooth a curl from Kalee's forehead. "But sometimes fighting isn't the only way. Sometimes... the dragon just needs to be talked to."

Kalee giggled. "Dragons don't listen, Mama. They roar too much."

Dani smiled, pulling the little girl close. "Maybe. But maybe they roar because they're scared too."

The words slipped out before she could catch them, and for a moment Dani felt the weight of her own truth settle heavy in her chest. She hugged Kalee tighter, burying her face in the warm scent of her daughter's hair.

Kalee squirmed, laughing. "Mama, you're squishin' me!"

"Good," Dani said, planting a kiss on her cheek. "You need to be squished sometimes, so you remember how loved you are."

Kalee tilted her head back, her eyes wide and serious in that way only children could manage. "Mama? Are the boys outside the dragon?"

The question pierced straight through Dani's heart. She hesitated, forcing her smile to hold. "No, baby. They're just boys. Not dragons."

"But they're loud," Kalee insisted. "And they look mean."

Dani swallowed hard. "That's just how they act. But you don't need to worry about them. Daddy and I will keep you safe. That's our job."

Kalee seemed satisfied with that, her grin returning as she pressed the doll into Dani's hands. "Then you be the princess, okay? She needs help."

Dani laughed softly, taking the doll. "Princess, huh? I don't know if I'm the princess type."

"You are," Kalee said simply, with the conviction only a child could give. "You're my princess."

The words melted Dani's heart. She pulled her daughter into her lap, holding her close as the dolls lay forgotten between them. For a few precious minutes, the world outside—the gangs, the sirens, the shadows gathering on the block—didn't exist. There was only the warmth of her child's laughter and the fragile, glowing cocoon of love they had built inside these walls.

Later, when Kalee finally grew tired of her dolls and curled into bed for an afternoon nap, the apartment slipped into that hushed stillness only children could create—the kind that felt fragile, temporary, like a bubble waiting to burst. Dani lingered at the doorway, watching her daughter's chest rise and fall, her tiny hands clutching the worn blanket she refused to sleep without.

The word "dragon" lingered in Dani's mind. Kalee had spoken it so easily, with that child's certainty that monsters were real and castles needed defending. But Dani knew the dragons outside didn't breathe fire or flap wings across the sky. They leaned on lampposts, wore hoodies in the heat, and laughed too loud when mothers passed with grocery bags. They spread across corners and sidewalks, taking pieces of the neighborhood like teeth sinking into flesh.

She eased the door shut and stepped back into the hallway, her bare feet silent against the worn linoleum. The apartment felt both too small and too big at once— walls pressing close while the silence stretched heavy. She thought of Henry, steady as stone, shouldering burdens she wished she could lift from him. He had always been the one to quiet her fears, the one to remind her of the love they built inside these walls. But even stone cracked under enough pressure.

The dragons weren't at the edge of the city anymore. They were circling closer, testing the walls of her home. She could feel their heat in the stares, in the whispers of neighbors, in the sirens that passed more often now, like wolves pacing outside a gate.

Dani crossed to the window again, parting the curtain just enough to see the block below. The two boys had gone, but in their place sat a bottle tipped on its side at the curb, glittering shards of glass catching the sun. Someone's trash bag had split open, spilling wrappers and bones into the gutter. A stray dog nosed through it, unbothered. Life carried on, messy and unkind.

She pressed her forehead against the glass, closing her eyes. "Dragons don't listen, Mama," Kalee had said. Maybe her daughter was right. Maybe the noise outside wasn't born of fear, but of hunger—of boys trying to prove something with their teeth bared. And maybe no words, no reason, no kindness would turn them back.

But still, Dani wanted to believe in talking to the dragon. She wanted to believe that the walls of her home, the laughter of her child, the steady hands of her husband, were enough to keep the fire out.

Her reflection in the glass looked back at her, tired but unbroken. She placed a hand over her chest, steadying her breath. For Kalee's sake, she had to believe. For Henry's sake, she had to hold the line.

The rattle of keys at the front door startled her, pulling her back from thought. Henry was home. And with his return, the cocoon of family would close around her again—for a little while, at least.

Henry fit the key into the lock with the same steady hand he always did, but his shoulders carried a weight that didn't show in the motion. The walk from the bus stop had been like every other—eyes following him, voices carrying just enough edge to set his jaw tight. A police cruiser had rolled slow past the block, its spotlight lingering on him a second too long before sliding away. By the time he reached the stoop, his body was wound tight as a cable, every muscle braced for the next slight, the next confrontation.

The door clicked open, and the scent of home reached him before the light did—coffee gone cold, faint detergent, the sweetness of Kalee's bubblegum shampoo lingering in the air. He stepped inside and let the door close behind him, pressing the city out. The tension in his chest eased, just a fraction, like air hissing from a valve.

Dani was there in the small living room, straightening a cushion she had already fluffed twice. Her eyes found him immediately. She didn't ask how his day was; she didn't need to. She could read it in the set of his shoulders, the way his brow carried a heaviness that work alone couldn't explain.

"You're home," she said softly, as though naming it made it true.

Henry exhaled, setting his lunch pail down by the door. "Yeah. I'm home."

Her smile was faint, but it reached her eyes, and that was enough. She crossed the room, brushing her hand against his arm in that quiet way that always grounded him. It wasn't dramatic, wasn't demanding—it was just there, steady, reminding him that here, in these walls, he wasn't a target. He was hers.

Kalee barreled down the hallway before he could take another step, her socked feet sliding on the floor as she threw herself into his legs. "Daddy!"

Henry laughed, the sound breaking free from a place he hadn't realized was locked tight all day. He scooped her up easily, pressing his face into her curls. The tension slid further away, replaced by the small weight of his daughter's arms locked around his neck.

"Hey, princess," he murmured. "You takin' care of Mama today?"

Kalee nodded solemnly, her little face serious. "I told her dragons don't listen. But she said maybe they roar 'cause they're scared. Is that true, Daddy?"

Henry blinked, caught off guard by the words, then glanced at Dani. She stood with her arms folded lightly, her eyes watching him. Something unspoken passed between them, but he let his focus stay on Kalee.

"Maybe Mama's right," he said slowly. "Sometimes the things that roar the loudest are the ones hurtin' the most."

Kalee considered this with the weight of a judge, then grinned and tucked her head against his shoulder.

In that moment, with his daughter safe in his arms and Dani's gaze steady on him, Henry felt the day's tightness unspool. Outside, the city pressed hard against their door, but here—inside these four walls—he could breathe again.

Henry carried Kalee over to the couch, her laughter bubbling as he swung her gently into the cushions. She bounced once, then scrambled upright, tugging at his sleeve. "Daddy, play princess with me. Mama said you gotta help fight the dragon."

He chuckled, loosening the laces of his boots. "Oh, so that's my job now, huh? Fightin' dragons?"

Kalee nodded fiercely, curls bobbing. "You're the knight. Mama's the princess. I'm the queen."

"Queen, huh?" Henry's smile spread wide, the day's weight dissolving with every word. "Well, if the queen commands it..." He gave a mock bow, and she erupted in giggles.

Dani stood in the doorway watching them, arms folded loosely, a smile tugging at her lips. The sight of Henry down on one knee, letting their daughter crown him with a plastic tiara from her toy chest, made something ease in her chest. For a few minutes, it was as though the world outside had no claim on them.

Henry let Kalee direct the game, slaying imaginary beasts with a broom handle held like a sword. He roared and stumbled when she struck him, falling dramatically onto the couch while she laughed so hard she could barely breathe. Dani finally stepped in, declaring with a playful sternness that the knight couldn't bleed all over her clean cushions.

The laughter carried them through dinner. It wasn't anything special—rice, beans, leftover chicken—but Henry made a show of pretending it was a feast, lifting each bite as though it were the finest meal he'd ever tasted. Kalee beamed at the attention, insisting on telling a long story about her dolls' castle adventure. Henry listened intently, nodding as though every twist of her tale was the most serious matter in the world.

Dani watched them, her heart pulled in two directions. On one hand, she wanted to stay here forever, wrapped in the glow of her husband's smile and her daughter's bright chatter. On the other, she couldn't ignore the truth Yvonne's words had carved into her that afternoon—the world outside was shifting, and this fragile cocoon might not hold forever.

After dinner, Henry helped Kalee with her homework at the kitchen table while Dani washed dishes. He leaned over her little notebook, patient as she stumbled through spelling words, his large hands turning the pages with surprising gentleness.

"You're gettin' smarter every day," he told her. "Soon you'll be teachin' me."

Kalee grinned, proud. "Then you gotta listen real good, Daddy."

"I always do, my princess."

When bedtime came, Henry carried her into her room, tucking the blanket around her shoulders. She demanded two kisses—one from Mama, one from Daddy—before closing her eyes. Her breathing softened quickly, drifting into sleep.

Henry lingered a moment, watching her small chest rise and fall, before closing the door quietly. He turned to Dani, meeting her eyes in the dim hallway. For a heartbeat, nothing needed to be said.

In that silence, Henry felt it again: the home they had built, fragile but fierce. Here, he was not just a man against the world. He was a husband, a father, a knight. The apartment had settled into its nighttime rhythm, soft and steady. Kalee's gentle breathing drifted from her bedroom, the hum of the refrigerator filled the silence, and the faint tick of the hallway clock marked each passing second. Henry leaned back into the couch, his body loosening after the long day, while Dani folded herself against him, her head resting on his shoulder. For a moment, it felt like peace.

Then the sound came—sharp voices outside, carrying up from the street. Laughter at first, then something harsher, the kind of tone that made the hairs on Henry's arms stir. Before he could rise, the sudden flash of blue light streaked across the walls, followed by the blip of a horn. The police cruiser rolled slow, its presence filling the block like a warning.

Dani straightened, her hand tightening on Henry's arm. She crossed quickly to the window, parting the curtain with careful fingers. The flash of lights spun against the buildings, painting brick and glass in shifting blue. She leaned forward, trying to see past the glare, but the cruiser's spotlight shifted away before she could make sense of what it was chasing. Only shadows and echoes remained, leaving her with more questions than answers.

"What is it?" Henry asked from the couch, his voice low but steady.

Dani let the curtain fall back into place, shaking her head. "I don't know. I couldn't see. The lights—everything looked blurred. Then they moved on."

Henry watched her cross the room, her movements sharp with unease. She sat beside him again, but her eyes kept darting toward the window as though the blue glow might return at any second. He reached for her hand, large and warm, closing around hers with a quiet strength.

"Don't trouble yourself over what you didn't see," he said softly. "That's their noise out there, not ours. In here, we keep our peace."

Dani searched his face, her lips pressing tight. "But what if it don't stay out there? What if it finds its way in?"

Henry leaned closer, his forehead brushing hers. His voice was steady, anchored, the same tone he used when guiding Kalee through her fears. "Then it'll find me waitin'. And you know I don't break easy."

She closed her eyes, drawing in a long breath, letting the weight of his words settle into her bones. His calm didn't erase the unease curling in her stomach, but it softened it, dulled the edge enough for her to breathe again.

Outside, the cruiser's engine faded into the distance, swallowed by the night. The voices on the block quieted too, whether dispersed by the lights or simply tired of the game. The silence that returned was heavier than before, but it was silence nonetheless.

Henry kept her hand in his, squeezing once, firm and sure. "We hold the line," he murmured. "That's what we do."

Dani nodded, leaning back into him. For now, it was enough. The blue light had gone, but its echo still clung to the walls. Dani stayed pressed against Henry, her hand resting over his heart as if to anchor herself in the steady rhythm beneath. The city might rattle their windows, but inside this small apartment, his presence was the fortress.

For a long moment, neither spoke. The silence wasn't empty—it was full of everything they both carried but rarely named. Finally, Dani tilted her face up, her eyes searching his. "Sometimes I feel like the world's just waiting for us to slip," she whispered. "Like no matter what we do, it's already decided what we are."

Henry's jaw tightened. He had felt that truth all day—on the bus, in the store, under McCaffrey's gaze at work. But hearing it in Dani's voice struck deeper than all of it.

He brushed his thumb over the back of her hand.

"World don't get to decide who we are. Not here. Not in this home. We choose that."

Her eyes glistened, reflecting the dim light. "And if it comes knocking?"

"Then we answer together." His tone was quiet, but it carried weight. "I won't let nothin' touch you or Kalee. That's my word."

Dani wanted to believe the promise was enough, and in that moment, wrapped in his steadiness, it almost was. She laid her head back on his shoulder, drawing strength from the way he simply existed, unbent despite the pressure pressing in from every direction.

Henry let his gaze drift to the closed hallway door where Kalee slept. He thought of her laugh, of the way she had crowned him a knight earlier, and felt a pang in his chest. Children had a way of naming truths without knowing. Dragons, she'd said. Maybe that's what the streets were—monsters dressed in the skin of boys, roaring because they wanted to be feared.

He exhaled, long and low, then looked back at Dani. Her hair brushed his cheek, and he kissed her temple, lingering there. "You and me," he murmured. "We've been through storms before. This one won't be no different."

Dani turned toward him, her eyes steady now, the fear softened but not gone. "I don't want to lose what we got, Henry."

"You won't," he said simply. "Not while I'm breathin'."

The conviction in his voice wrapped around her like armor. They sat that way for a long time, hands clasped, bodies leaning together against the quiet. Outside, the city continued its restless churn—cars passing, a dog barking down the block, someone shouting in the distance. But inside, in that fragile circle they had built, the noise fell away.

For Dani, the fear dulled into something manageable. For Henry, the tension in his chest loosened another notch. They both knew the storm was coming. But for tonight, they had each other, and that was enough to push the darkness back one more time.

The apartment was quiet long after Dani drifted into sleep, her breathing soft and even beside him. But Henry's eyes stayed open, tracing the faint cracks in the ceiling above their bed. The silence pressed heavy, not comforting now but expectant, as though the city itself were holding its breath.

He turned onto his back, folding his hands across his chest. The sounds of the block seeped in through the thin walls—distant engines revving, laughter too sharp, the occasional pop of something that could have been fireworks but made his muscles tense all the same. He knew the difference, though. Fireworks didn't echo off brick like that.

His mind slipped backward, unbidden, to a different night under a different sky. Afghanistan. The desert air had been bone-dry, carrying the smell of dust and diesel. He remembered lying flat in the dirt, his rifle pressed close, the stars cold and endless above him. Around him, men had waited in silence, the kind that made every rustle sound like thunder. Waiting for the next strike. Waiting for the unseen enemy to decide when the night would break.

The feeling was the same now. Lying in his own bed, in his own city, beside the woman he loved, Henry felt that same taut line in his chest, that same awareness of danger pressing close but just out of sight. The block outside wasn't a battlefield, not officially. But the tension smelled the same. The way voices carried through the night, the way shadows seemed to hold more than just darkness—he knew those signs. Trouble was circling.

He glanced at Dani, her face soft in sleep, the worry lines eased for now. He envied her that rest, but he couldn't share it. Soldiers didn't sleep easy when the air felt like this.

His thoughts drifted to Kalee, tucked safe in her bed. She was too young to understand how close danger could creep, too innocent to know that monsters sometimes wore familiar faces. Henry had seen boys barely older than her cousins carrying rifles overseas, eyes burning with a fire they didn't yet understand. And he had seen the wreckage left behind when fire wasn't enough to fill the hunger.

He exhaled slowly, forcing his body to stay still, to keep the tension from waking Dani. But his eyes never closed. He kept watch the way he had years ago in the desert—alert, restless, unwilling to trust the quiet. He told himself it was different now, that this was home, that no strike would come crashing through their door in the dark.

But the truth pressed against him like the weight of the ceiling above: Boston had its own wars, its own enemies waiting in the shadows. And if the night broke, if the storm finally came pounding at their door, he knew he'd have to fight it the same way he always had—steady, unflinching, refusing to bend.

Henry stared into the darkness, listening, waiting. Sleep never came.

The morning sun slanted through the blinds, pale and thin, unable to chase away the weight of the night. Henry rose quietly, careful not to wake Dani, and moved through the apartment with the measured steps of a man who hadn't slept but refused to show it. Kalee stirred only when he leaned down to kiss her forehead before she sat at the table with a bowl of cereal, her hair wild and her eyes still heavy with sleep.

By the time Henry stepped onto the stoop, the block was already buzzing. A cruiser idled at the corner, its blue lights muted but still flashing, washing the brick rowhouses in a weary pulse. Two officers stood on the sidewalk, clipboards in hand, moving from door to door. Their voices carried low, clipped, rehearsed.

Across the street, Mrs. Alvarez clutched her robe tight, shaking her head quickly at whatever was being asked. The younger officer scribbled notes, while the older one scanned the street like he expected the pavement itself to give him answers.

Henry squinted toward the commotion down the block. Yellow tape sagged between two lampposts near the CVS. The front windows were gone, glass scattered like ice across the sidewalk. A car—what was left of it—sat halfway lodged in the wall, its hood crumpled, smoke stains blackening the brick above. Word spread fast through the murmurs of neighbors: someone had driven straight through the storefront in the night, hooked chains around the ATM, and dragged it out like a prize. Henry felt his stomach tighten. Bold. That wasn't desperation—it was a statement.

One of the officers glanced up, eyes narrowing as they landed on him. They crossed the street together, the younger one flipping to a fresh page on his clipboard.

"Morning," the older one said, his tone flat, official. "You live here?"

Henry kept his stance relaxed, his hands at his sides. "Yeah."

"See or hear anything around three, four in the morning?"

Henry shook his head. "No. Just heard sirens after it was done."

The younger officer studied him longer than necessary, pen poised over paper but unmoving. Henry met his eyes evenly, refusing to shrink or flare. He'd been looked at like that before—overseas at checkpoints, back here on sidewalks. He knew what suspicion felt like when it had nothing to stand on but skin.

Finally, the older officer cleared his throat. "Alright. If you remember anything, give us a call." He held out a card, which Henry accepted without looking at it before slipping it into his pocket.

They moved on, knocking at the next door.

From behind him, Dani's voice carried softly through the open window. "What happened?"

Henry turned just enough to meet her worried eyes. "Smash-and-grab at the CVS. Took the ATM."

She exhaled, shoulders sagging. "That close..."

Henry stepped back inside, closing the door behind him. "Yeah," he said quietly, his jaw set. "Too close."

Henry closed the door with a firm click, shutting out the sight of flashing lights and nervous neighbors. The sound of it made Dani flinch, though she tried to cover it by moving toward the counter, picking up a dish towel she didn't need. Her eyes followed him as he set his keys down, his shoulders stiff beneath his shirt.

"What kind of people do that?" she asked, her voice sharp but trembling underneath. "Drive a car into a store? Like the world's theirs to take?"

Henry pulled out a chair at the table and sat heavily, running a hand over his face. "The kind that don't care who watches. That's the point. Bold like that—it ain't just about money. It's about lettin' everyone know they runnin' the streets."

Dani sank into the chair across from him, the towel still clutched in her hands. "So now what? We just... live with it? With people smashing stores, dragging ATMs down the block like trophies?"

Henry met her eyes. "We don't got much choice, Dani. We keep our heads down. We look after each other. That's how we make it through."

Her lips pressed tight, a storm brewing in her gaze. "That's what Yvonne said yesterday. Keep our heads down. Don't show fear. But what if that's not enough anymore? What if keeping quiet just lets them get closer?"

Henry didn't answer right away. He stared at the tabletop, tracing the faint scratches and knife marks etched into the wood over the years. The table had seen family dinners, Kalee's first scribbled drawings, late nights when bills stacked higher than paychecks. It was the heart of their home, and now even it felt like it carried the weight of the streets pressing in.

Finally, he lifted his head. "I've seen what happens when you try to fight every battle head-on. Back overseas, some nights you had to hold position, no matter how much you wanted to strike back. If you broke cover too soon, you lost everything."

Dani's eyes softened, but the fear didn't leave. "And if holding position means the fight comes through our door?"

Henry reached across the table, prying the towel gently from her hands and taking them into his own. His grip was steady, grounding. "Then it finds me first. Not you. Not Kalee. Me."

Her throat tightened, tears threatening. She shook her head. "You can't carry it all alone, Henry."

"I can carry enough," he said firmly.

The silence between them stretched, broken only by the hum of the refrigerator and the distant murmur of voices outside. Dani squeezed his hands back, searching his face for something—an answer, a promise, maybe just the steadiness she always found there.

"I just don't want her growin' up thinking this is the way the world is," she whispered.

Henry leaned forward, his voice low, certain. "Then we teach her different. No matter what's out there, in here she learns love first. That's what she carries with her."

For a moment, the storm outside receded, and all that remained was the fragile strength between them.

By late afternoon, the block had settled into its uneasy rhythm—kids shouting down the sidewalk, the hum of radios from open windows, the faint smell of fried food drifting out of a corner kitchen. But beneath it all, Henry felt the shift. He always did. The city had a way of telling on itself if you knew how to listen.

He stood on the stoop, lunch pail in hand, waiting for the bus that groaned down the avenue every half hour. His eyes wandered across the street, down toward the narrow alley that cut between their brownstone and the next. It was a service lane really, meant for city workers hauling trash bins and delivery trucks easing through

with boxes for the corner stores. But now it wasn't
empty.

Three boys leaned against the wall, their hoods up, the
glow of a cigarette ember flaring as it passed between
them. Their laughter was low, sharp, not the kind that
belonged to kids killing time but the kind that belonged
to boys who thought they owned whatever ground they
stood on. Henry's jaw tightened. That alley had been
nothing yesterday, just cracked pavement and the stink
of garbage. Now it was theirs.

He shifted his stance, watching without staring. One of
the boys glanced up, meeting his gaze for half a second
before smirking and turning back to the others. A
message in the look: *We see you. This is ours now.*

The growl of an engine drew Henry's attention just as a
black SUV rolled slowly into the mouth of the alley. Its
windows were tinted dark, the kind that gave nothing
away. The boys straightened, their postures changing,
alert now. Henry's chest tightened as the SUV idled, its
grill glinting under the afternoon sun. Something was
exchanged—he couldn't see what, only the shift of
hands, the faint movement of shadows behind the
glass.

He leaned forward slightly, trying to catch more, every
instinct sharpening the way it used to when he was on
patrol overseas. He didn't need details to know what it
meant. SUVs like that didn't cruise alleys for small talk.

The hiss of brakes pulled his attention away. His bus
screeched to a stop at the curb, the doors folding open

with a wheeze. Henry hesitated, one foot on the first step, his eyes still drawn toward the alley. The SUV hadn't moved. The boys hadn't either.

He climbed aboard, the driver giving him a nod. As the bus rumbled forward, Henry turned in his seat, leaning low to peer out of the window. The angle was bad, the glass streaked and dirty, but he searched anyway. Nothing. The alley stretched back into shadow, empty as if it had swallowed whatever he'd seen whole. The SUV was gone. The boys too.

Henry sat back slowly, his hand tightening around the rail beside him. The city had a way of showing you just enough to let you know trouble was real—then snatching the rest away, leaving you with questions and the weight of knowing.

The bus rumbled forward, its engine grumbling like an old man's cough, but Henry barely heard it. His mind stayed in that alleyway, replaying the flash of shadows inside the SUV, the cocky tilt of the boys' shoulders as if they'd just been knighted. He leaned against the window, the city sliding past in blurs of brick and neon, and let his thoughts dig into old memories.

He had seen this kind of thing before. Not just in Afghanistan, where convoys slipped in and out of villages like ghosts, dropping off supplies that turned boys into soldiers overnight. He had seen it right here in Boston too, long before he wore a uniform.

Back then, he was just a kid on the block, watching the older boys ride by in cars too clean, shoes too new, pockets too heavy to come from any nine-to-five. They were kings of the sidewalk, and they knew it. They carried themselves like the world owed them a crown, and the neighborhood—hungry, desperate—bowed without ever saying a word.

Henry remembered the way the corner shifted when those cars pulled up. One minute, kids playing ball, women gossiping, men smoking and talking work. The next, silence. Eyes turned. Everyone knew better than to stand too close when money or goods changed hands. Even as a boy, Henry had understood that nothing was free. Every bag dropped in an alley, every handshake with something folded inside—it all came with a price. Now, staring out the dirty bus glass, he recognized the same rhythm in the boys leaning against his brownstone. They weren't just hanging out. They were being groomed, tested, pulled into something bigger. The SUV was a signal, same as those clean cars he remembered—someone above them was watching, investing.

The bus hit a pothole, jolting Henry in his seat. He rubbed his jaw, feeling the tension coiled tight there. His instincts told him the block was shifting faster than most folks realized. Smash-and-grabs at the CVS, cops canvassing in daylight, SUVs feeding kids in alleys—it wasn't random. It was a chain, each link locking tighter around the neighborhood.

He thought of Dani's words at the table, of her fear spilling out despite all her strength. He thought of Kalee asking about dragons, her innocence still whole but already sensing shadows. Henry pressed his hand against the cool glass of the window, watching the streets roll by, crowded with faces that looked weary, distracted, beaten down.

This wasn't just noise anymore. It was organization. It was the kind of move that said the gangs weren't satisfied with corners—they wanted the block, the stores, the fear. They wanted it all.

Henry exhaled slowly, his breath fogging a small patch of glass. The city gave him no answers, only more questions. But one truth settled heavy in his chest: the storm wasn't creeping anymore. It was coming fast, and sooner or later, it would force him to choose how he'd meet it.

The plant smelled of steel and sweat when Henry walked in, same as always. Forklifts whined in reverse, boots scraped on concrete, and the steady grind of machinery filled the cavernous space. Yet beneath the noise, Henry carried the silence of that alley with him. It clung to him like the smoke that never left his clothes after a long shift.

Wilson spotted him first, tossing a wave as he stacked crates. "Man, you look like you didn't sleep a wink. That kid of yours keepin' you up?"

Henry shook his head, setting his lunch pail down. "Wasn't her. Streets been loud."

Steven strolled over, wiping his hands on a rag, his eyes sharp. "Ain't just your block, bro. Word is, it's happenin' everywhere."

Henry paused, lifting a brow. "Everywhere?"

Steven leaned closer, lowering his voice beneath the machinery's grind. "Mass Ave to Fields Corner—folks sayin' the same thing. High-end cars rollin' up on corners, slow and clean. Windows blacked out, like they don't want nobody seein' faces. Boys standin' around one minute, actin' like kids. Next minute, those SUVs show, and suddenly they standin' taller, actin' like they just got crowned."

Wilson let out a low whistle. "Hell, even in Roxbury last night. My cousin swears he seen a black Escalade pull up outside his building. Kids was laughin' like they just hit the lotto. Said they walked away with sneakers fresh out the box."

Henry tightened his grip on the crate in his hands, the wood digging into his palms. He thought of the smirk on the boy's face in the alley that morning, the quick shift of hands near the SUV's window. His gut told him it was all connected.

Steven kept talking, his words coming in a rush. "This ain't no random handouts either. They ain't just givin' kids gifts outta kindness. Nah, this is recruitment. Same way the gangs always done it, just bigger now. Flash the money, the cars, the power—make 'em feel like kings before they even earn their stripes."

Henry set the crate down harder than he meant to, the thud echoing over the machinery for a moment. "And once they're in, there ain't no gettin' out."

Steven nodded grimly. "Exactly. They ain't playin' small no more. They want whole neighborhoods tied up."

Wilson spat to the side, shaking his head. "Cops act like they don't see it. Or maybe they do and just don't care till it's too late. Either way, it's gettin' bold."

Henry rubbed the back of his neck, feeling the weight settle heavier on his shoulders. He thought of Dani's fear, of Kalee's innocent question about dragons, of the way silence had followed that SUV's arrival like the whole block knew to hush.

If this was true—if it wasn't just his block but the city itself being swallowed one corner at a time—then the storm was bigger than he'd imagined. And waiting it out, holding position like he had told Dani, might not be enough.

The clang of a dropped wrench echoed off the concrete floor, followed by a curse that was quickly swallowed by the grind of machines. Wilson, Steven, and Henry huddled near the loading dock, voices low enough not to carry. The talk didn't stop once it started; it spilled fast, like water pushing through cracks.

"My uncle works nights near South Bay," Wilson said, leaning against the pallet jack. "Swears he seen two different rides pull up in the same hour. Mercedes this time, not no old junk. Boys walked away with pockets fat. He told me straight—Boston's bein' carved up block by block."

Steven shook his head, his brow furrowed deep. "It's the same pattern everywhere. First they give a taste—sneakers, cash, maybe a phone. Then they come back askin' for favors. Run a bag across town, keep a lookout, don't ask questions. By then the kids already hooked."

Henry listened, but his mind was half elsewhere. The SUV in the alley. Dani's nervous eyes at the window. Kalee's voice asking about dragons. He rubbed the back of his neck, feeling the ache of sleeplessness gnaw at him, but what kept him restless wasn't just fatigue. It was knowing that bold moves didn't stay contained—they spread.

Wilson leaned closer. "You know what's worse? Folks actin' like it don't matter 'cause it ain't on their doorstep yet. But it don't take long. One corner at a time. That's how it always starts."

Henry's hand found his phone in his pocket before he realized he'd made the decision. He stepped away from the noise of the dock, thumbing the worn screen, pressing Dani's number. The ring buzzed in his ear, each second heavier than the last.

Finally, her voice answered, warm but a little hurried. "Henry? Everything alright?"

He closed his eyes, letting the sound of her settle him. "Yeah, I just—wanted to check in. How's everything?"

There was a pause, then the faint sound of traffic behind her words. "It's fine. I dropped Kalee off at school already. I'm on my way in now. Why, what's wrong?" Henry shook his head though she couldn't see it. "Nothin'. Just needed to hear your voice."

She softened, her tone gentler now. "You didn't sleep, did you?"

"Not much," he admitted, his voice low. "But I'm good. Long as you two are good."

"We're fine," she assured. "Go on with your day. Don't worry yourself sick."

Henry let out a breath he hadn't realized he'd been holding, the tension loosening a notch in his chest. "Alright. Be safe."

"You too," Dani said, and the call ended.

He stood there a moment longer, phone still in hand, the hum of machines filling the silence left behind. Relief washed through him, thin but real, like a patch of sunlight breaking through cloud. But beneath it ran the deeper current of unease, the knowledge that safety was fragile, and every day the line holding it together grew thinner.

Henry slipped his phone back into his pocket, drawing a steady breath before turning toward the floor again. The relief of hearing Dani's voice still lingered, but it sat fragile in his chest, easily shaken by the noise and weight of the warehouse.

"Hey!" The bark came from across the aisle. McCaffrey. His stocky frame was planted near the forklift, arms crossed, his voice carrying over the machines with practiced disdain. "You takin' a break on company time, Mann? Or you plan on actually earnin' that paycheck?"

A few heads turned. Henry felt the eyes but kept his expression flat, calm. He walked back toward the pallet without hurry, gripping the dolly's handle with quiet precision. "Made a quick call," he said evenly. "Back at it now."

McCaffrey snorted, shaking his head as though the very sound of Henry's voice irritated him. "Always an excuse." He turned to the younger workers nearby, his tone sharp and performative. "Lesson for you boys— some folks think showin' up is enough. But real men put in the work."

Henry clenched his jaw but said nothing. Words were wasted on men who needed to step on someone else just to feel tall. He shifted another crate onto the dolly, muscles straining, letting the rhythm of labor smother the sting of insult.

Wilson sidled up as McCaffrey stalked off, muttering under his breath. "Man's a damn vulture. Picks at you 'cause he knows you won't bite back."

Henry adjusted the crate, setting it firm. "Let him. I'm not here for him."

Steven joined in, hefting another box onto the stack. "Yeah, but we see it. Don't matter how much he runs his mouth—ain't a soul here works harder than you, Henry."

Henry gave a short nod, grateful but unwilling to let the words linger. Praise didn't lighten the load; it just reminded him there was a load to bear. He bent his back to the work, sliding into the grind, his breath steady and measured.

For the next hour, the warehouse swallowed him whole. The noise, the weight, the sweat—it all blurred into a single rhythm. He welcomed it, letting the strain burn through the restless energy left over from the night. Every crate lifted was something he could control. Every stack finished was proof he still held the line, even if the world outside spun faster and meaner than before.

But the rhythm couldn't silence everything. Now and then his mind slipped back—to the boys in the alley, the dark tint of the SUV window, Dani's voice on the phone, telling him they were fine. Each memory was a thread, tying the grind of his day to the storm gathering outside. Henry lifted another crate, setting it with precision. The work didn't care about worry. The work demanded his body, his time, his strength. And for now, that was enough to keep him moving forward.

The hum of copy machines and the soft clatter of keyboards filled the office, a rhythm Dani had come to rely on. Order, schedules, paperwork—things she could measure and control. But this morning, that rhythm was broken.

By the time she returned from the breakroom with her mug of coffee, a small group of women from her team had gathered near the filing cabinets, their voices hushed but urgent. Dani paused, leaning against the doorframe to listen.

"You hear about that CVS on Tremont?" one woman said, her eyes wide. "Drove a car right through the glass. Like somethin' out of a movie."

"I heard it was an ATM," another replied. "Hooked chains to it and dragged it out like nothin'. Broad daylight after too—neighbors saw everything."

A third woman shook her head, clutching her sweater tight around her shoulders. "It ain't just Tremont. My cousin over in Dorchester says crews are runnin' wild on Fields Corner. And the cops? They show up late, same as always. Like they don't care 'til it's over."

The others murmured agreement, worry etched into their voices.

Dani took a sip of coffee, letting them talk. She wasn't one to squash conversation outright, not when it was clear these women needed to vent. Fear had a way of spreading faster than fact, and sometimes letting it spill out was better than bottling it.

Still, as she listened, her stomach knotted. The same fears Yvonne had voiced, the same unease Henry carried in his shoulders, were now here—in the office, in the voices of women who just wanted to get through a workday without looking over their shoulders.

Finally, Dani straightened, her voice cutting gently into the group. "Alright, ladies. I know it's got everybody's nerves on edge, but let's get back to it. We've got deadlines, and the work won't finish itself."

They nodded reluctantly, dispersing back to their desks. The hum of machines and typing returned, but it wasn't the same as before. The edge lingered, like a shadow no one could shake.

Dani stood by her desk, her mug still warm in her hands, staring at the screen in front of her without seeing the words. She thought of Kalee, small and bright, heading off to school with her backpack bouncing against her shoulders. She thought of Henry, his silence holding more than he let show. And now, here were women with no stake in her block, no reason to gossip for gossip's sake, carrying the same worry.

It wasn't just her neighborhood. It wasn't just Henry's burden. The city itself was shifting, bending under something bold and dangerous that crept through alleys and crashed through storefronts.

Dani drew in a long breath, steadying herself before sinking into her chair. She told herself she needed to focus, to keep her team on track. But the unease clung to her all the same, whispering that the storm outside was bigger than she wanted to believe.

By midday the office had settled back into its routine, the sound of typing and phones ringing steady again. But Dani's focus wouldn't come. Her fingers moved across the keyboard, but her eyes blurred over the screen, the words refusing to stick. The whispers by the filing cabinets replayed in her head—*Dorchester, Fields Corner, the CVS... cops showing up late.* Different voices, same story.

When the lunch bell chimed and her team drifted off toward the breakroom, Dani stayed at her desk a

moment longer, staring at the phone on the corner.
Finally, she reached for it, scrolling to Yvonne's number.
"Girl, you at work?" Yvonne's voice came through quick,
lively as always, but with that undercurrent Dani knew
too well—worry dressed up as attitude.
"Yeah," Dani said, keeping her voice low. "On break. Just
needed to hear you."
"Mm-hmm. That don't sound like a break, that sound
like you stressin'."
Dani leaned back in her chair, pressing her palm against
her forehead. "Women here were talking this morning.
About the CVS, about kids getting pulled in by these
cars showing up on corners. Same stories you told me
yesterday, only now it's everywhere."
Yvonne exhaled loud through the phone. "Told you it
wasn't just your block. This city's gettin' chewed up one
piece at a time. Folks act like it don't touch them, but
wait—they gon' find out."
The words settled heavy, though Dani already knew they
were true. "I keep thinking about Kalee," she admitted.
"She's so small still. Innocent. But how long before she
starts seeing things I can't hide from her?"
Yvonne's tone softened. "That's why you and Henry
gotta hold it down. Kids read us before they read the
world. If you steady, she steady."
"I don't always feel steady," Dani confessed.
"Sometimes I think I'm one more siren away from
breaking."

"You won't break," Yvonne said firmly. "You might bend, but you won't break. And you ain't alone. Don't forget that."

The line went quiet a moment, just the faint hum of background noise on Yvonne's end. Dani let her friend's words settle, grounding herself in the familiarity of them. Yvonne had always been the one to sharpen her when she dulled, to remind her that fear didn't get to have the last word.

Still, when Dani finally ended the call and set the phone down, the silence of the office felt heavier than before. She glanced toward the window, the city skyline hazy in the distance. The streets below were filled with people going about their day, but Dani knew better now. Trouble wasn't just creeping in alleys and breaking glass storefronts. It was moving, bold and deliberate, weaving itself into every corner of Boston.

She straightened in her chair, forcing her hands back to the keyboard. She had work to finish, a daughter to raise, a home to protect. But no matter how steady she tried to be, the question kept pressing against her heart: *How long before the storm hit their door for real?*

The rest of the day dragged, the hum of the office offering no real comfort. Dani kept her head down, finishing reports, answering calls, moving through the motions as though muscle memory alone could carry her. When five o'clock finally came, she gathered her things quickly, eager to leave the stale air of the office behind.

The city felt different on her walk to the school. People moved fast, eyes a little sharper, voices edged with caution. Sirens wailed somewhere in the distance, not unusual but louder in her mind after the morning's talk. She held her purse close, her steps steady, her gaze forward.

At the school gates, Kalee's face lit up as soon as she spotted her mother. She came running, backpack bouncing, her curls wild from a long day. Dani bent to scoop her up into a hug, the weight of her daughter grounding her against the noise of the city. "How was my queen's day?" she asked softly.

"Good! We did drawings and I got a sticker," Kalee announced proudly, pulling the wrinkled star from her pocket.

Dani smiled, tucking it safely into her bag. "That's going on the fridge tonight."

They walked hand in hand through the neighborhood, Dani keeping her stride measured so Kalee's smaller legs could keep up. The sun was dropping low, shadows stretching long across the cracked sidewalks. The familiar row of brownstones came into view, and with it, the narrow alley beside their own building.

Dani's chest tightened.

A cluster of teens leaned against the brick, the same alley Henry had watched that morning. Their voices carried low, sharp laughter rising in bursts. The smell of smoke drifted out toward the street. Dani's grip on Kalee's hand tightened, but she didn't slow her pace.

"Hey there, pretty lady, I'd tap that all night long" one of them called, his tone dragging, bold. Another followed with a whistle, the sound echoing off the walls. They were crude and bold. Though they didn't look much older than 17, they acted like immature men.

Dani kept her eyes forward, her face calm, her steps steady up the worn stoop. She didn't give them the satisfaction of a flinch. Kalee looked up curiously, but Dani squeezed her hand before the question could form, ushering her toward the door.

The laughter trailed after them, a sound meant to stick like a thorn. Dani unlocked the door with quick fingers, pulling Kalee inside and shutting it firmly behind them. The lock clicked into place, but her heart was still racing.

Inside, she forced her shoulders to ease, her voice calm as she helped Kalee with her shoes. "Go wash up, baby. Dinner soon."

Kalee skipped down the hall without a care, humming softly. Dani leaned against the door for a moment, pressing her palm flat against the wood, listening to the muffled laughter fading outside. She said nothing, not to Henry when he came home later, not to Yvonne when she called again. But the weight of it settled deep inside her, heavier than the catcalls themselves.

The storm was closer now. It had a face, a laugh, a shadow in her own alley.

The bus hissed to a stop, its brakes sighing like an old man settling into a chair. Henry stepped down to the cracked pavement, the evening air carrying the faint smell of fried food, exhaust, and the lingering smoke of cigarettes. He adjusted his lunch pail in his hand and began the familiar walk toward home, his stride steady, his eyes scanning as they always did.

Halfway down the block, he slowed. The alley beside his brownstone was alive with shadows. The same group of teens loitered there, shoulders hunched against the brick, their voices carrying in bursts of sharp laughter. But this time it wasn't just them.

The black SUV was back.

It idled deep in the mouth of the alley, its grill glinting beneath the streetlight. The windows were tinted black, giving nothing away. Henry felt the tension climb up his spine. He stopped just short of the stoop, letting his gaze settle on the scene without turning his head too much. He knew better than to stare openly—it was a lesson learned long ago, both on Boston's blocks and in deserts half a world away.

From where he stood, he couldn't see what passed between the vehicle and the teens, only the subtle shift of bodies, the way one boy straightened as though suddenly taller, prouder. Another laughed too loud, a sound that echoed down the alley like a dare.

Henry tightened his grip on the handle of his lunch pail. He wanted to step closer, to catch more, but the shadows and the angle betrayed him. Whoever was inside the SUV stayed hidden, watching, feeding the boys like pieces on a board.

Then one of the teens noticed him. The boy's eyes locked on Henry's broad frame in the dim light. His voice cut sharp through the laughter:
"What?"
The others turned, snickering, emboldened by his bark. Their laughter spilled over each other, a chorus of mockery that carried down the block.
Henry held their gaze for a heartbeat, steady and unreadable. He'd learned long ago that sometimes silence was louder than words. Without breaking stride, he shifted his weight and started up the sidewalk again, his pace even, deliberate.
The laughter followed him, a jagged sound that scraped at his back. He didn't speed up, didn't give them the satisfaction of seeing tension in his step. But every muscle in his body was taut, every instinct screaming that the SUV wasn't just a car—it was a sign, a message, a promise of what was coming.
When he reached his stoop, he paused just long enough to glance once more at the alley. The SUV was still there, its engine humming low, its windows impenetrable. The boys had already turned back, their bodies angling toward the dark interior, their laughter fading into something quieter, more serious.
Henry unlocked his door and stepped inside, the noise of the block shutting out behind him. But the image stayed burned into his mind—the gleam of the SUV, the boldness of the boys, and the question hanging

unspoken: how long before that shadow reached all the way into his home?

Henry stepped inside and closed the door with deliberate care, as though sealing the world out took more strength than it should. Dani was in the kitchen, setting plates on the table, her movements neat and controlled. She looked up when he entered, reading the tension in his face before he said a word.

"You saw somethin'," she said softly.

Henry set his lunch pail down by the door, his jaw tight. "Kids in the alley again. Same ones. And that black SUV was back, sittin' there like it owned the place." He shook his head. "Didn't see who was inside. Windows too dark. But the way those boys straightened up—like they were standin' for inspection—it wasn't just small talk."

Dani's hand lingered on a fork she'd just set down. She forced her shoulders to stay loose. "I saw them too," she said carefully. "Nothin' happened. They were just there."

Henry studied her, eyes sharp, as though he could peel back the truth she didn't offer. Dani held his gaze, steady but quiet, giving him only the surface. She wasn't ready to tell him about the catcalls, about the way their laughter had chased her and Kalee up the steps. Not tonight. He carried enough already.

He sighed, rubbing the back of his neck. "SUVs pullin' up on corners across the city. Wilson and Steven been hearin' the same. Feels like somethin' bigger's movin' in."

Dani crossed the room, laying a hand against his arm. "Then you don't need to be carryin' it in your bones every second you walk through that door. You home now. Let it wait out there."

Henry let out a low chuckle, humorless but soft. "Easier said than done."

"Maybe," Dani replied, her voice firmer now, "but you can start by takin' a quick shower before dinner. Wash the day off. Relax a little." She squeezed his arm, coaxing him gently. "For me."

Henry looked at her a long moment, then nodded. He knew what she was doing—easing the tension off him, keeping the cocoon intact a little longer. He didn't argue. "Alright. For you."

As he moved toward the bathroom, Dani exhaled slowly, her hand falling back to her side. She listened to the creak of the floorboards under his heavy steps, the soft thud of the bathroom door closing.

She turned back to the table, finishing the place settings with practiced care. The clink of silverware steadied her hands, but inside, the unease still sat heavy. She had given him part of the truth, but not all. Not the sharp voices, not the laughter, not the way she'd felt Kalee's hand tighten in hers.

Some truths could wait. Tonight, her family needed warmth, not more shadows.

The bathroom was small, the tiles worn smooth from years of use, but it was one of the few places Henry allowed himself to let go. He twisted the knob, the pipes rattling before a steady stream of water hissed to life. Steam began to fill the room, curling against the mirror, softening the edges of everything.

Even with the door shut, the alley's noise seeped in. Shouts and laughter, sharp and bold, carried through the thin walls. The kids outside weren't just hanging around anymore—they were claiming the block one yell at a time. Henry stood there for a long moment, jaw tight, listening as his fists curled at his sides.

Then he stepped into the stream, the hot water crashing over his shoulders, beating down the tension knotted into his muscles. He closed his eyes, letting it wash over him, drown out the sounds beyond the walls. The hiss of the shower became louder than the voices, louder than the SUV's engine that seemed to haunt his memory, . louder even than McCaffrey's bark from earlier.

For the first time all day, his body began to loosen. The heat seeped into his skin, unwinding the tightness in his back, easing the ache that had built from work and worry alike. He let his head fall forward, the water cascading over his face, trailing down his chest in rivulets. His breathing slowed, deepened, matching the rhythm of the stream.

But then it hit.

A sharp bolt cut through his body—pain sudden and deep, ripping through the steadiness he tried to hold. His face twisted, eyes flying open as the strength went out of his legs. The tile blurred, steam curling thick around him, and before he could catch himself his knees buckled.

He caught the wall with one hand, his shoulder slamming hard against the wet tile. The water beat down relentless, mixing with the hiss of his breath. His heart thudded heavy in his chest, too fast, too loud. His other hand clutched at his side, as if pressing against something unseen might hold him together.

Henry grit his teeth, forcing the sound of pain back down into silence. Not here. Not where Dani might hear, not where Kalee might wake and come running. His body trembled under the spray, his breath shallow, ragged. The strength that had carried him through long shifts, long nights, and years of war felt like it was slipping, betraying him in this smallest of spaces.

He pressed his forehead against the wall, the cool tile grounding him as the heat of the water cascaded down. His knees shook, fighting to hold him upright. For a moment, the fear wasn't the SUV, the gangs, or the laughter outside—it was his own body, giving way when his family needed him most.

And in that moment, Henry realized the storm wasn't just outside the door. It was inside him too.

Henry's hand shot out, slick with water, trying to grip the tile. For a split second his palm found purchase, but the strength bled from his arm as fast as the pain tore through his body. His legs buckled again, this time giving way completely. He hit the shower floor hard, the impact rattling his ribs.

Steam closed in around him, hot and suffocating, the spray of water now pounding directly against his chest. His vision blurred, white and gray, and then—suddenly—sand.

The hiss of the shower turned to the whine of wind through the Afghan desert. The tile under his back became dry, cracked earth. His body remembered this feeling: the weight pressing him down, the heat burning into his skin, the sharp fire tearing through muscle and bone.

He gasped, his breath catching as memory fused with the present. Back then, the firefight had erupted without warning, rounds cracking overhead, men shouting, the ground shaking under mortar blasts. He had dropped fast, adrenaline blazing, then felt it—the searing punch in his side. For a heartbeat he hadn't understood. Then the wet warmth spreading across his uniform told him the truth.

Now, in the shower, that same truth cut through him again. His eyes dropped, wide, to the water swirling around the drain. It wasn't clear anymore. Dark streaks mixed with the runoff, spiraling in lazy circles before disappearing. Blood.

His breath came hard, ragged, panic pressing at the edges. He pressed a hand against his side, half expecting to feel the fabric of fatigues, but there was only skin slick with water—and still, the heat, the sting, the undeniable wetness of blood.

"No…" he muttered under his breath, teeth clenched. His voice sounded strange in the cramped echo of the bathroom, half-strangled by fear.

The memories crashed into him—shouts of "Man down!" in the desert, the weight of a brother-in-arms dragging him back to cover, the blur of medics working fast as his vision dimmed. He had lived through it then, survived by a thread.

But now?

Henry tried to push himself up, but his arm trembled, slipping against the wet tile. The water still fell relentless from above, splashing into the pool of red that spread wider beneath him. His breath grew shorter, harsher, each inhale a battle.

The alley's noise outside had faded into nothing. There was only the roar of the shower and the thud of his heart pounding in his ears. He was back in Afghanistan and here at the same time, caught between past and present, knowing with bone-deep certainty that something inside him had given way.

The soldier in him fought to stay upright, to breathe steady, to hold on. But the father, the husband, the man who had promised Dani he would never let anything touch her or Kalee—he felt the ground slip beneath him as the red water swirled down the drain.

Henry's body trembled as he pressed his palms against the slick tile, forcing himself onto his side. The water kept beating down, hot needles against skin that felt colder by the second. His breath came in jagged pulls, each one sharp enough to cut.

With a low groan, he dug his elbow into the floor and pushed. His shoulder screamed in protest, his legs weak beneath him, but he managed to drag himself toward the edge of the tub. His fingers scraped against porcelain, knuckles splitting against the hard edge, but he didn't stop.

Dani… Kalee…

Their names burned through his head louder than the roar of the shower. He could see them—Kalee's curls bouncing as she laughed, Dani's steady eyes meeting his across the dinner table. Were they safe? Did they hear him fall? Were those kids outside still in the alley? The SUV? The danger wasn't supposed to be here, inside his walls.

His chest heaved as he clawed his way forward, slipping and catching himself again. The floor outside the shower looked a mile away, blurred by steam, but it was the only thing that mattered. He had to reach the door. Each inch felt heavier, his strength bleeding out faster than the water carrying red spirals toward the drain. His vision tunneled, the edges darkening, but he refused to give in. He pressed his body against the tub wall, lifted one arm, then another, dragging himself over the lip until his chest hit the cold tile of the bathroom floor. The shock of it stole his breath. He gasped, the sound raw, wet, rattling in his throat. His hand slapped against the floor, fingers stretching toward the door as though he could will it closer.

"Dani..." His voice cracked, barely more than a rasp. "Kalee..."

No answer.

The silence pressed in harder than the steam, heavier than the pain. He tried again, forcing the words out through gritted teeth. "Dani!" The shout tore his throat raw, echoing off the tiles before dying in the small room. Still nothing. No footsteps, no rushing voice, only the steady hiss of the water he had left running.

His lungs burned, every inhale shallow, desperate. His body wanted to give, to sink into the cool floor and stop fighting. But his mind clung to them—the promise he had made at the kitchen table, the vow he'd whispered in Dani's ear, the kiss he'd pressed to Kalee's forehead that morning. He couldn't break now.

Henry's hand clawed at the tile, dragging him inches closer to the door. His chest heaved, his vision flickered, but still he fought, every muscle screaming. He didn't know if he would reach it, didn't know if he would be heard.

But he knew this: he would not stop calling for them until the last breath left his body.

Henry's body moved on sheer instinct now, each crawl forward tearing more from him than he thought he had left. His arms shook violently, his breath wheezing in shallow bursts, but still he pulled himself across the bathroom threshold and into the narrow hall. The tile floor gave way to linoleum, cool beneath his chest, slick beneath his palms.

Every inch was agony. The wound in his side burned, hot and wet, blood smearing behind him in a broken trail. His vision blurred, black creeping at the edges, but the thought of Dani and Kalee waiting just beyond—them not answering his calls—drove him harder. He dragged himself forward, teeth clenched, a growl tearing from his throat with every pull.

The hall stretched longer than it ever had before. The sound of the shower was still hissing behind him, but faint now, distant. Ahead, the kitchen light spilled across the floor, golden and steady. He clawed toward it, willing his legs to move, forcing his arms to keep working.

When he finally reached the doorway, he lifted his head—and the world shattered.

Dani lay crumpled near the table, her arm outstretched as though she had tried to reach for something that wasn't there. Her blouse was soaked through, dark red spreading in cruel shapes across the linoleum. Beside her, Kalee's small body was still, her curls matted, her tiny hand slack against the floor. The pool of blood beneath them spread together, glistening under the kitchen light like a reflection of a nightmare.

Henry's breath caught, his chest convulsing. For a heartbeat he thought it wasn't real, that his mind was tricking him, mixing memory with fear. But the copper smell hit him, sharp and undeniable. His vision tunneled on their bodies, and the sound that ripped from his throat was half roar, half sob.

"No!"

His voice shook the walls, raw, violent, tearing from the deepest place inside him. Rage surged through his veins hotter than the pain, stronger than the weakness dragging him down. His hands clawed against the floor, trying to reach them, to pull them into his arms, to undo what his eyes told him was true.

But his body betrayed him.

The strength drained out in an instant. His arms gave way, collapsing beneath him. His chest hit the floor with a heavy thud, his face turning toward Dani and Kalee, the sight of them burning into him. The rage still thundered inside, but his body no longer obeyed. His vision blurred, the golden kitchen light dimming to a faint haze.

The last thing he felt was the cold spreading beneath him, his own blood joining theirs, merging into one dark pool. His eyes fluttered, his breath shuddered, and then the world went black.

Chapter 3

The sterile brightness of **Boston Medical Center**'s waiting area felt suffocating. The walls were clean, the air conditioned, but the space carried a **cheerless weight**—the hum of vending machines, the scratch of shoes across tile, the muted coughs of the grieving. A television bolted to the corner wall cycled through local news, and the top story was theirs: *"Triple shooting in Dorchester leaves one dead, two injured. Sources confirm a child among the victims…"* The anchor's voice was detached, professional, and yet it cut into the room like broken glass. Every relative there stiffened when Dani's name was read aloud.

Yvonne sat rigid, her face collapsed into her hands, whispering prayers that were half-sobs. Beside her, Dani's brother and cousins shifted uncomfortably, too restless to sit still, too broken to speak. The family had arrived together, bundled by shock, clinging to scraps of hope. They'd been told nothing concrete yet—just that *Henry had survived the surgery,* Dani had not made it, and Kalee remained in critical condition, unresponsive. Police officers in plain clothes hovered near the nurses' station, waiting for the chance to interview Henry once he regained consciousness. Their notebooks rested on their knees, eyes flicking occasionally toward the family, knowing they were intruding on sacred ground but bound by duty to press for answers.

Every few minutes, the automatic doors sighed open, letting in more bodies: a friend of Henry's from work, another from the neighborhood, both pale and stunned. They crossed themselves or muttered curses under their breath, joining the silent cluster in the waiting room. Nobody knew what to say.

The television droned on, reporting crime statistics in Boston, speculation from neighbors who claimed they heard "kids running through the alley." The relatives tried not to listen, but their eyes couldn't help darting upward, searching for details, craving some kind of explanation. None came.

Then a nurse entered, clipboard in hand, scanning the room. Every head lifted at once. The air snapped tight, and even the television seemed to go quiet.

The room didn't stay quiet long. A woman from the neighborhood, wrapped in a headscarf, leaned over to Dani's cousin and whispered fiercely, loud enough for others to hear.

"These streets ain't safe no more. Kids with guns running wild. Cops don't do nothing until somebody's already bleeding."

Another man, a local resident who had followed the news and rushed over, shook his head bitterly. *"Every damn week, it's the same. A mother, a child, gone. What's it take for them to care about us?"*

Yvonne's sobs thickened, her hands trembling. Dani's brother rubbed her back in circles, trying to console her though his own jaw was tight with anger. The family murmured among themselves—half prayers, half memories. Dani's aunt whispered about how she used to sing at every family cookout, while one cousin repeated, "She didn't deserve this," as if saying it might change the fact.

The television continued its cruel broadcast. A reporter outside their apartment complex gestured toward flashing police lights, reciting, "Neighbors say the violence began with a confrontation in the alley. No suspects in custody yet."

The words "no suspects" sent a ripple of frustration through the room. One of Henry's coworkers cursed under his breath, pacing near the vending machines.

"All these cameras in the city, and still no one caught nothing? Bullshit."

The officers by the nurses' desk tensed but said nothing. They had heard this all before. They were waiting for Henry—the one surviving adult—who might be the only person able to describe what really happened.

Relatives huddled tighter, trying to be strong for one another. One of Dani's younger cousins scrolled endlessly on his phone, searching for updates, while another rocked back and forth in the hard plastic chair. They spoke in fragments, unfinished sentences, tears filling the gaps.

- *"Kalee's strong, she's gonna make it."*
- *"Dani was supposed to be here next Sunday, we were cooking together."*

- *"She always kept that little girl so neat, always with a bow in her hair..."*

Every voice rose and fell against the sterile quiet of the hospital, weaving grief with rage, consolation with disbelief.

Then the automatic doors hissed again. This time it wasn't family or friends—it was a uniformed chaplain. His presence made the air heavier, and for the first time, nobody spoke. All eyes shifted from the television to the chaplain's face, waiting for him to either bring peace or confirm the weight of what they already feared.

The chaplain's shoes clicked softly against the tile as he entered, hat held in both hands. He was older, face lined with years of funerals, shootings, overdoses. His eyes swept the room—over Yvonne hunched in her seat, the cousins pressed together, the neighbors pacing with nervous energy. He didn't say anything at first. Just his presence made people straighten, bracing themselves. Finally, he lowered his voice. "I came to sit with you all while we wait. Sometimes it helps to pray, or just to have someone hear your grief."

Yvonne shook her head hard, tears streaking her cheeks. "Don't need no prayer. I need my daughter back." Her voice cracked into a wail. "My baby's gone." Her words unraveled the thin thread of silence. One cousin jumped up, pacing. "We should be outside the precinct, demanding answers, not sitting here like this."

A neighbor answered from across the room, voice rising. "And what? March on them? They'll just tell us it's 'an ongoing investigation.' Always the same line."

The television flicked to a live shot of a police spokesperson giving a statement. *"We are canvassing the area and speaking with witnesses. This is an active scene, and we ask for patience as we—"*

"Patience?" someone muttered bitterly. "If this was in the suburbs, they'd have ten squad cars chasing kids down already."

The two plainclothes detectives by the nurses' station shifted uncomfortably, pretending to focus on their notes. Their presence was a constant reminder—help and scrutiny in the same breath. They weren't there to mourn. They were there to question, to catalog, to assign blame once Henry opened his eyes.

Henry's coworker Wilson arrived then, breathless, still in his work uniform. He paused at the doorway, seeing the room thick with sorrow. "How's he doing? Anybody know?" His voice carried too much hope.

One of Dani's cousins turned toward him, voice flat. "Alive. But Dani's gone. Kalee... she's still fighting."

Wilson sat down heavily, pressing his palms together, eyes red already. "He was just talking about taking Kalee to the zoo. Just last week." His head dropped. "Man... Henry doesn't deserve this."

Another friend, Steven, showed up minutes later, his face a mask of anger. "Where the hell were the cops? Where the hell's the city? They let these gangs run wild, but they'll pull Henry over for a broken tail light. Tell me that makes sense."

Murmurs of agreement rippled, frustration sharpening the grief. The chaplain raised a hand gently, as if to settle the storm. "I know the anger. I know it well. But tonight—tonight is for mourning what has been lost, and praying for what may still be saved." His voice carried calm, but the room still bristled.

Yvonne clutched a tissue, twisting it in her hands. "I just want to see my granddaughter. Just let me hold her hand."

The nurse behind the desk glanced up at the detectives, then back at the family, hesitant. Hospitals had rules. Police had their procedures. Everyone here knew how tangled it could get when tragedy and justice collided. The waiting room became a patchwork of voices:

- Dani's uncle quietly promising they'd raise money for Kalee's care.
- A neighbor recounting how Dani always stopped to help carry groceries.
- One cousin talking about leaving Boston altogether—"Ain't nothing here but death."
- A young nephew insisting, "Kalee's strong. She's gonna wake up. She has to."

The television droned on, replaying flashing lights, crime scene tape, blurred images of officers in the alley where Henry and his family had been found. The news ticker scrolled grim statistics: *Boston shootings up 14% this year.*

Through it all, the detectives stayed seated, their notebooks resting on their knees, eyes occasionally flicking toward the family. They said nothing, but their silence weighed heavy—like wolves waiting for the chance to pull apart the story.

When the automatic doors hissed again, everyone turned. This time it was a doctor in scrubs, face tired but composed. He held the clipboard against his chest as if bracing himself.

Every sound in the waiting room cut out at once—the television, the vending machine hum, the pacing footsteps. All that remained was breath, shallow and quick. The doctor's eyes found Yvonne first.

The doctor stopped just inside the doorway, scanning the crowded room. His lips pressed into a thin line, and for a long moment he didn't speak. The clipboard shifted against his chest as he adjusted his grip.

Everyone froze. Even the detectives straightened, pens poised but unmoving. The chaplain lowered his head, murmuring something under his breath.

Finally, the doctor cleared his throat. "I need to speak with the immediate family." His voice was calm, professional, but heavy with the kind of weight only bad news carried.

The words scattered through the room like broken glass. "Immediate family." Everyone knew what that meant, but no one wanted to be the one to stand. Yvonne's hands shook as she reached for her daughter's brother,

her voice cracking. "Come with me." A cousin rose too, clinging to her arm.

The doctor nodded gently. "This way, please."

He didn't elaborate, didn't give anything away. He just turned toward the hall, leading them past the sliding doors into a smaller consultation room. The rest of the waiting room sat in suspended silence.

The television droned on, but nobody looked. A neighbor swore under his breath, pacing harder now, muttering about how "no news is worse than bad news." Wilson buried his face in his hands, elbows on his knees. Steven leaned against the wall, jaw set tight, glaring at the detectives as if daring them to say something.

The detectives kept still. They'd been here too many times before, seen this scene play out in too many hospitals. The grief, the anger, the suspicion—it was always the same. They glanced at each other briefly, then back down at their notebooks.

From behind the consultation room's half-closed door came muffled voices. A sharp cry. Then another, louder. Yvonne's grief tore through the thin walls, reaching everyone in the waiting room. Some of Dani's cousins flinched as if struck. One young nephew covered his ears.

The chaplain closed his eyes, whispering another prayer, but the rest of the room just sat in stunned silence. The reality had been confirmed—not yet in words for everyone else, but in the sound of a mother's heartbreak that told the truth more brutally than any doctor could.

The door stayed shut. The waiting room became a limbo—grief on one side, waiting on the other.

The cry on the other side of the door pierced the sterile quiet like a blade. Yvonne's voice—raw, unrestrained, animal—tore through every person in the waiting room.

"My baby... my baby's gone!"

The words were muffled, but clear enough. They struck harder than the newscast, harder than the chaplain's prayers, harder than all the whispered fears.

Silence fell. The vending machines hummed. The television continued to play, the anchor droning about statistics, but nobody heard it anymore. The waiting room froze, suspended in that single, devastating moment.

Wilson let out a long, shaky breath, his hands slipping from his face. Steven pressed his fist into his mouth, eyes glassy, as if he'd been punched in the gut. One of the younger cousins leaned forward suddenly, head between his knees, whispering, *"No, no, no..."* on repeat.

A neighbor who'd been muttering anger all night now stared at the floor, jaw clenched, unable to speak. The sharp edges of fury dulled, replaced by a heavy, suffocating weight of loss.

The detectives exchanged a glance, their pens unmoving. Even they looked momentarily human—eyes lowered, shoulders heavy—before professionalism masked it again. They stayed quiet, their notebooks closed in their laps.

The chaplain folded his hands, whispering something so soft only those nearest could hear: "Lord, have mercy." Minutes stretched. No one seemed to know how to move, what to say, how to breathe in a room where grief had just taken over completely.

Then, slowly, the reactions began to ripple outward.

- One of Dani's cousins whispered, *"She was only thirty-two..."* as if repeating the number would make sense of it.
- Another cousin began sobbing openly, her face buried into the shoulder of whoever sat next to her.
- A man from the neighborhood shook his head over and over, muttering, *"Boston's eating its own. Always the good ones."*

The television tried to reclaim the space, flipping to a live press conference from the mayor, who promised "an increased police presence" and "a commitment to justice." The words sounded hollow, political. Nobody in the waiting room reacted, except Steven, who muttered, "Too late now," under his breath.

The door to the consultation room remained shut, but Yvonne's grief had already done what no doctor's words could—it confirmed the truth. Dani was gone.

The weight of that truth pressed down on every soul in the waiting room, binding them in shared silence.

Henry woke to a sound he couldn't place at first. A steady rhythm, like drums deep underwater. Beeping. Machines. His head felt heavy, his body numb in places and burning in others.

The ceiling above him was white, too bright. The smell of disinfectant stung his nose. He tried to move, but pain lit up his side like fire, pinning him down. A groan escaped his throat, dry and cracked.

For a moment, he thought he was back in Afghanistan—caught between morphine haze and battlefield dust, listening to medics bark orders in the background. His chest tightened at the memory. He blinked hard, forcing the blur of the hospital lights into focus.

Boston. He wasn't overseas. He was here. Home.

A nurse leaned over him, adjusting tubes and lines. She gave him a quick glance, startled that his eyes were open. "Mr. Mann? Can you hear me?"

His lips parted, but words came slow, like pushing stones uphill. "My... my wife? My daughter?" His voice rasped, almost unrecognizable to his own ears.

The nurse pressed a hand to his shoulder gently. "You need to rest, sir. Please—don't strain yourself."

But Henry's eyes locked on hers. Desperation gave him strength he didn't have. "Tell me."

The nurse hesitated, eyes flicking toward the door. She wasn't the one meant to give him this news, but his demand cut through protocol. Still, she didn't answer. She only smoothed the blanket across his chest and murmured, "The doctor will be in shortly."

Henry turned his head, wincing at the pain that shot down his neck. Through the half-open door of his room, he caught sight of movement—a cluster of figures down the hall, some weeping, some pacing. He thought he saw Yvonne, Dani's mother, clutched tight between two cousins.

Grief hit him before confirmation. His body went rigid. He tried to sit up, but the agony in his side dragged him back into the mattress. "No..." The word broke in his throat. "Dani..."

His chest heaved, and for a moment he fought against the wires and tubes, desperate to tear them out, to get up, to see his family. The nurse called out for help, pressing him down gently but firmly.

"Mr. Mann, please—you're safe, you're alive. But you have to stay still."

Her words meant nothing. Safety didn't exist. Not anymore.

Henry's breaths came ragged, each one dragging pain through his chest. The nurse had called for help, and another appeared briefly in the doorway, murmuring something about checking vitals. They moved efficiently, professionally, but Henry's mind was elsewhere.

From the hall, voices filtered in. Fractured. Muffled. But unmistakable.

Yvonne's sobs rose and fell, uncontrolled. He heard her say Dani's name, again and again, like a prayer broken in half. "Dani... oh God, Dani..."

Another voice—male, sharp—cut in, trying to hold her steady. Dani's brother maybe. *"Ma, you gotta sit down. Please. Don't do this to yourself."*

The words reached Henry like shards. His pulse quickened, the beeping beside him rising in tempo. He gritted his teeth, trying to force his body up again, but the pain in his side shoved him flat.

He closed his eyes, listening harder, as if he could will himself through the wall.

More voices. Softer this time. One cousin whispering, "The baby... still in a coma." Another: "Henry don't even know yet. How's he gonna take it?"

Henry's stomach dropped. His fingers twitched at the sheets, clutching them until his knuckles whitened. Dani's name echoed in his skull, colliding with the phrase *still in a coma*. He tried to stitch them together into something that made sense, but all that came was panic.

A chair scraped in the hall. Then Steven's voice, low but furious: "He's gonna blame himself. I know Henry. He's gonna take this all on his back."

Wilson's reply was quieter, almost choked: "Man already carried a war on his shoulders. Now this..."

Henry's throat tightened. His chest shook with shallow breaths. He wanted to scream for answers, for someone to come in and tell him straight, but his voice betrayed him—dry, cracked, weak. All he could do was stare at the ceiling as grief pressed in through the walls like smoke.

The door to his room opened slightly wider. The nurse leaned back in, giving him a fleeting glance before stepping out again, her voice hushed to someone outside: *"He's awake. But not stable enough for questioning yet."*

Another voice—firm, clipped—answered: *"Doesn't matter. We'll need his statement soon."*

Henry's eyes narrowed. Police. They were waiting like vultures, ready to pick apart what little strength he had left.

But all Henry could think of was Dani's voice—her laughter, her warmth—and Kalee's tiny arms around his neck. He tried to summon those sounds, those touches, to fight the silence of the hospital room. Yet outside the door, the muffled grief kept pulling him back toward a truth he wasn't ready to face.

The door opened wider, and this time it wasn't the nurse. A doctor stepped in, his blue scrubs creased, his eyes carrying the weight of too many nights like this. He closed the door softly behind him, shutting out the sounds of the hallway.

Henry's gaze snapped to him. His throat worked, but no words came. The doctor didn't rush, but his face told Henry everything before his mouth did.

He pulled a chair close to the bed and sat, resting the clipboard on his lap. "Mr. Mann..." His voice was steady, but low. "You came through surgery. You're alive, and we're monitoring your recovery closely."

Henry's eyes burned, his chest heaving against the tubes and bandages. "My... wife. My daughter."

The doctor inhaled slowly, choosing his words with care. "Your wife, Dani... she didn't make it."

The room fell into a silence that wasn't silence at all—it was a roar inside Henry's head, a crushing weight that pushed the air from his lungs. His mouth opened, but no sound escaped.

The doctor's voice softened, but it didn't ease the blow. "Your daughter, Kalee—she survived the initial trauma. She's alive, but she's in a coma. She's stable for now, but we don't know if—or when—she'll wake."

Henry's body convulsed with a broken gasp. His vision blurred, the sterile lights overhead smeared into white streaks. He shook his head weakly, as if denial alone could undo the words. "No... no, no, no..." His hand clawed at the sheets, gripping them until the stitches in his side screamed.

The doctor leaned forward, voice firm but gentle. "Mr. Mann, I need you to stay calm. Your body has been through a trauma. We'll have counselors available to help. You're not alone in this."

But Henry wasn't listening. His chest rose and fell in ragged bursts. Dani's face flashed in his mind—her smile at the dinner table, her laugh in their bedroom, the way she brushed Kalee's hair back with motherly care. Gone. All gone.

His eyes shifted to the corner of the room where shadows gathered, as though grief itself had taken

shape there. He whispered her name once—"Dani..."—
and the sound of it nearly shattered him.

The doctor sat quietly, giving him space. Outside the door, muffled sobs and voices lingered, but in here, Henry was alone with the truth.

Cold, undeniable, merciless truth.

Henry's breaths came jagged, as if each one scraped his chest raw. The doctor's words looped in his head, refusing to fade: *Dani didn't make it. Kalee is in a coma.* His heart pounded. Every beat was another hammer strike of reality. He turned his face away from the doctor, toward the blank white wall, because looking at another human being felt impossible right now.

A flood of memories crashed against him, violent and unstoppable.

- Dani laughing at the kitchen counter, teasing him about burning the rice.
- Kalee tugging at his pant leg, holding up her crayons, demanding he sit on the floor and draw with her.
- Dani's touch on his shoulder last night, warm, alive, so real.

All ripped away in a single night of violence.

The guilt hit next. Heavy, suffocating. His fault. Somehow, all of it was his fault. He should've heard the kids in the alley sooner. He should've checked the lock twice. He should've fought harder, shielded them, taken every bullet himself. He'd lived through firefights overseas, trained to survive ambushes—and yet, when

it mattered most, in his own damn home, he failed
them.

His fists clenched around the sheet, nails digging into
his palms. His jaw locked so tight it ached. The monitors
beside him beeped louder, faster, echoing his spiral.

The nurse slipped back in quickly, eyes widening at the
numbers on the screen. "Mr. Mann, please—you need
to calm down. Breathe slow. In through the nose—"

Henry barked a sound, half laugh, half sob, bitter and
hollow. "*Calm?* My wife's dead. My baby girl's..." His
voice cracked. "She's just a little girl. And I'm lying here."

The nurse froze, lips pressed tight, unable to argue with
the truth of it.

The doctor stood, motioning to her quietly, signaling for
medication. Henry caught the exchange, and rage flared
in his chest. "Don't you put me to sleep. Don't you dare.
I need to see her. I need to—" His words broke into
coughing, pain stabbing his side, but he pushed through
it. "I need to hold her hand."

The doctor's voice stayed calm, but firm. "You'll see
your daughter, Mr. Mann. But not tonight. You need to
heal enough to stand, or you won't make it to her
bedside at all."

Henry's eyes blazed, wet with tears, locked on the man
who had just condemned his world to ash. He wanted
to swing, to smash, to scream until the whole hospital
shook—but his body betrayed him, weak and broken. All
he could do was lie there, choking on rage and grief.

Finally, his head dropped back against the pillow, tears sliding into his hairline. The rage gave way to a crushing hollowness, a weight so vast it felt like the bed itself was swallowing him whole.

He whispered again, almost too soft to hear. "Why her? Why them? Why not me?"

No answer came—only the steady beeping of the machines, the smell of antiseptic, and the unbearable truth that he was alive when Dani was not.

The consultation room door finally opened. Yvonne emerged, flanked by her son and a cousin holding her steady. Her face was streaked with tears, her body trembling, but her voice carried a sharp edge now, a demand cutting through her grief.

"I want to see my granddaughter," she said to the nearest nurse at the desk. Her tone left no room for hesitation. "Right now. Take me to her."

The nurse's expression tightened, caught between policy and compassion. "Ma'am, the pediatric ICU has strict visitation—"

"Don't you dare tell me about rules." Yvonne's voice cracked, but the fire in it blazed. "That's my baby's baby lying in there. My Dani's gone. Don't you tell me I can't hold her hand."

The room went still. Even the cousins who had been pacing stopped in their tracks, watching. The detectives glanced up from their notes, their faces unreadable, but their attention fixed on the exchange.

The chaplain stepped closer, placing a hand lightly on Yvonne's arm. "We'll make sure you see her," he said gently. "Sometimes it takes a moment to clear the way, but you will see her."

Yvonne's chest heaved as she nodded, tears spilling again, but her resolve unbroken. "I need to see her before anything else."

The nurse picked up the phone, murmuring into it quickly, eyes flicking nervously between Yvonne and the hallway. After a moment, she nodded. "They'll allow one at a time for now. You can come with me."

Yvonne's knees buckled, but she straightened, pulling herself upright with a will that came from somewhere deep. Her son stayed at her side, steadying her as she followed the nurse down the hall.

As they disappeared, the room stirred again. Dani's cousins whispered among themselves, some crying openly, others sitting stiff, hands clenched in their laps. A neighbor muttered, "That little girl's all they've got left."

Steven leaned back against the wall, arms folded, his jaw tight. "And Henry," he said, voice low but firm. "He's still here. Don't forget him."

Wilson nodded, though his eyes were distant. "Yeah. But when Yvonne's done with Kalee, she's gonna want to see Henry."

The truth of it hung in the air. Everyone knew that meeting would come, and no one knew how it would go.

The hallway to the pediatric wing was hushed, sterile, almost sacred in its quiet. Machines hummed softly behind glass doors, their steady beeps a fragile rhythm of life. The nurse led Yvonne and her son past rows of closed rooms until she stopped at one.

Inside, little Kalee lay still in the hospital bed. Her small body seemed swallowed by the white sheets, tubes trailing from her arms, a machine beside her breathing with slow, mechanical certainty. Her face was pale but peaceful, her curls brushed back neatly by some nurse who had tried to preserve her dignity amid the wires and tape.

Yvonne froze in the doorway, her breath catching. For a moment she couldn't move. Her legs trembled, and her son had to steady her again. Then, with a shudder, she pressed forward.

She reached the bedside and gripped the rail, lowering herself into the chair. Her hand found Kalee's tiny fingers and held them, though they didn't squeeze back.

"My sweet girl," Yvonne whispered, her voice breaking. "Grandma's here now. You hang on, you hear me? You hang on."

Her thumb brushed gently over Kalee's hand, careful not to disturb the IV lines. Tears slipped down her cheeks, dotting the sheet. She bent forward until her forehead rested against the child's hand.

"You look just like your mama," she sobbed. "Just like her. She'd sing you to sleep, remember? I'll sing now, baby. I'll sing for both of us."

Her voice trembled into a hymn, half-prayer, half-lullaby. The words wavered, but the melody carried a weight of love that filled the small ICU room. Nurses passing by slowed for a moment, their faces softening. Her son stood back, leaning against the wall, wiping at his own eyes. He looked at his niece, then at his mother, and whispered, "She's fighting, Ma. You can see it. She's not letting go."

Yvonne lifted her head, nodding fiercely through her tears. "She's Mann blood. She's strong. Just like her daddy. Just like her mama."

For a long time she sat there, stroking Kalee's hand, whispering to her about the family waiting outside, about how much she was loved, about how her mama would always watch over her.

Finally, the nurse touched Yvonne's shoulder softly. "I'm sorry, but we have to limit the visit tonight. She needs her rest."

Yvonne turned, eyes blazing with grief. "Rest? She's in a coma, and you're telling me she needs rest?" But her anger dissolved as quickly as it came. She bent forward, kissed Kalee's forehead gently, and whispered, "I'll be back tomorrow. You don't leave me, you hear? You don't leave me like your mama."

She stood with effort, letting her son guide her back toward the hallway. Her shoulders sagged, but her eyes were sharper now, filled with grim determination.

As they walked, she whispered to him: "Now take me to Henry. I need to see him."

Henry lay propped against the pillows, eyes glazed and unfocused, when the door opened again. The sound of quiet footsteps reached him first, followed by the faint rustle of fabric. He turned his head slowly, every movement pulling pain through his side.

Yvonne stood there. Her face was lined with grief, her eyes red and swollen, but her posture was rigid, as though sheer will alone was keeping her upright. For a long moment she didn't move, didn't speak. She just looked at him — the man lying in a hospital bed while her daughter lay in a morgue.

Henry swallowed hard, guilt slamming into him. His lips parted, voice hoarse. "Yvonne..."

She raised a hand, not to stop him, but to steady herself. Then she crossed the room, her movements trembling but sure. She sat in the chair by his bed, folding her hands tightly together in her lap.

Her eyes glistened as she finally spoke. "I saw her. I saw Dani's baby girl. She's so small in that bed, Henry. So still. Machines doing what God used to do." Her voice broke, but she caught it in her throat and forced it back down. "But she's alive. She's fighting."

Henry's face contorted. His jaw clenched against the sob that threatened to break loose. "I should've—"

"No," Yvonne cut him off sharply, her tone snapping like a whip. "Don't you put this on yourself. Don't you dare." Her eyes burned into his. "This ain't your fault. This is this city's fault. This neighborhood. This broken society that lets children run around with guns while mothers bury their daughters. That's who I blame. Not you." Henry's chest shook, and a tear slid down into his beard. For the first time since waking, he let himself cry openly.

Yvonne reached for his hand. Her fingers gripped his tightly, her strength surprising for someone so wracked with grief. "You fought a war for this country. You gave everything. And what did it give you back? A city that couldn't keep your family safe in their own home." Her voice softened, grief swallowing the fire. "My Dani deserved better. You both did."

Silence stretched between them, filled only by the rhythmic beeping of Henry's monitors. He couldn't speak, his throat too tight, his mind too broken.

Yvonne wiped at her eyes with the back of her hand, steadying herself again. "Henry... that little girl. She's all we got left now. She's the last piece of Dani." She paused, letting the words settle. "I'll be there for her. Whatever it takes. She needs a woman's hand now. A steady home. You... you need to heal. You need to rest." Her words weren't accusatory. They weren't even firm yet. But the implication hung in the air between them — that perhaps Henry, broken and grieving, wasn't enough on his own. That maybe Yvonne was already picturing herself stepping into the role of primary caretaker.

Henry turned his face toward the wall, tears streaking silently. He didn't argue. Couldn't. Deep inside, a part of him feared she might be right.

Henry stayed silent for a long moment, staring at the wall. His chest rose and fell unevenly, the weight of Yvonne's words pressing down on him like another wound. Finally, his voice came low, raw, but firm: "Kalee's mine, Yvonne. She's my little girl. My blood. Dani's blood. I don't care if I'm broken in this bed, I'll crawl if I have to—but I'll be the one to raise her."

Yvonne's lips trembled. She gripped his hand tighter, her thumb pressing into his knuckles as though testing the strength left in him.

"Henry," she whispered, "I don't doubt your love for her. Lord knows I don't. But look at you. You're fighting for your life in this bed. And Kalee... she's in a fight of her own. That little girl's gonna need so much, more than one man can give. Especially now."

Henry's jaw set. His eyes, wet but steady, turned back to her. "I'm her father. That's what I swore to Dani, that no matter what, I'd take care of our girl. I couldn't protect Dani... I couldn't stop what happened. But I'll be damned if I let anyone take Kalee from me."

The monitors picked up his rising heartbeat, a quickening beeping that filled the silence.

Yvonne's breath hitched, her grief battling against her pride. For a moment she looked like she might argue, might press harder — but then her shoulders sagged, and her grip softened.

"You're right," she admitted, her voice breaking. "She's yours. And she always will be. I'm just... I'm just so scared, Henry. I already buried my daughter tonight. I can't bury my granddaughter too. I can't."

Henry closed his eyes, his face twisting with pain. Slowly, he lifted his hand from the sheets and laid it over hers, weak but steady. "We'll keep her safe. Both of us. You hear me? She's gonna need all the love we got left. I'll fight for her with whatever I got."

For the first time that night, Yvonne let out a long, shaky breath that wasn't a sob. She nodded, pressing her free hand against his arm. "Alright then. We fight together. For her."

The room fell into silence again, but it was different now. Not just grief and loss, but a fragile pact — a promise born from the ashes. Both of them knew the road ahead would be brutal, but neither was ready to let go of the little girl who carried Dani's light.

Outside in the hall, the muffled sounds of the waiting room carried faintly — the restless shuffle of feet, quiet weeping, detectives murmuring low. But here, in this hospital room, the center of it all narrowed to two broken souls and the one child left between them.

The door creaked open before either Henry or Yvonne could speak again. Two men in plain clothes stepped inside, their shoes tapping lightly against the tile. The first, older, with silver streaks through his cropped hair and deep lines around his eyes, carried himself with quiet authority. The second, younger and restless, kept glancing between Henry, the monitors, and his notebook.

The older man stepped forward. "Mr. Mann," he said, voice steady but heavy with weariness. "I'm Lieutenant Ronald Mitchell. This is Detective Costa. I wish we didn't have to do this now, but... there are questions we need to ask while things are still clear."

Yvonne's head snapped toward them, fury in her grief. "Are you serious? He just woke up from surgery. His wife's gone. His baby's in a coma. And you think now's the time to play twenty questions?"

Mitchell nodded slowly, his expression sincere. "I understand, ma'am. Believe me, I do. If it were my family, I'd want everyone left the hell alone. But these cases... they go cold fast. We can't let that happen here."

Costa, standing stiffly at his side, chimed in, voice clipped. "Mr. Mann, we need you to tell us if you recognized any of them. Faces, clothing, voices—anything."

Mitchell shot him a quick look, then softened his tone back toward Henry. "Take your time. Don't push yourself. Just tell us what you remember."

Henry swallowed hard, his chest rising with uneven breaths. His mind dragged him back against his will—the muffled shouts in the alley, the burst of laughter, the deafening cracks of gunfire. Dani's body crumpled, Kalee's stillness.

His fists clenched into the sheets. "I didn't see faces. Just voices... kids, teenagers. Running. Laughing like it was a damn game." His voice cracked. "Then the shots."

Costa's pen scratched furiously across his notebook. "Any idea of the number? Three? Four? More?"

Mitchell lifted a hand, stopping him. "Easy, Costa. Let the man breathe." He turned back to Henry, his gaze steady, almost fatherly. "You're doing fine, Henry. Anything you can give us helps. We'll do the legwork."

Yvonne leaned forward, her voice sharp with rage. "So what—you're telling me kids with guns can shoot up a family home, murder my daughter, put my grandbaby in a coma—and you've got no suspects? No names? No nothing?"

Costa stiffened. "We're canvassing, ma'am. Pulling camera feeds, checking prior incidents—"

"Camera feeds," Yvonne spat, glaring. "What good are cameras if they don't stop bullets?"

Mitchell placed a hand gently on the back of her chair, his voice softer. "She's right to be angry. She has every reason. But we *will* follow this, ma'am. We don't walk away from cases like this." His eyes, tired and heavy, told her he'd seen this kind of promise break before— but that he still believed it had to be made.

Henry's jaw tightened, his voice low. "I'm not your witness. I'm her husband. Her father. You want to catch them? Then do your damn job. Don't put this on me."

Costa's lips parted as if to argue, but Mitchell raised a hand again, stopping him. He gave Henry a small, steady nod. "You're right. That's on us. We'll be back when you're stronger, but if anything comes to you before then—anything at all—just let us know. You've carried enough already."

The two men turned to leave. Costa closed his notebook briskly, his jaw set in irritation, while Mitchell gave Yvonne a faint nod of respect before stepping out. The door shut softly behind them, leaving the room once again filled with the quiet rhythm of Henry's monitors and Yvonne's uneven breathing.

Yvonne shook her head, muttering bitterly, "They'll talk and talk, but they don't care. Dani will just be another headline to them."

Henry closed his eyes, Dani's face etched on the inside of his eyelids. "Mitchell might," he whispered hoarsely. "But he can't fight the whole city."

Chapter 4

The basement reeked of sweat, smoke, and gun oil. A single bulb swayed from the ceiling, casting shadows over the gathered men. Crates were stacked against the walls, their labels scrubbed off, but the scent of grease and steel betrayed their contents.

The African Lords were arguing, voices bouncing off the cinderblock walls like ricochets.

"Man, that shit in the alley was sloppy," snapped **Reggie "Stone" McClain**, his broad shoulders tense as he paced. "Stray fire in a buy? You out your damn minds? That wasn't supposed to go down like that."

"It wasn't *us*, it was them Hell's Gentlemen fools," barked **Antwan**, younger and quick to flash his teeth in defiance. "They spooked, started waving iron around, like we some punks. What you want me to do—just stand there and get lit up?"

"Don't matter who pulled first," Stone shot back, his voice booming. "Bullets flew. Now we got bodies in the street. Innocent ones. You think cops ain't gon' be crawling all over our business now? Every corner, every alley watched. They don't care it was an accident. Heat is heat."

Big Leon, the unofficial elder of the crew, leaned forward from his chair, his gold chain catching the light. His voice was slower, more deliberate, carrying weight. "Stone right. Don't nobody care whose finger squeezed.

All they see is dead folks. Mothers crying. That's the kind of noise get the city riled up, get detectives sniffin'." The room fell quiet for a beat. Even Antwan swallowed his reply.

From the corner, **Darius**, one of the younger runners, shifted uneasily. "I heard one of them that got hit was a woman. Another was a little kid." His voice cracked under the weight of the words.

The silence thickened, then Stone slammed his fist on a crate. "This is what I mean! That shit don't just wash off. You hit a cop, you hit a rival, you hit someone who knew what game they was in—that's business. But a woman? A child? That's trouble that don't go away."

Antwan finally looked down, muttering, "Wasn't supposed to happen like that..."

Leon's gaze swept the room, measuring each man. "Supposed to or not, it did. And now the name of the African Lords is in people's mouths for the wrong reasons. We either fix this, or we get buried in it."

The silence didn't last.

"I'm tellin' you, Stone," Antwan snapped, raising his voice again, "we wouldn't even be in this if you hadn't vouched for doin' business with those Hell's Gentlemen in the first place. They some sloppy-ass clowns, not soldiers. Can't trust 'em to hold a line, can't trust 'em to keep cool."

Stone's jaw flexed as he stepped forward. "Watch yourself, boy. You ain't been in this game long enough to talk about who I bring to the table. I been running these streets before you even knew how to cock a nine."

Antwan squared up, his bravado clashing with the older man's authority. "Don't matter how long you been runnin'—you ain't cleanin' up the mess neither! I seen the way them cops rolled up after. Whole neighborhood lit up with sirens. What's your big plan now, huh?"

"Plan?" Stone barked a humorless laugh. "Plan is to make sure you little hotheads don't sink us deeper."

Darius muttered from the side, "Sound like we already sunk."

That earned him a glare from both Stone and Antwan. Big Leon raised his hand for calm, but the room had already broken into overlapping shouts. Fingers jabbed. Someone kicked over an empty beer bottle.

Accusations flew—too much heat, too little discipline, wrong alliances, wrong leadership.

The argument was reaching its boiling point when the door creaked open.

The sound alone was enough.

Mykelti stepped in.

Tall, lean, with the cold eyes of someone who didn't need to shout to be heard, he carried himself like the room already belonged to him. His leather coat brushed the floor as he walked, and the cigarette smoldering between his fingers cast a thin curl of smoke around his face.

The noise died instantly.

Nobody wanted to be the last man heard talking when Mykelti entered.

He scanned the room, taking in the tipped bottle, the flared tempers, the guilty silence that followed. A slow smirk tugged at his mouth.

"When," he said, his voice smooth but sharp as glass, "are we gonna stop fussin' like bitches and get what we came for?"

He flicked ash onto the floor and leaned against a crate. "Tell me, when we gettin' them guns from the Hell's Gentlemen? Or should I say…"—his smirk widened—"the *Hellmans*?"

A few nervous chuckles rippled around the room, but no one laughed too loud.

Mykelti let the silence stretch, his eyes moving from man to man, watching them squirm. Then he dropped the cigarette to the concrete floor, grinding it out beneath his boot.

"All this noise about accidents, about who pulled first, about who's scared of cops," he said evenly. "That's small talk. That's coward talk. We ain't here to argue about who slipped up—we here to *own* this city."

Stone shifted uneasily. "But the heat—"

"The heat don't scare me," Mykelti cut him off, his voice rising just enough to shut the room down. "You think the police, the papers, the weeping mothers—they matter? They don't. They've always been in the way. The only thing that matters is that every block, every corner, every set knows whose name holds weight. And that name is African Lords."

He stepped closer to the center of the room, his coat swaying, his presence tightening the air.

"The Piranhas," he said, his lips curling in disdain. "First ones to go. They flashy, loud, think they run half the Southside with their green bandanas and dime-store muscle. We cut off their heads, take their stash, their corners—everybody sees what happens when you stand against us. No more Piranhas. No more noise."

A murmur of agreement moved through the room, though it was laced with fear as much as respect.

"And them Hell's Gentlemen?" Mykelti sneered, deliberately mocking the name. "They just middlemen playin' tough. They ain't gentlemen, and they sure as hell ain't family. I'll take their guns, then I'll take their lives if I feel like it. Don't nobody call the shots in this city but me."

He looked around the room again, daring anyone to speak.

"No more bickering. No more pointing fingers. Collateral damage? That's the cost of doing business. But hesitation—*hesitation* is the cost of losing. And I don't lose."

The younger men—Darius, Antwan—averted their eyes, chastened. Even Stone, hardened as he was, dipped his chin slightly, unwilling to challenge Mykelti outright.

Big Leon gave the faintest nod, more acceptance than approval. He knew what Mykelti was, and what it meant for all of them.

Mykelti finally sat, claiming the only empty chair as if it had been waiting for him. "So here's the order. We finish the deal with the Hellmans, take their steel, then sweep the Piranhas off the map. Clean. Loud. Final. Anybody got a problem with that?"

Silence answered him.

Mykelti leaned back in the chair, satisfied with the silence that followed his decree. He let the weight of his words hang in the air a moment longer, then clapped his hands together once, sharp and final.

"Good," he said, his voice carrying the finality of a verdict. "Now let's get dem dogs fighting for tonight. We need more cash for dem guns."

A ripple of energy moved through the room—nervous for some, eager for others. The younger men perked up, their eyes lit with the promise of fast money and savage entertainment. Stone's jaw tightened, but he didn't speak. Leon merely folded his arms, his silence a reluctant seal of agreement.

Darius shifted, uneasy again. Dog fights meant noise, bodies packed tight in the warehouse, blood on the floor. It drew gamblers, hustlers, sometimes even outsiders sniffing for a score. But it also meant quick money—and money was what Mykelti demanded.

"Make sure the word spreads," Mykelti continued. "I want every fool with a dollar to burn packed into that pit.

Let 'em cheer, let 'em lose, let 'em bleed their pockets dry. By sunrise, we'll have the cash to grease the Hellmans' palms and put their steel in our hands."

He smirked, the fire of ambition burning in his eyes. "And once we hold that steel, the Piranhas won't last the week."

The men nodded, some more eagerly than others. Orders were orders. And under Mykelti's rule, disobedience was unthinkable.

The basement meeting broke apart with a low hum of voices, each man moving with renewed purpose. Orders were already being carried out before Mykelti had even risen from his chair.

By nightfall, the warehouse on Forty-Third was alive with motion. Corrugated steel walls rattled under the bass of a portable speaker someone had dragged in, the smell of beer and smoke rolling heavy in the air.

A chain-link cage had been bolted into the center of the floor—its mesh already stained with dark streaks from past nights. Around it, folding chairs scraped against concrete as the first wave of bettors took their seats.

"Get the boards up!" Stone barked, his voice carrying over the noise. Two younger Lords scrambled to mount plywood sheets against the windows, hammering them in place to block out wandering eyes. Outside, cars pulled up one after another, headlights sweeping across the lot before vanishing as engines cut.

Antwan strutted through the crowd with a wad of cash in his fist, calling out odds and collecting bills. "Two to one on Razor! Five to one if you stupid enough to bet on Killer! Line up, line up!" His grin was wide, his eyes feverish—he lived for this part, for the chaos of easy money.

At the far end, Leon oversaw the pit dogs being led in. Muscled brutes with ribs like iron, their handlers straining to keep them apart as they lunged and snapped, froth flying from their jaws. The animals' growls filled the space with a primal thunder, pulling nervous laughs and hungry shouts from the crowd. Darius kept to the edges, his stomach tight as he watched. He'd seen plenty of dirt in his short years, but the way the dogs tore at each other still unsettled him. He avoided looking into their eyes, knowing full well they had no choice in the violence.

Mykelti arrived last, and when he entered, the noise shifted again—like the air itself recognized his authority. He walked to the cage, brushed ash from his sleeve, and smiled thinly at the sight of money already changing hands.

"This," he said, his voice low but carrying, "is how kings are crowned. Blood makes the world turn, gentlemen— animal or man, it don't matter. Long as it pays."

The crowd roared its approval.

Inside the cage, the handlers unclipped the chains. The dogs exploded forward.

The warehouse erupted in cheers, curses, and the rustle of dollar bills changing hands. For the African Lords, the night had just begun.

The cage rattled with the violence inside it. Razor clamped down on Killer's throat, shaking until blood spattered against the mesh. The crowd surged forward, men hollering, women clutching fists of cash, the air thick with beer, sweat, and the sharp scent of blood. Bills passed hand to hand, the volume rising with every snap of bone, every howl of pain.

Antwan barked odds like a carnival barker, waving bills above his head. Stone kept a watchful eye on the doors, scanning faces for cops or outsiders. Mykelti sat back in a folding chair, calm as a king at court, a glass of whiskey in his hand.

Then the energy shifted.

A man near the edge of the cage shoved back his chair, his face twisted in fury. His crumpled betting slips dangled from his fist. "This shit rigged!" he spat, voice cracking under rage. "Ain't no way that mutt supposed to lose!"

A few in the crowd laughed, others jeered, but he didn't stop. His face reddened, sweat running down his temples as he tore the slips in half and flung them to the floor. "I put everything on Killer! Everything!"

Antwan snorted. "That's on you, fool. Nobody told you to be stupid with your rent money."

The man's eyes darted across the room, wide and feverish. His chest heaved, his hand trembling as it slipped inside his jacket. Nervous energy rippled through the onlookers.

Then came the flash of steel.

The man ripped a pistol free, raising it with both hands. The music cut as someone yanked the plug. Shouts died into a tense silence, the only sound the labored growls of the bloodied dogs still locked in combat.

"I ain't goin' home broke!" the man yelled, his voice cracking, desperate. "You hear me? I can't! My kids need food, rent's due—what I'm supposed to tell 'em? I can't go home with nothin'!"

The crowd froze. No one moved, no one dared breathe too loud. A handful of gamblers raised their hands, backing away. Antwan cursed under his breath, his bravado shrinking fast. Even Stone tensed, ready but unsure which way it would break.

Mykelti didn't flinch. He swirled the whiskey in his glass, his gaze fixed on the man like a predator watching wounded prey.

The gun wavered, swinging from the cage to the crowd, the man's hand slick with sweat. "Somebody gon' pay me back! Somebody!"

The man's voice cracked, carrying over the tense stillness. His gun hand trembled as he shouted, eyes darting wildly between the crowd and the cage.

"Y'all don't know the shit I'm in!" he barked. "I can't find no work. My bills piling up, every damn day! My woman left me—took my kids, won't even let me see 'em!" His voice faltered, catching between rage and despair.

"What I'm supposed to do? Huh? Somebody tell me what the hell I'm supposed to do!"

The crowd murmured uneasily, shifting back and forth. Some faces showed pity, others contempt. A few slipped toward the exits, not wanting to be anywhere near a man on the edge.

The gun wavered higher as his breathing grew ragged. "I ain't leavin' here empty—"

He never finished.

With a blur of motion, Mykelti rose. A wooden **Louisville Slugger**, dark with old stains, swung in his grip. The crack of wood on bone rang louder than any gunshot. The man's eyes went wide as his skull caved under the blow. He collapsed sideways, the pistol clattering from his limp hand. Blood spilled fast, pooling across the concrete floor.

Gasps rippled through the crowd, followed by a stunned silence.

Mykelti stood over the twitching body, his chest rising slow, deliberate. He let the bat rest on his shoulder, his voice carrying across the room with cold precision. "Nigga," he said, his tone laced with mocking calm, "do I look like Doctor fucking Phil?"

A nervous ripple of laughter broke through the silence— hesitant, uneasy, but no one dared keep quiet. The message was clear: weakness, excuses, tears—none of it mattered.

Mykelti tapped the bat twice on the floor, then turned his back on the dying man as if he were nothing more than a distraction. "Get this mess outta here," he ordered. "And somebody clean the floor before it stains the bets."

The crowd exhaled as one, the tension giving way to cheers, whistles, and money flashing back into the air. The fight in the cage raged on, but the real lesson of the night had already been taught.

The man's body twitched once, then lay still. Blood spread outward, inching across the concrete floor in a widening pool.

Mykelti prodded the corpse with the toe of his boot, then gave it a sharp kick that rolled the head limp to one side. He sneered down at the man, his lip curling.

"Y'see?" he said, his voice cutting through the low murmur of the shaken crowd. "This...this right here is what keeps our African brother weak. Worryin' 'bout bills, worryin' 'bout bitches. Cryin' about what life owe him instead of takin' what's his."

He paused, then slowly placed his hands over his own face, fingers spread like a mask. His shoulders shuddered once, twice, as though he were about to sob. The crowd held their breath, uneasy, unsure of whether to laugh or to mourn.

When he pulled his hands away, his eyes were dry, his mouth twisted into a cruel smile.

"If this is what I must do," he said softly, almost sorrowful, "to keep our people strong..." He let the words hang, then dropped his hands to his sides. "I'm good with that."

He swept his gaze over the gathering, his voice growing louder, sharper, feeding off the tension in the room.

"This here ain't just some fool who lost a bet. This—" he jabbed the bat toward the body—"this is another black man who let the system beat him down. Another statistic. Driven to walk away from his woman, his kids, his whole damn life, 'cause he thought a job or a paycheck was gonna save him."

A few men in the crowd nodded, some with conviction, others just because they were afraid not to.

Mykelti's voice hardened. "You want that to be you? Huh? You wanna be the next sad story, the next nigga cryin' over light bills and court papers? Or you wanna be a man that takes what's his—no excuses, no tears, no weakness?"

The roar that answered him wasn't unanimous, but it was loud enough. Some cheered because they believed him. Others because they had to.

Mykelti grinned, satisfied. He pointed the bat toward the cage, where the dogs still tore at each other, fur and blood flying.

"This is life. You fight. You bite. You win—or you get put down. And me? I ain't never been put down."

The crowd erupted again, louder this time, feeding on the violence, the money, and the power in Mykelti's voice. The man's body was dragged away, forgotten before the blood had even dried.

The cheering crowd went back to their gambling, their shouting, their drinking. The cage rattled as the handlers pried the mangled dogs apart, blood smeared across the mesh.

Mykelti set his bat against the wall and poured himself another drink. Out of the haze of smoke and noise, **Switch** drifted over. Lean, wiry, with a half-burned eyebrow that gave him a permanent smirk, Switch was one of Mykelti's most reliable men—the one who handled the books when others only thought in fists.

"Mykelti," Switch said low, handing over a bundle thick with bills. "We pulled near twenty-k tonight, maybe more when the last bets get counted."

Mykelti flipped through the stack, the corners of his mouth twitching upward. "Good. That'll keep the wheels greased."

Switch hesitated, then asked the question everyone else was avoiding. "We still dealin' with the Hellmans?" The way he said the word carried the same mocking tone as Mykelti had used earlier.

Mykelti's smile thinned. "Don't mistake me, Switch. I despise those clowns. They strut like roosters, dress like bums, and think sellin' scraps of iron makes 'em kings. But kings don't sell—they conquer."

He leaned back, sipping his whiskey, eyes drifting past the cage as if looking at something far beyond the warehouse walls.

"When I was a boy," Mykelti began, his voice dropping into something colder, darker, "I saw rebels trade with the very men they swore to kill. Soldiers in rags, with guns older than their fathers, buyin' bullets from the same traders who armed their enemies. You know why?"

Switch shook his head, listening intently.

"Because business was business. And when your goal is bigger—when you want not just to fight, but to *win*—you take what you need from whoever has it. Pride don't buy you power. Only money does. Only firepower does." He tossed the bundle of cash back into Switch's hands. "So yeah, we deal with the Hellmans. We take their guns, we take their time, we take their lives when I'm finished with 'em. But for now? They got what we need. And what we need comes first."

Switch nodded slowly, his smirk fading into something closer to awe. "Business before pride."

"Exactly," Mykelti said, his grin sharp again. "Business before pride, until pride can be paid in blood."

The noise of the warehouse swelled behind them—dogs snarling, men shouting, bills being waved. Mykelti looked back at the cage, eyes hard, already thinking past the Hellmans, past the Piranhas, past tonight's blood money.

The hum of machines filled the ICU, steady and cold, each beep and hiss a reminder that life itself was now tethered to wires and tubes. The air was heavy with antiseptic and sorrow.

Henry stood at the doorway, staring at the small figure on the hospital bed. **Kalee.**

Her face was pale beneath the bruises, her tiny chest rising and falling with the rhythm of the ventilator. A crown of bandages wrapped around her head, too large for her fragile frame. The tubes in her arms, the IV stand beside her—it all looked monstrous against her small body, as though she'd been swallowed into a world that had no business touching her.

Henry stepped forward slowly, his breath catching as he drew near. His hand trembled as he reached out and laid it gently over her tiny fingers. They were warm but limp, resting in his palm as if the life had been drained away.

His throat closed. He wanted to speak, but words felt like betrayal in a room like this. He leaned forward, his lips brushing her forehead, the scent of antiseptic stinging his nose, tears blurring his sight.

"I'm here, baby girl," he whispered hoarsely. "Daddy's here."

The machines kept their rhythm, oblivious.

Henry's grief swelled until it felt like his chest might burst. But inside that grief, something else grew darker—harder. His tears slowed, replaced by the fire in his gut that had been smoldering since the moment he saw Dani and Kalee's blood on the kitchen floor.

He clenched her hand tighter, lowering his head until his forehead pressed against hers.

"I swear to you," he muttered through gritted teeth. "I swear to you, Kalee—I'm gonna find who did this. I don't care if it takes the rest of my life. They're gonna pay for every drop of your blood."

The words were a vow, forged in grief and sharpened by rage.

As he stood there, the door opened softly behind him. The quiet tread of footsteps entered the room, and Henry didn't need to look up to know it wasn't a nurse. It was the detectives.

he door clicked softly shut, and Henry turned just enough to see them step inside.

Lt. Ronald Mitchell entered first, tall but stooped, his suit rumpled at the edges, tie loosened. The lines on his face carried years of long nights and heavier memories. His eyes went to Kalee in the bed, and for a brief moment the weariness softened into something closer to sorrow.

Behind him came **Detective Costa**, younger, sharper, moving with an edge of impatience. His notebook was already in his hand, pen poised as if he'd been itching to start scribbling before he even walked in.

Mitchell gave Henry a respectful nod. "Mr. Mann," he said, his voice low, carrying both sympathy and gravity. "I'm sorry to come in at a time like this. I wish we didn't have to. But...we need to ask you some questions."

Henry turned back to Kalee, his jaw tight, his hand still cradling hers. "Now? While she's lying here?"

Costa stepped forward, ignoring the edge in Henry's voice. "Now's when details are sharp, Mr. Mann. We're tryin' to piece this together before things go cold."

Mitchell shot Costa a look, a silent correction, then approached the bed slowly, giving Henry space. His voice was softer when he spoke again. "We know this is hard. But anything you can tell us—anything you heard, saw, remembered—might help us find the people who did this."

Henry let out a bitter laugh under his breath. "Find them? You really think you're gonna find them before I do?"

Mitchell didn't flinch. "That's what we're here for. And I get it—you don't trust that. Maybe I wouldn't either, in your shoes. But I've been doing this a long time, and I've seen what happens when men take justice into their own hands. It doesn't end the way they think it will."

Henry turned then, his eyes red, fixed on Mitchell. "She's eight years old," he hissed. "My little girl. You telling me I'm supposed to just sit back while some bastard walks away laughing?"

Costa cleared his throat, stepping in briskly. "We're not telling you to sit back. We're telling you to help us. What did you hear before the shots? Any voices? Cars? Anything you can give us narrows this down."

The machines kept their steady beeping between the words, a cruel reminder of Kalee's fragile state. Henry squeezed her hand again, torn between the urge to scream and the need to cling to what little calm he had left.

Henry exhaled slowly, forcing his voice steady. He looked at Mitchell, not Costa, when he began.

"I was in the bathroom when it started," Henry said quietly. "Could hear the kids out in the alley, same ones always hangin' around. Then...then the noise changed. Yelling. Different voices—deeper, older. Not kids this time."

Costa scribbled notes, head down. Mitchell gave a slow nod. "Go on."

Henry's hand never left Kalee's. "Then the shots. Loud—close. Like they were right outside the window. I didn't think it was real at first, thought maybe it was back in Afghanistan, thought it was just in my head..." His voice trailed off before he forced himself onward. "But then I felt the pain. My leg gave out. I saw the blood in the shower. And when I crawled out—"

His voice broke, just for a moment. He glanced at Kalee, his throat tightening before he pressed through it. "When I crawled out, Dani and Kalee were already down. Dani..." He swallowed hard. "She was gone. Kalee was still breathing. I don't remember much else after that. Just crawling. Holding them. Trying not to pass out."

The pen in Costa's hand slowed. He flicked his eyes up at Mitchell, then back to Henry. "You catch any words? Accents? Anything from those voices outside?"

Henry closed his eyes, replaying the chaos in his mind. "It was fast. Angry. Two men, maybe three. Sounded young, but not kids. They weren't just yelling at random—they were arguing. Like something went wrong out there. And then the shots..."

Mitchell leaned forward slightly, his voice steady, measured. "Could you tell if they were shooting at someone, or just firing wild?"

Henry's eyes opened, burning now. "Didn't matter. Bullets came through my window, through my walls. Hit my family. That's all that mattered."

The room fell quiet except for the machines. Costa tapped his pen, then shut the notebook with a soft snap. "That's enough for tonight."

Mitchell lingered, studying Henry's face. "We'll follow up. If you remember anything more—even the smallest detail—you call me. Day or night." He placed a card on the tray beside the bed.

Henry glanced at it but didn't pick it up. His focus was still on Kalee, her small hand in his.

Mitchell's voice softened. "She's strong. Stronger than she looks. Don't give up on her."

The detectives turned to leave. Costa was already halfway to the door, but Mitchell gave Henry one last look—a look that carried weariness, but also something else. Respect.

When the door closed, Henry bowed his head once more, whispering so low only Kalee could hear.

"They'll hunt you," he muttered. "But so will I. And when I find you, you'll wish them cops got to you first."

The hallway outside the ICU was quieter, but the hum of hospital life still pressed in—the shuffle of nurses' shoes, the distant squeak of a gurney, the muted voices of families holding on to hope.

Mitchell closed the door behind them and let out a slow breath, rubbing his eyes with thumb and forefinger.

Costa flipped his notebook open again, jotting down quick lines.

"Well?" Costa asked. "You buying his story?"

Mitchell gave him a tired look. "It ain't a story. It's a man barely holding himself together."

Costa shrugged. "I'm not saying he's lying. But grief makes people say things they didn't see, or twist what they heard. We need facts. Forensics, shells, angles. You know that."

Mitchell started walking down the hall, Costa falling in step beside him. "Facts, yeah. But don't ignore what his gut picked up. He heard arguing outside. That tells me this wasn't some random spray. Something went wrong out there. A deal, maybe."

Costa tapped his pen against the notebook. "A deal between who?"

Mitchell's jaw tightened. "African Lords. Hell's Gentlemen. Maybe both. You been here long enough to see how the lines cut?"

Costa gave a small shake of his head. "Still catching up."

Mitchell slowed, leaning against the wall by a vending machine. His voice dropped, steady and deliberate, like he'd told this story before but wished he didn't have to. "The African Lords been around since the nineties. Started small, corner crews. Graduated to muscle-for-hire, then they figured out their own hustle. Dogfights, dope, guns—you name it. They're disciplined when they want to be, but lately?" He shook his head. "New blood. Hotheads. Quick to pull triggers. That's bad for them, worse for the rest of us."

Costa scribbled notes. "And the Hell's Gentlemen?"

Mitchell gave a humorless laugh. "Don't let the name fool you. They're no gentlemen. White boys mostly, old biker trash mixed with young punks. Been movin' guns through this city for years. Sometimes they fight with the Lords, sometimes they deal with 'em. Depends on the week."

"And the Piranhas?" Costa asked.

Mitchell's eyes darkened. "Small-time gang, flashy, noisy. Southside. They like to mark their territory with bodies. Problem is, bodies bring headlines. And headlines bring us. I wouldn't be surprised if they're next on somebody's list."

Costa clicked his pen shut, frowning. "So what we're looking at is—what? A turf war? Bad deal gone worse?"

Mitchell straightened, slipping his hands into his pockets. "We're looking at the beginning of something. And if I know anything about men like Mykelti running the Lords, it won't stop at stray bullets. This city's about to bleed."

The Piranhas' hideout was a converted auto shop at the edge of South Boston, its windows blacked out, the air thick with stale smoke and grease. The overhead lights buzzed weakly, throwing long shadows across the graffiti-smeared walls. The place stank of oil, sweat, and cheap liquor.

At the center sat **Rico "Piranha" Salazar**, their leader. Stocky, tattooed from knuckles to throat, his teeth glinted with silver caps filed into points. He lounged in a battered recliner that looked like it had been dragged off a sidewalk, a half-empty bottle of rum on the armrest. In one hand he held his phone, scrolling lazily. Then he stopped. His eyes scanned the screen, and a laugh bubbled up from deep in his chest. A cruel, rasping sound.

"¡Mira esto!" Rico barked, waving the phone. "Look at this shit! Stray gunfire, a woman dead, little girl in the ICU. Whole neighborhood cryin'." His laughter echoed in the dim shop. "Boston cryin'!"

He reached into a cooler beside him and pulled out a raw steak, blood dripping onto the concrete. With no hesitation, he sank his teeth into it, tearing a chunk free and chewing noisily, the juice running down his chin. Gang members lounging nearby—some cleaning guns, others rolling dice—looked up, grinning at the display. Rico stood suddenly, his stocky frame commanding the room. He tossed the phone onto the chair, the steak still in his fist.

"Listen up!" he barked, his voice echoing off the corrugated metal walls. One by one, the Piranhas straightened, their laughter dying, eyes fixed on their leader.

Rico raised the steak high, the blood dripping onto the floor. His voice grew louder, fevered, carrying the cadence of a preacher at war.

"Boston thinks it's seen blood? Thinks it remembers war? The Revolution, muskets in the streets, redcoats and patriots? That was a picnic compared to what's comin'! Boston will bleed more than the Revolutionary War ever brought to this city. And we, hermanos, we are the ones to spill it!"

The room erupted—cheers, gunfire into the ceiling, boots stomping the floor. The Piranhas roared like a pack of wolves smelling blood.

Rico dropped back into his recliner, laughing, his teeth glinting as he chewed another mouthful of raw meat.

"Let the city cry. 'Cause we're just gettin' started."

The **Hell's Gentlemen** crowded inside their usual haunt, a dim pool hall tucked into Dorchester's backstreets. Neon beer signs flickered weakly in the windows, throwing pale blue light across peeling wallpaper. The air reeked of cigarettes and spilled whiskey, the kind of place nobody came to play pool anymore—only to deal.

At the center table sat **Jason Farokmanesh**, their leader. Anglo-American, slicked-back hair gone slightly thin on top, a pinstripe vest stretched over his gut. He dressed like a throwback to Prohibition, trying to sell the image of an old-time gangster in a modern world. A fedora hung on the back of his chair, and a thick gold ring glinted when he reached for his glass.

In front of him lay an open briefcase: handguns, ammo, and two small blocks of military surplus C4 cushioned in foam. Jason ran his hand across the contents with the tenderness of a jeweler showing diamonds.

"These African Lords," Jason muttered, his voice nasal but slick, "they talk big, they posture bigger. But when it comes to business? They damn near botched the whole deal last night. Stray gunfire in a buy? That's amateur hour."

Across from him, **Knox**, one of his lieutenants, leaned forward, elbows on the table. "We could've walked out with lead in our backs. Mykelti's boys can't control their tempers."

Jason chuckled, low and dismissive, like he'd heard it all before. He plucked a toothpick from a glass and chewed on it as he spoke. "That's the problem with these so-called 'street kings.' They forget the one rule that kept men like Capone alive: keep the streets calm, keep the money flowing. Violence is a tool, not a tantrum."

He leaned back in his chair, letting the toothpick dangle. "Now, do I trust 'em? No. Do I want their money? Hell yes. Because every dollar they spend on my merchandise makes them lean on me a little harder. And when a man leans, he gets dependent. That's when you own him."

The men around the table nodded, though some shifted uneasily.

Knox scratched his neck, eyes darting to the case. "And if they don't pay up?"

Jason's smile sharpened. He tapped the block of C4 with his ring, the *clink* echoing on the wood. "Then we sell elsewhere. Piranhas got cash, reckless as they are. And the Irish boys in Southie? They'll take explosives off our hands without blinking. Business goes on. Always does."

He sat forward again, adjusting his vest like a man preparing for a photo. "The African Lords think they're building an empire. Mykelti thinks he's Caesar, strutting around with his little speeches. But in this city? Nobody eats without the Hell's Gentlemen setting the table."

Jason raised his glass, amber whiskey catching the neon glow. "To business, gentlemen. And may Boston bleed enough to make us rich."

Jason swirled the whiskey in his glass, the ice clinking softly. Around him, the men of the Hell's Gentlemen leaned in, watching his face, waiting for direction.

"You see, boys," Jason said, voice slow and deliberate, "the trick ain't about who's toughest. It's about who pays longest. The Lords?" He wagged the toothpick for emphasis. "They're flashy. They want everything now— guns, corners, respect. That kind of hunger makes a man dangerous... but it also makes him sloppy. Mykelti's got vision, sure. But he's too proud to see he's already dancing to my tune."

Knox smirked. "And the Piranhas?"

Jason laughed, shaking his head. "Ah, Rico Salazar—calls himself Piranha like it's supposed to scare somebody. That man's nothing but teeth and noise. He's unpredictable, but that's useful. You keep feeding a dog scraps, pretty soon he's fighting in your yard. He wants blood, he'll pay for the tools to spill it."

He leaned forward now, eyes narrowing with a gleam. "Here's the game. We sell to both. Enough to keep 'em stocked, never enough to let 'em win outright. Let the Lords and the Piranhas beat the hell out of each other, tear this city apart. While they're busy spilling blood, we count bills and hold the real power."

The men around the table muttered their approval, one letting out a low whistle.

Jason smiled like a stage actor hitting his mark. He picked up his fedora, dusted it off, and set it carefully on his head. "This city... Boston's always been a battleground. Redcoats, patriots, Irish, Italians—it's just new uniforms now. But history don't change. It belongs to the men who know how to make chaos profitable."

He drained his glass, then jabbed the toothpick at the case of weapons. "So we give Mykelti his toys, let Rico have a taste too. They think they're playing war; I'm playing banker. And in the end, when the smoke clears? The Hell's Gentlemen will own this city without firing a shot."

The room erupted in laughter, rough voices echoing off the walls. Jason laughed with them, loud and theatrical, like a man who believed the city was already his.

The laughter of the Hell's Gentlemen rolled on, echoing in the smoke-stained hall. Jason tipped his fedora at them, flashing that easy grin he'd practiced for years in the mirror. He looked every bit the self-styled mob boss, a man in command of the table, of the city, of fate itself. But when the meeting broke apart and the men drifted off to the bar, to the tables, to their vices, Jason lingered. The pool hall quieted, leaving him alone with the dim jukebox hum and the faint rattle of pipes in the ceiling.

He refilled his glass with a heavy hand and stared into the amber liquid. His reflection wavered on the surface—a middle-aged man with thinning hair, a gut he couldn't shake, and a costume borrowed from dead gangsters who never really won.

Jason's jaw tightened. He set the glass down, rubbing the bridge of his nose. For all his bravado, a thought gnawed at him.

Mykelti.

He'd seen men like Mykelti before—charismatic, brutal, visionary. But Mykelti wasn't just another street boss. There was something in his eyes when they met last night, something Jason hadn't seen in decades of hustling. A kind of coldness, a kind of fire. The look of a man who didn't bluff.

Jason shivered despite himself, the memory creeping in like a chill. He thought of the stories—Mykelti coming up from Africa, the whispers about what he'd seen as a boy, the rebels, the blood. Men like that weren't built on make-believe. They carried horror with them, and worse, they embraced it.

Jason downed the whiskey in one swallow and wiped his mouth, forcing the thought away. He adjusted his vest, straightened his fedora, and put the mask back on. "Business is business," he muttered to himself, as though repeating a prayer. "Business before pride. Always."

But in the back of his mind, no amount of whiskey could quiet the truth: business only mattered if you survived long enough to spend it.

And Jason Farokmanesh wasn't sure he'd survive Mykelti.

The paperwork seemed endless—form after form signed with a shaky hand, the words blurring together until Henry barely knew what he was agreeing to. Discharge instructions. Prescriptions. Insurance details. He nodded when the nurse explained his medication schedule, but the truth was, he wasn't listening. He heard only the faint hiss of oxygen tanks, the constant beep of monitors down the hall, the background noise of lives clinging on.

When they finally set the crutches against him, Henry pushed himself up. His stitched leg burned with a sharp, insistent pain, but he refused to show it. The hospital gown was gone, replaced by a pair of worn jeans and a T-shirt Yvonne had brought from home. They felt foreign on him, as though they belonged to another man—the one who'd kissed Dani that morning before work, the one who had read Kalee her bedtime story the night before.

That man was gone.

Yvonne walked at his side, her purse clutched tight, her eyes fixed ahead. She didn't speak much. When she did, her voice was clipped, carrying both grief and something harder. "Take it slow," she told him as they reached the elevator. "You push too hard, those stitches'll tear. Doctor said rest. You hear me?"

Henry didn't answer. He didn't look at her, only at the dull steel doors reflecting back a gaunt version of himself. He barely recognized the hollow eyes, the unshaven jaw. A soldier's face, but not the one who had come home.

The elevator ride was silent, the air heavy with everything unsaid. Yvonne reached once for his arm, but he shifted away, his grip tightening on the crutches. She sighed softly but said nothing.

When they reached the exit, the brightness of the outside world hit him like a blow. Cars passed. People walked. Life moved on, indifferent to the hole blown into his own.

He stopped just outside the sliding doors, gripping the crutches, his chest tight. For a moment, he thought he couldn't move forward. The weight of it all—the hospital, Dani, Kalee—pressed down so heavy he felt his knees might buckle.

But then Yvonne's voice cut through. "Henry."

He blinked, forced a breath, and moved forward. One step. Then another. Every stride was pain, but he welcomed it. Pain reminded him he was alive. Pain reminded him why he couldn't stop.

He didn't say it aloud, but the thought burned inside him: *This isn't over.*

The funeral home smelled faintly of lilies, but underneath was something harsher—varnish, polish, the sterile scent of death made presentable. Henry sat stiff in a leather chair across from the director, the caskets displayed in the adjoining room like furniture in a showroom.

The man across the desk wore a dark suit, his voice practiced, polite. "White oak is traditional. Very clean finish. But mahogany—well, mahogany carries more weight, more permanence. Families often—"

Henry cut him off, his voice flat and toneless. "Which one closes the tightest?"

The director blinked. "Sir?"

Henry's jaw worked, his eyes fixed on the glossy wood displayed through the doorway. "The casket. Which one closes tightest. I don't want dirt getting in."

Silence hung between them. Yvonne shifted in her chair beside Henry, her hand brushing his arm. "Henry..."

He pulled away, his gaze never breaking. His voice cracked just slightly. "Dani hated dirt. Always fussed at Kalee for tracking mud into the house. She'd lose her mind if she thought—" His throat closed off the rest of the sentence.

The director cleared his throat gently. "White oak, sir. The seal is... secure."

Henry nodded once, sharp, as if that settled everything. He pushed himself upright on the crutches, ignoring the flare of pain in his leg. "Then that's the one."

Yvonne followed him into the showroom, her eyes wet, her hands wringing the strap of her purse. She looked at the mahogany, at the steel options, at the white oak Henry had chosen, and she sighed. "She deserved better," she whispered.

Henry's lips pressed thin. "She deserved *life*. But this is what we got."

The director stepped forward, beginning his quiet explanations of pricing, lining, floral arrangements. Henry heard none of it. He saw only the smooth lid of the oak casket, its polished surface reflecting a distorted version of himself. The image swayed as his vision blurred with unshed tears.

He forced his eyes away. His face hardened. The fire inside him burned hotter.

The church was filled, every pew taken. Neighbors, coworkers, Dani's family—all gathered in silence. The air was thick with perfume and sorrow, the murmurs of grief swelling and breaking like waves.

Henry sat in the front row, crutches propped against his seat. Kalee's absence weighed heavier than any cast or stitch. The pew beside him, empty, screamed louder than the preacher's words.

He did not cry. Not once. His eyes stayed fixed on the oak casket at the altar. The preacher spoke of peace, of heaven, of Dani's kindness. But Henry heard none of it. To him, the words were empty sounds in a room full of meaningless noise.

When the service ended, mourners filed past, offering hands and embraces. Some whispered prayers, others muttered platitudes about "justice" and "time." Henry nodded, said nothing. His face was a mask, unyielding, his jaw tight as stone.

At the cemetery, the sky was a flat gray, the kind of colorless day that swallowed light. The ground was soft, damp from rain the night before. Henry stood at the edge of the grave as the casket lowered, the ropes creaking, the oak lid vanishing inch by inch into the earth.

Yvonne wept openly beside him, clutching a tissue, her shoulders shaking. Other family members sobbed, the sound raw and unfiltered. But Henry's eyes burned, dry, unblinking. His crutches sank into the soil, his knuckles white on the handles.

When the last shovel of dirt fell, muffling the casket below, the others drifted away, their voices fading into the distance. Henry stayed. Alone, except for the cold wind.

He stared at the fresh mound, his body rigid, his breath short and uneven. His lips parted, whispering so low the words were almost swallowed by the breeze.

"They think they ended me."

He lowered his head, pressing his forehead against the crutch's padded grip, his teeth clenched until his jaw ached.

"They only woke me up."

The vow hung in the air, a promise etched into the silence of the cemetery.

Henry stood there long after the others had gone, the fire in him coiling tighter with every beat of his heart.

The house was silent when Henry opened the door. Too silent. The kind of silence that presses in on you, alive and suffocating. He stood in the threshold a long moment, one hand gripping the crutch, the other on the doorknob, staring into the space that had once been full of laughter and life.

The curtains were half-drawn, a strip of afternoon light cutting across the living room floor. Toys lay scattered where Kalee had left them—her favorite doll, a jumble of crayons, a board game half-packed away. Dani's sweater still hung on the back of the couch, folded neatly, as though she might return at any moment to slip it on.

But she wouldn't.

Henry's chest tightened as he stepped inside, each movement echoing through the emptiness. He lowered himself into the chair by the window, the one Dani always teased him for calling his "spot." From there, he could see into the kitchen. The stains had been scrubbed, the floor washed, but he could still see it— Dani on the linoleum, Kalee small and crumpled beside her. His mind replayed it in flashes he couldn't control. The blood mixing with the water from the shower. The crawling. The helplessness.

He gripped the armrests until his knuckles whitened, forcing himself to breathe.

The refrigerator hummed. A clock ticked somewhere in the distance. These ordinary sounds mocked him. Life inside the house carried on as if nothing had changed, but every corner was a ghost.

When the sun dipped lower, Henry rose and limped to the bedroom. The bed was made, untouched since that night. He sat at the edge, the mattress dipping beneath his weight, and opened the drawer of Dani's nightstand. Inside lay a handful of her things—lip balm, a paperback novel, her rosary beads tangled at the bottom. He picked them up, turning them in his fingers, the beads cold and smooth against his skin.

"Keep her safe," he muttered, though he didn't know if he was praying or cursing.

He placed the rosary back, then opened the drawer of his own nightstand. Inside was a small wooden box. He hadn't touched it in months, maybe years. He lifted the lid.

His service pistol lay inside, wrapped in a cloth. The metal gleamed faintly in the dim light, familiar and heavy. His reflection stared back at him in the barrel—hollow eyes, unshaven jaw, a man broken and remade. Henry's hand hovered over it, trembling. For a long moment, he didn't move. The old part of him, the soldier who had seen too much already, whispered that picking it up would be the end of him. That once he stepped back into this life, there would be no return.

But then he saw Dani's face in his mind. Kalee's tiny body in that hospital bed.

His hand closed around the grip.

The weight steadied him.

He exhaled slowly, slipping the cloth back over the pistol and returning it to the box. Not yet. Not tonight. But soon.

Henry closed the drawer with a sharp click and sat in the dark, the fire in him no longer smoldering but beginning to burn.

He wasn't ready. But he would be.

Night fell heavy over the house. Henry didn't turn on many lights—just a lamp in the corner of the living room, throwing a weak circle of yellow across the floor. The rest stayed dark. He sat in his chair, staring at nothing, his crutches leaned beside him. The house creaked occasionally, settling in its old frame, but otherwise it was silent. Too silent.

Every sound outside carried to him with sharp clarity: the muffled roar of a motorcycle on the avenue, a burst of laughter from teenagers walking past, the faint bark of a dog. Each one reminded him the world kept moving, that life outside his walls hadn't stopped. But his had. His gaze drifted to the corner where Kalee's backpack leaned against the wall, straps tangled, one zipper half open. A piece of paper stuck out—a drawing she'd made, crayon strokes of blue sky and a house with smoke curling from its chimney. A stick figure family stood in front, smiling. Daddy, Mommy, Kalee. He felt his throat tighten until it hurt.

Henry pressed his palms into his eyes, his breath catching. He had been in Afghanistan, he had seen men torn apart by IEDs, friends shot down beside him, but nothing—nothing—felt like this. There he'd known the enemy. Here, faceless shadows had crawled into his life, stripped it bare, and left his daughter clinging to life. And it was his fault.

The thought pressed harder than the pain in his stitched leg. If he'd been quicker, if he hadn't stepped into that shower, if he had checked the window when he heard the voices—maybe Dani would still be alive. Maybe Kalee wouldn't be in that hospital bed. The guilt sank into him like a stone, pulling him down, and no amount of breath could lift it.

He leaned forward, elbows on his knees, hands gripping his hair. Images crowded his mind—the way Dani's face lit up when she laughed, the way she teased him about his stubbornness, the warmth of her hand on his cheek. Kalee's voice calling him "Daddy" in that half-sung way children have, her little feet racing down the hallway in the mornings. The memory was too vivid, too cruel.

A tear slipped free despite him. He wiped it quickly, angry at himself for letting it show, even alone.

Henry's chest rose and fell sharply. He thought of Kalee, hooked to machines, her small body fighting battles she never asked for. What if she didn't wake up? The fear clawed at him, digging deeper than grief. He couldn't lose her too. He wouldn't.

His hand drifted unconsciously to the nightstand, to the drawer where the pistol waited. Not to take now, not yet. Just knowing it was there steadied him, like a lifeline.

He whispered into the empty room, voice low, almost trembling. "I'll protect you, Kalee. I'll protect what's left. No matter what it takes."

The silence swallowed his vow, but inside Henry, the fire grew hotter, spreading through every vein. He was a man undone, but also a man sharpening—guilt, grief, and fear pressing him into something harder, something dangerous.

He wasn't ready to move yet. But when he did, he knew there'd be no turning back.

The knock on the door came just after dusk. Henry froze where he sat, shoulders tightening. For a moment he thought about ignoring it, letting the silence stretch until whoever it was gave up. But the knock came again— firm, familiar.

He pushed himself up with his crutches, leg aching with every step, and opened the door.

Wilson and Steven stood on the porch, framed in the pale light of the streetlamp. Both men wore the same uneasy expression—half concern, half reluctance, as though they weren't sure they had a right to intrude.

"Hey, brother," Wilson said softly, his deep voice carrying its usual calm. "We just wanted to check in. Bring you some food." He held up a paper bag, grease spots bleeding through. "Fried chicken. Dani always said you liked it the next day, cold."

Steven shifted his weight, eyes darting past Henry into the dim house. "We didn't wanna bother you, man. Just... figured you shouldn't be sitting here alone."

Henry swallowed, jaw tight. Forcing his voice steady, he stepped aside. "Come in."

The two men entered quietly, setting the bag on the kitchen counter. The house felt even smaller with their presence, the walls pressing closer around Henry. They tried small talk at first—work, the neighborhood, even a game on TV—but their words fell flat. Wilson's eyes lingered on the photos still hanging in the hallway: Dani's smile, Kalee's gap-toothed grin. Steven tapped his fingers against the table, restless, the silence between questions heavier than the questions themselves.

"You holding up?" Wilson finally asked.

Henry gave the smallest shrug. "Best I can."

Steven leaned forward, his voice low but insistent. "You know if there's anything we can do—anything—you just say it. You're not alone in this, Henry."

Henry's stomach twisted. He wanted to tell them the truth—that he wasn't thinking about healing or moving on, that every breath was spent feeding the fire of vengeance building inside him. But he couldn't. Not here. Not with them.

He forced a tight smile instead. "I know. And I appreciate it. Really."

The three sat in silence a moment longer, the air heavy with unspoken words. Finally, Henry exhaled and pushed himself up, leaning on his crutches. "Listen, I'm tired. Been a long day. I should get some rest."

Wilson stood, nodding slowly. "Of course. We just wanted to see your face. Make sure you ate something."

Steven hesitated, then clapped Henry's shoulder gently. "We'll be around, man. Don't shut us out."

Henry's throat ached. He managed a quiet, "Thank you," and walked them to the door.

When it closed behind them, the silence rushed back in like a wave. He leaned his forehead against the wood for a moment, eyes shut tight, fighting the weight pressing down on him.

Then he turned, moving back to the kitchen. He opened the bag of food, pulled out a piece of chicken, and set it aside. His eyes weren't on the meal. They were on the drawer where his pistol waited.

Henry lowered himself into his chair, pulled a notepad from the side table, and laid it flat. His hand hovered over the blank page, then began to move. Names.

Places. Loose threads of memory—voices outside, the alleyway, fragments of what he'd told the detectives.

It was messy at first, scattered. But slowly the words began to take shape. A plan. A direction.

For the first time since Dani's death, Henry felt steady. Not whole. Never whole. But steady.

The fire inside him had found its purpose.

The notepad sat on the table, scattered with half-formed thoughts, names, and fragments of memory. Henry stared at it for a long while, the pen still in his hand, until the lines blurred together. His chest rose and fell in short, heavy breaths.

Finally, he pushed back the chair and rose to his feet. His leg screamed at him, the stitched wound pulling, but he ignored it. He moved down the hallway, past the photos on the wall, past Kalee's empty bedroom with the door ajar. His steps took him to the hall closet—a place he hadn't opened in years.

The hinges creaked as he pulled the door wide. Stacked behind boxes of winter coats and old shoes was a heavy olive-drab footlocker, its paint scuffed and peeling but still solid. His name—*Johnson, H.*—was stenciled across the top, faded but legible.

Henry crouched, grunting with the strain in his leg, and dragged it into the light. He sat back, hands resting on the cold metal for a moment. Memories pressed at him—dust, heat, the smell of diesel and gunpowder, the endless desert sky. He snapped the latches. The lid creaked open.

Inside lay the remnants of another life.

His old fatigues, neatly folded. A worn pair of desert boots. A Kevlar vest, edges frayed. And beneath them, wrapped carefully in cloth, his personal gear—the tools he'd carried through fire and blood overseas.

Henry unwrapped them slowly, reverently. A combat knife, blade nicked but sharp. A sidearm holster. Extra magazines still loaded with brass that gleamed faintly. A multitool he had used for everything from fixing Humvees to prying open crates.

He set each item out on the floor in front of him, lining them up with the same precision he had learned years ago.

Then he peeled back the bandages on his leg. The stitches were red, angry, the skin tender. He cleaned them carefully with alcohol, the sting biting deep, before wrapping them tighter, firmer. He looped the bandages again and again until the wound felt locked into place, no longer something fragile but something reinforced.

He flexed his leg. It hurt, but it held.

Henry slid the knife from its sheath, tested the balance in his hand, then laid it on the table beside the pistol from his nightstand. The two weapons sat there together like a pair of old companions waiting for him to speak first.

He ran a hand over the fatigues, the fabric rough against his fingers. He didn't put them on—not yet. But he knew he would. Soon.

The clock ticked somewhere in the silence. He glanced around the dim house, its shadows heavy, and realized he felt different now. Not whole. Not healed. But steadier, sharper. Like the soldier he used to be, called back to life by blood and loss.

Henry lowered himself into the chair again, staring at the gear spread out before him. His jaw tightened. His hands curled into fists.

He whispered into the silence, as if Dani could still hear him:

"They won't see me coming."

Henry was still at the table, the gear spread out before him like ghosts of another life, when the knock came. It wasn't the hesitant tap of a neighbor or the pounding of someone impatient—it was firm, measured. The kind of knock from a man who knew authority when he used it.

Henry's chest tightened. He hesitated, staring at the pistol resting on the table. For a moment he thought about sweeping everything back into the footlocker, hiding the past he'd just dragged into the present. But the knock came again, steady, patient.

With a grunt, Henry pushed himself up on the crutches and moved to the door.

Lt. Ronald Mitchell stood there, his trench coat collar turned up against the night chill, his eyes as weary as ever. He gave Henry a small nod, the kind that was part courtesy, part test.

"Evening, Henry," Mitchell said. "Mind if I come in a minute?"

Henry hesitated, then stepped aside. "Yeah... sure."

Mitchell entered quietly, his gaze taking in the dim room. His eyes lingered on the kitchen, the photos in the hallway—then landed on the table.

The knife. The pistol. The fatigues folded beside them. Henry's stomach clenched, but he forced a casual shrug. "Just... cleaning up some old stuff. Closet was getting crowded."

Mitchell stepped closer, hands tucked in his coat pockets, his eyes flicking across the array. He gave a low whistle. "Hell of a collection you got there. That standard issue, or you brought some of this home on the sly?"

Henry smirked faintly, masking the tension in his shoulders. "Perks of service, I guess."

Mitchell picked up the knife, weighing it in his hand, turning it over under the lamplight. He raised an eyebrow. "Sharp as the day they gave it to you. Most vets I know keep medals in their closets, not hardware that could gut a man."

Henry's jaw tightened. "Different kind of memories."

Mitchell set the knife down gently, his eyes lingering on Henry longer than the words warranted. Then, with a small chuckle, he leaned back. "Well, if I ever need somebody to cut through red tape—or drywall—you're my guy."

The joke hung there, half-hearted, a way to ease the air. But Henry didn't laugh.

Mitchell let the silence stretch a moment, his expression unreadable. Then he patted the edge of the table lightly and stepped back. "Just came by to check on you. See how you're holding up after the service." Henry shifted on his crutches, gesturing toward the door. "I appreciate it. Really. But I'm... tired. Trying to rest."

Mitchell gave him a long look, something sharp behind the weariness. Then he nodded once, pulling his coat tighter. "I'll let you get back to it."

At the door, he paused. "Henry—if you ever need to talk, you got my number."

Henry managed a tight smile. "Yeah. Thanks, Lieutenant."

Mitchell stepped out into the night, the door closing softly behind him.

On the sidewalk, he paused under the streetlight, lighting a cigarette with slow, deliberate care. Smoke curled in the cold air as he looked back at the apartment window, eyes narrowed.

He didn't say a word. But in his gut, Mitchell knew. Henry wasn't just mourning. He was sharpening.

The silence after Mitchell left pressed harder than before. Henry stood by the door a long moment, his hand still on the knob, listening to the retreating footsteps fade into the night. Only when he heard the car start down the block did he finally turn away.

His eyes went back to the table. The pistol. The knife. The fatigues folded neatly, just as Mitchell had seen them.

Henry cursed under his breath, slamming a fist against the wall. How could he have been so careless? It wasn't like him—never had been, not in the field, not in his life. Carelessness got people killed. Dani. Kalee.

He limped back to the table, lowering himself slowly into the chair, his stitched leg aching as he bent. He gathered the items, one by one, wrapping the knife back in its cloth, sliding the pistol into the holster, folding the fatigues tighter. He packed them into the footlocker with the precision of a soldier breaking down camp before dawn.

But this time, he didn't bury them.

The locker stayed open, sitting at his side like a companion. He stared into it, chest heaving, the old instincts prickling to life inside him.

Mitchell's face floated in his mind—the half-smile, the way his eyes lingered, the weight in his voice when he said Henry had his number. The Lieutenant had seen too much not to suspect. Henry respected that. Hell, part of him even liked Mitchell. But respect didn't mean trust.

From now on, Henry told himself, nothing would sit out in the open. He couldn't afford to let anyone see what was coming—not Yvonne, not Wilson or Steven, not the cops.

He rose slowly, dragging the locker across the floor to the back room. There, he pried up the old floorboard beneath the rug, the one spot he'd once used to stash savings when work was lean. The space was narrow, dark, but it would do.

Piece by piece, he lowered the gear inside—the pistol, the knife, the magazines, the fatigues. He left only the bandages and the alcohol kit out, resting them neatly on the dresser. He pulled the board back into place, pressed the rug down, and sat back on his heels, listening to his breath.

Hidden, but not forgotten.

Henry leaned against the wall, sweat damp on his temples despite the chill. He realized then that Mitchell's visit had given him clarity. He could no longer let grief drive him blindly. If he was going to do this—if he was going to make them pay—it had to be quiet. Patient. Controlled.

He thought of Dani, of her voice calling him stubborn, of Kalee's laugh. The fire inside him steadied, focusing into a sharp point.

"I'll be smarter than them," he whispered into the dark. "Smarter, faster. They won't see me coming."

He tightened the bandage around his leg until the pain sharpened his senses, until he felt his body align with his mind.

From this night forward, Henry promised himself one thing: no more mistakes.

The house sank into darkness as the hours dragged on. Henry didn't turn on the lights. He sat in the living room, the glow from the streetlamp outside cutting thin stripes of pale light across the floor. The world felt suspended, like time itself was holding its breath.

His eyes wandered to the photos on the wall. Dani's smile in their wedding picture, her head tilted, laughing at something he'd whispered just before the flash went off. Kalee's school portrait with her missing front tooth and that proud, gap-toothed grin. He stared until his vision blurred, but the images didn't fade—they sharpened, stabbing at him.

The guilt crept in again, heavy and merciless. He pressed his palms into his eyes, but it didn't block the thoughts. *If you'd come out sooner. If you'd heard them in time. If you'd been faster.*

Instead he'd been in the shower, drowning out the noise, trying to wash away the tension of another day. His family had bled while he let the water run. He'd fought in war zones, walked through ambushes, patched men together under fire—but he hadn't been able to protect his wife in his own home. The thought hollowed him out.

He rose slowly, crutches digging into the floor, and made his way to Kalee's bedroom. The door creaked as he pushed it open.

Her small bed was neatly made, the pink comforter pulled tight, her favorite stuffed rabbit tucked under the pillow where she'd left it. The smell of her still lingered—

shampoo, crayons, the faint sweetness of bubblegum. Henry stepped inside, his throat constricting. He lowered himself onto the edge of the bed, the mattress barely shifting under his weight.

His hand rested on the rabbit, its fur worn thin from years of clutching. He remembered Kalee holding it to her chest, peeking over its ears as he read her bedtime stories. "One more page, Daddy," she'd always begged, eyes wide, voice soft. And he always had—one more page, every night, until her breathing slowed and her hand went slack.

A sharp ache twisted in his chest. What if she didn't come home? What if this room stayed empty forever, frozen in time?

Henry bent forward, his forehead pressing against the rabbit. "Hold on, baby girl," he whispered, voice breaking. "Just hold on for me. Daddy's not done yet. You hear me? Daddy's not done."

The silence answered him.

He stayed there a long time, rocking slightly, the rabbit clutched in his hands, memories of Dani's voice and Kalee's laughter chasing each other through his mind. The weight of it nearly buckled him, but the fire inside steadied him once again.

He wiped his eyes with the back of his hand, sharp and rough. Rising carefully, he closed Kalee's door behind him.

The house was still. The ghosts hadn't left, but he'd made a promise to them now.

Tomorrow, he told himself, the first step would come. Morning light crept through the blinds in thin bands, striping the living room. Henry hadn't slept much—his body restless, his mind relentless—but the house felt different when the sun was up. Less haunted. More purposeful.

He sat at the table, the notepad open in front of him, the phone in his hand. The paper was covered now with scribbled names and half-thought notes, arrows connecting fragments of memory, all circling back to one word: *vengeance.*

His thumb hovered over a number he hadn't dialed in years. **Caleb Hart.** A man he'd shared sand and fire with, someone who had pulled him out from under shrapnel once and never asked for thanks. The last time they spoke, Caleb had been in Pennsylvania, running a mechanic shop, married, kids. Normal life. Henry wondered if Caleb knew—if word had traveled from Boston about Dani, about Kalee.

He drew in a slow breath and pressed *call.*

The line rang twice before a gravelly voice answered. "Henry? Damn, brother, I heard some things but didn't want to believe 'em."

Henry closed his eyes, jaw tight. "It's true."

There was silence, then a sigh on the other end. "Jesus. I'm sorry. I don't know what to say."

Henry swallowed, forcing the words past the lump in his throat. "I'm not calling for sympathy, Caleb. I need... help."

Another pause. Then Caleb's tone shifted, lower, firmer. "No questions. What do you need?"

Henry leaned forward, his hand gripping the edge of the table. "I'm trying to track down some people. Bad people. The kind that don't care who they hurt. I need eyes. I need... options."

Caleb's voice carried no hesitation. "You got it. Whatever I've got, it's yours."

Henry almost broke then—almost let the weight of brotherhood and loyalty crack the shell he was building. But he held steady. "I can't promise I'll be able to explain everything. Hell, I don't even know how far this is gonna go."

"Henry." Caleb's voice was steady, unyielding. "You don't owe me explanations. We bled together once. That's all that matters. You call, I show up. Simple as that."

The silence stretched between them, not awkward, but heavy with shared history. Henry nodded, though Caleb couldn't see it. "I'll be in touch. Soon."

"Any time, brother. Day or night. You ain't alone."

Henry ended the call, setting the phone down slowly. His hand lingered on it, trembling just slightly. He exhaled, long and uneven, then looked back at the notepad. Caleb was there. Others might be too. A network buried in the past, but not gone.

For the first time since the night of the shooting, Henry felt the faintest echo of strength—not just his own, but borrowed, shared. He wasn't just a grieving father. He was a soldier again, with brothers who would stand beside him if called.

He closed the notepad, slid it aside, and reached for the footlocker. The next step was coming.

And this time, he wouldn't be walking into it alone.

Henry didn't call Caleb again that day. Or the next. He didn't need to. The line was open now, the bond reestablished. And Caleb had understood immediately: no questions, no explanations, no guilt. Just readiness. Henry leaned on that. It gave him strength.

Over the next few days, more quiet messages trickled in. A text from **Marcus**, another vet from his unit: *Heard about Dani. Anything you need, brother. No questions.* A missed call from **Torres**, no voicemail but Henry knew what it meant. Even an email from **Anders**, typed in clumsy all caps: *I GOT YOU MAN. JUST SAY WHEN.*

Henry never replied with details. He gave them distance, gave them deniability. He told them he was "working through it," that he was "just trying to keep Kalee strong." That was enough.

But beneath the surface, they all knew. He could hear it in their voices, see it in the short, clipped words they left behind. They knew Henry wasn't just grieving. He was sharpening himself for something.

And they approved.

That was the unspoken truth: every message carried the same quiet cheer, the same solidarity. A nod from one soldier to another. *Do what you have to. We've got your back.*

Henry carried their faith like a hidden weapon.

At night, when the house was still, he replayed Caleb's voice: *You ain't alone.* It echoed through him as he sat at the table, the footlocker open, the gear spread out once again. His hands moved slowly, methodically, disassembling his pistol, cleaning each part until it gleamed, reassembling it with the precision of ritual.

His leg wound still ached, but he tightened the bandages himself each morning, firm enough that the limp grew steadier. Pain was a companion now, one he welcomed.

He studied maps of the neighborhood, printouts he'd pulled from an old stack of utility bills and junk mail that had sketches of alleys, streets, back routes. He scribbled notes about line of sight, about escape paths, about where a man could hide and where he couldn't. When he closed his eyes, he could hear the voices again—angry, quick, young. He tried to separate them, to mark their tones, to fix them in his mind. Three men, maybe four. He wrote it down. He circled it.

Sometimes, when the weight of guilt pressed too hard, he picked up the rabbit from Kalee's bed and held it in his lap as he worked. The contrast was sharp and painful, but it grounded him.

Henry never told his old friends what he was doing. He never would. But their silence and their offers hung like a shield around him.

They would deny knowing if asked. But in their hearts, they were with him. And that was enough.

The city looks different when you aren't a part of it anymore.

Henry sat in his car, an old sedan with a dented fender and a sputtering heater, parked two blocks off the avenue. The windows were rolled down just enough to let the night air slip inside, carrying with it the smells of fried food, motor oil, and cigarette smoke. He sat still, hands on the wheel, eyes scanning the street the way he used to scan ridgelines overseas.

This wasn't Afghanistan. No sand, no convoys, no IEDs buried under dirt. But the rhythms of danger were the same. You learned to watch how people moved, who controlled the corners, where the shadows gathered thicker than they should.

From his spot, he had a view of three separate intersections. On each, young men lingered—hoods up, hands deep in pockets, their laughter sharp and quick. The same faces rotated out every few hours, like shifts on watch. Henry noted the hand signals, the way cars slowed and pulled close, how bills passed quick and low, how palms never stayed empty long.

He wrote down times. Movements. Headcounts.

He didn't need to step into the alley where his family had bled. He knew the cops had been there, knew the city workers had washed away the blood and patched the holes in the brick. That place was sanitized now, useless to him. The truth didn't linger in empty walls; it lived in the men who prowled the streets after dark.

Henry shifted slightly, his stitched leg aching. He pressed the pain down and kept his gaze steady. Across the way, two men met under the buzz of a failing streetlamp. He recognized the colors—green bandanas tied sloppy at their waists. The **Piranhas.** Young, reckless, their voices loud enough to carry even through the car's cracked windows. He watched one pull a wad of bills from his pocket, slapping it into another's hand. A cigarette sparked, the smoke curling up into the night. Not far down the block, a different group clustered by a corner bodega. No bandanas, but Henry caught the subtle rhythm of their posture, the way they scanned every passing car, the tension under their easy laughter. **African Lords.** More disciplined, less flashy, but the control was obvious. The block moved around them like the world knew who owned it.

Henry leaned back, his jaw tight. These were the players. The names the detectives had circled around, the gangs Mitchell had hinted at when he said the city was about to bleed.

Henry didn't write down the names—not yet. He just watched, committing the patterns to memory. He knew patience was everything. He wouldn't strike blind. He'd move only when he was certain.

Hours passed. The crowds shifted. Streetlights buzzed, cars came and went, the city breathed. Henry sat through it all, silent, his body rigid, his eyes sharp.

By the time he drove home, the first threads of a map had already begun to form in his mind.

He wasn't chasing ghosts anymore. He was hunting men.

The nights bled together, one after the other, until Henry's days revolved around two things: sitting by Kalee's side at the hospital, and watching the streets once the sun went down.

He didn't move fast. He knew better than that. You don't rush into an ambush blind—you wait, you study, you learn the rhythm of your enemy until you know them better than they know themselves.

From the driver's seat of his dented sedan, Henry became part of the background. A car idling at the curb wasn't strange in Boston; people were always waiting for someone, always killing time. He adjusted his seat low, wore a cap pulled down over his face, and let the city flow around him.

Each night, he picked a new vantage point.

One night, he parked near the edge of Dorchester, where a pool hall bled neon light onto the sidewalk. He didn't need to step inside to know it was tied to the **Hell's Gentlemen**—their patched jackets and leather cuts told the story as they drifted in and out. White boys with biker swagger, loud voices, and the careless arrogance of men who thought they owned the world. Henry noted how they moved in groups, how cash exchanged hands quickly, how more than one car trunk carried the weight of crates.

Another night, he settled near the Southside. The **Piranhas** ran it like a carnival, loud and chaotic. Their hangout was an old auto shop with bay doors that never closed, music thumping through blown-out speakers, men spilling into the street with bottles in their hands. Green bandanas marked them, but they didn't need colors—their noise gave them away. Henry watched as they dragged in a kid no older than sixteen, slapping him on the back, handing him a pistol like it was a toy. He wrote it down. Young recruits. No discipline. Dangerous in numbers, but sloppy.

And then there were the **African Lords.**

Henry kept his distance, careful not to draw eyes. They were more subtle, their corners watched like checkpoints, their gatherings quieter. But their control was visible in the way people deferred, crossing the street to avoid them, dropping their eyes when they passed. Henry noted their warehouse on Forty-Third, how men filtered in and out with a purpose, not the swagger of punks but the stride of soldiers. Mykelti's hand was everywhere, even if the man himself stayed out of sight.

Each observation added another thread to the map Henry kept tucked in his notepad. Three groups, three styles of chaos. Different masks, same disease. And somewhere in that web, were the men who had fired wild into his home.

Henry sat with the engine off, the cool night air cutting through the open window. His eyes traced the faces in the street, committing them to memory. Not just the bosses, not just the soldiers—everyone. Lookouts.

Runners. Drivers. He was building a picture, one piece at a time.

He knew patience was his greatest weapon now. When the time came to move, he wanted to know the city better than the gangs themselves.

For now, he just watched.

And he burned.

It was near midnight when Henry caught it.

He had been parked two streets off from the African Lords' warehouse, the glow of his dashboard clock ticking slow, when two men stepped into the open. He recognized one immediately—**Switch**. Wiry, cocky, the kind of man who strutted even when no one was watching.

The second man was younger, barely more than a boy, his shoulders hunched like he was still learning the weight of the gang life. They leaned against a rusted fence, voices low but sharp enough to carry in the still air.

"...should've kept that shit tight," Switch muttered, shaking his head. "Mykelti don't like heat. Cops sniffin' around ain't good for business."

The kid shifted nervously. "Ain't our fault. The Hellmans came wild. Bullets went everywhere—"

Switch cut him off with a laugh, thin and mean. "Fault don't matter. People dead. That's the only story anybody cares about. Now every block's lit. We keep it moving, stay louder, stay meaner—then folks forget."

Henry's chest tightened. His grip on the steering wheel left his knuckles white. These were the voices from the night—the careless bravado behind the bullets that had torn his life apart.

He slid from the car, moving into the shadows. He trailed them at a distance, his crutches left behind— tonight he forced himself to walk, every step sharp with pain but silent on the cracked pavement.

Switch split from the kid two blocks down, cutting toward an unfinished housing development on the edge of the neighborhood. Half-built homes sat in skeletal rows, frames and drywall exposed, windows nothing but empty sockets staring into the night.

Henry followed.

The streets were empty here, no traffic, no eyes. Switch lit a cigarette as he walked, the ember flaring in the dark, his head down. Henry closed the distance, his body coiled tight, his breath slow and steady.

But Switch stopped suddenly. His head tilted, his body stiff. He turned, the glint of metal flashing in his hand. The gun barked once—loud, sharp, echoing off the unfinished walls. The bullet whined past Henry's shoulder, splintering wood behind him.

Henry didn't flinch. He moved forward fast, years of muscle memory taking hold, his body remembering things his mind hadn't wanted to. Switch cursed, stumbling backward into the frame of a half-built house, firing again. The shot went wide, tearing a hole through fresh drywall.

Henry barreled after him. The pain in his leg flared white-hot, but he drove through it, slamming his shoulder into the frame. Drywall cracked, gave way, and both men crashed through in a cloud of plaster dust. Switch scrambled, wild-eyed, trying to raise the gun again.

Henry lunged, his hand clamping down on Switch's wrist, twisting hard. The gun clattered to the floor. Switch snarled, swinging with his free hand, but Henry didn't let go. He crashed him into the studs, plaster crumbling around them, the sound of struggle filling the hollow house.

Finally, with a guttural roar, Henry drove him through another section of unfinished wall, the drywall exploding around them. He pinned Switch to the floor, dust thick in the air, his own breath ragged but steady. He had him.

Boston glittered beneath them, the city sprawled out in a grid of headlights and neon. The wind was sharp this high up, tugging at clothing, carrying the smell of steel and rain. Boston's Prudential building.

Switch trembled, his wrists bound tight with thick cord, his body pressed forward against the rails of a window cleaner's scaffold that swayed ever so slightly in the wind. The city yawned hundreds of feet below, the streets no bigger than veins of light.

Henry stood behind him, silent, his chest rising slow and steady. His face was hard, his eyes hollow, lit only by the faint glow of the city. He gave the scaffold a sharp jolt with his foot, and Switch gasped, the ropes biting into his arms as he lurched forward.

"Please, man," Switch stammered, his voice cracking against the wind. "You don't gotta do this. You don't—"

Henry stepped closer, his voice low, controlled. "You fired into my home. My wife is in the ground. My little girl's hooked to machines."

"I didn't—" Switch started, but Henry cut him off with another sharp kick. The scaffold rocked violently, the ropes groaned, and Switch screamed.

Henry leaned in, his mouth close to Switch's ear. "Don't waste my time. You talk, or I let go. 'that simple."

The younger man's breath came in ragged gasps, his body shaking against the ropes. He looked down again, Copley Square spinning beneath him, and then the words tumbled out.

"It was a deal! With the Hell's Gentlemen! Guns, man, crates of them. Mykelti wanted steel, big moves comin'. But it went bad. Shots everywhere. I swear, we didn't mean to hit no civilians—it was chaos! The Piranhas started sniffin' around too, makin' noise. Mykelti—he wants them gone. Wants the whole damn city under his thumb!"

Henry's jaw tightened, but he didn't move. He let the words hang, the wind carrying them off into the night. Switch went on, desperate now, words spilling fast. "We got a warehouse—Forty-Third Street. That's where it's movin' through. Guns, explosives, all of it. Mykelti calls the shots, but Leon and Stone—his lieutenants—they run the day-to-day. You wanna find who pulled the trigger? That's where they'll be."

Henry stared at him, cold and silent. Switch's chest heaved, his eyes wide, every nerve in him screaming panic.

Another pause. Another gust of wind. Then Henry reached down, untied the cord from the scaffold rail, and yanked Switch backward to safety. The younger man collapsed onto the platform, sobbing in relief, his face streaked with sweat and plaster dust.

Henry knelt, his face inches from Switch's. "You breathe a word about this," he whispered, "and I'll find you again and we will re-visit our little love nest up here. You understand me?"

Switch nodded frantically, his voice breaking. "Y-yeah. Yeah, I swear."

Henry rose, pulling the ropes loose, leaving Switch slumped and shaking. He turned away, his eyes fixed on the horizon where the city stretched endless and merciless.

For the first time since Dani's funeral, he had direction. A name. A place.

The hunt had begun.

Chapter 5

The quiet of the hospital pressed against Henry like a weight. The corridors were nearly empty at this hour, lit by the soft hum of fluorescent bulbs overhead. The scent of disinfectant lingered in the air, sharp and sterile, masking everything human. He moved slowly past the nurses' station, his boots sounding heavier than usual against the tiled floor, until he reached the ICU wing. Every visit was the same, and yet every visit hurt worse than the last.

Kalee's room sat at the end of the hall, her door cracked open as though waiting for him. He stepped inside and immediately felt the cold air of the machines, the steady beeping monitors that seemed louder in the silence. There she was — his daughter, his baby girl — pale against the sheets, small beneath the wires and tubes that kept her tethered to this world.

Henry's breath caught. No matter how many times he came, he was never ready for the sight of her lying so still. His large hands, scarred and rough, looked almost clumsy as he reached for her smaller one. It was warm but limp, her fingers unresponsive as he wrapped them in his grip.

"You should've seen me tonight," he said softly, almost whispering to her, as though she were simply asleep. "I got closer. I'm piecing it together, step by step. The men who did this to you — they're running scared now. I'll find them. I'll make them pay."

His voice cracked, just slightly, and he pressed his lips together to still the tremor. He couldn't cry here. He wouldn't let her see weakness, even in sleep. He leaned closer, brushing a strand of hair back from her forehead with surprising gentleness.

"You just keep fighting, sweetheart," Henry murmured. "Your old man's got this part covered."

The machines ticked on steadily, indifferent to his words. But Henry chose to believe, just for a moment, that some part of her could hear him. That she knew he was still out there, fighting for her.

He sat beside her bed for several minutes, lost in the rhythm of her breathing, watching the slight rise and fall of her chest. It was proof of life, fragile as it seemed. He remembered when she was younger, when he used to sit at her bedside waiting for her to drift off to sleep. She would grip his hand the same way he held hers now, refusing to let go until she was safe in dreams.

Henry closed his eyes, remembering the sound of her laughter, the way she'd shriek with delight when he tossed her into the air. Memories collided with the sterile reality in front of him. His daughter, vibrant and strong, reduced to this fragile form wrapped in tubes. Rage curled inside him, sharp as barbed wire.

But rage alone wouldn't bring justice. Discipline would. Control would. And Henry had both in spades. He bent closer, his voice firm now, almost like a report being given to a commanding officer.

"I know where they're moving," he said. "They're dealing rifles down in Chinatown. I'll cut the deal off at the knees. They won't see me coming. And when I'm done..." He exhaled, the words thick in his throat. "When I'm done, maybe you'll open your eyes and see the world's a little safer again."

His eyes stayed locked on her face, searching for the slightest flicker, the smallest sign of response. None came. Still, he nodded, as if she'd confirmed the plan. Henry rose to his feet reluctantly, letting her hand slip gently back to the sheets. He straightened his jacket, the weight of it heavy against his shoulders. He gave the room one last glance, imprinting her face in his mind like a sacred image, something to carry into the night ahead.

At the doorway, he paused. The city was waiting for him, pulling him back into its shadows, but leaving her behind tore something open in his chest. He wanted to stay, to guard her himself, but that wasn't what she needed. What she needed was a father who would burn down the world to keep her safe.

"I'll be back tomorrow," he said quietly, not for the machines or the walls but for her alone. "Don't give up, Kalee. Not now. Not ever."

Then he stepped out, closing the door softly behind him. The hallway swallowed him in its quiet again, but his mind was already turning. Chinatown. Rifles. The

Hell's Gentlemen. He had work to do, and the city was about to feel it.

The night outside struck Henry like a slap of cold water. The hospital's brightness gave way to Boston's darker pulse — the streets alive with neon, the glow of bars and late-night eateries, the hushed scuffle of shoes on sidewalks. A cab shot past, headlights glaring, the driver shouting at someone stepping off the curb too slow. Henry shoved his hands into the pockets of his jacket and moved down the street, letting the rhythm of the city fold around him.

Boston at night was a different animal. It prowled on half-lit corners and whispered in the alleys. Chinatown wasn't far, but already the signs of its presence bled into the air — the smell of roasted duck carried faintly on the wind, the spatter of foreign tongues mixing with the sharp crackle of English curses. Even the walls seemed to hum with layered history: immigrants and exiles carving out space, gangs staking claim where old traditions and new hustles overlapped.

Henry had always been good at blending in. Even now, with his shoulders broad, boots heavy, and his whole body screaming soldier, he moved with a subtlety that let him slip between clusters of strangers without drawing more than a passing glance. He was a man in a city of millions, just another shadow threading through neon light. But his eyes — those sharp, cold eyes — marked him different. He wasn't wandering. He was hunting.

At a corner, he stopped beneath the glow of a red lantern swinging over a doorway. Across the street, two men haggled loudly with a street vendor packing up his cart. The vendor waved them off, tossing his remaining dumplings into a bag and wheeling the cart into the dark. A group of teenagers hurried past Henry, laughing too loud, their sneakers slapping the pavement. None of it mattered. What mattered was what lay deeper in — the place he knew from whispers and Switch's confession, where suits with embroidered devils on their backs were making trades that poisoned the city. Henry drew a slow breath, tasting the damp night air. His daughter's face hovered at the front of his mind. Every step, every breath, every move he made tonight had to count. He wasn't just searching for vengeance anymore. He was cutting out rot before it spread further, before more families ended up staring at hospital monitors, clinging to hope in sterile rooms.

He adjusted the fit of his jacket and started walking again, deeper toward Chinatown's heart. The further he went, the louder the city grew. The metallic scrape of gates pulling down over storefronts. The thrum of bass from clubs where the night was still young. The low, private conversations at corners where deals were struck, words traded for money, for drugs, for guns. Henry's jaw tightened. He had spent enough years in uniform to know that the real battles weren't fought under flags or for medals. They were fought in places like this — nameless streets, dim corners, where predators feed on the weak. Tonight, he was taking the fight to them.

The streets narrowed as Henry pressed on, neon signs flickering above him like restless spirits. Dragons coiled in paint across brick walls, their scales chipped from years of weather but still fierce in the glow of the lights. Steam hissed from a grate beneath his boots, rising to curl against his face before disappearing into the night. Somewhere in the distance, a siren wailed — sharp, hollow — then faded as quickly as it came. Boston's pulse never stopped, it only shifted rhythms.

Henry slowed at an intersection where the shadows grew thicker. A noodle shop stood closed on the corner, its chairs stacked neatly on tables behind fogged windows. Across from it, a small group of men smoked outside a convenience store, their voices carrying in short bursts of Mandarin. They watched him pass but said nothing, eyes narrowing as if trying to place him. He ignored them, keeping his stride steady, his posture relaxed but not careless. He had learned long ago how to move like he belonged anywhere — enough presence to keep predators cautious, enough calm to avoid stirring curiosity.

Ahead, the city changed flavor. The clamor of bars and restaurants thinned into a quieter, heavier silence. The buildings leaned inward here, shutting out much of the neon and moonlight. This was the Chinatown no tourist maps showed — where deals were made in whispers, and doors opened only if you had the right knock.

Henry's senses sharpened. The faint rumble of bass
from a club subsided, replaced by the softer sounds of
shifting feet, a car door closing, the muted hum of an
idling engine somewhere ahead.

He paused at the mouth of an alley, back pressed briefly
against the cool brick. He inhaled through his nose,
steadying his breath, letting his eyes adjust to the dim
light. He could feel it — the tension that always lived on
the edges of gun trades. He'd seen it before, overseas
and back home. The same nervous glances, the same
hunger for money, the same weight of violence just
waiting to spill out.

Henry checked his jacket, the concealed bulk at his
side pressing reassuringly against his ribs. He wasn't
looking for a fight, but he knew Chinatown wouldn't give
him any other choice. The intel Switch had coughed up
painted the picture clear enough: Hell's Gentlemen
were moving rifles here tonight. That meant the
warehouse near the Summer Street waterfront,
guarded, crawling with men who thought a devil on their
back made them untouchable.

He stepped out of the alley, heading toward the glow of
street lamps that pooled on the far side of the block.
The night pressed close around him, the kind of close
that muffled sound and magnified every small detail —
a bottle tipping in the gutter, the faint scratch of a
lighter, the brush of fabric against brick. He caught it all,
absorbing it, turning it into a map in his head.

Every move forward brought him closer. Every step was a promise. He wasn't just following leads anymore. He was hunting wolves in their territory.

Down by the waterfront, the city wore a different face. The smell of salt and diesel hung thick in the air, mingling with the sour tang of garbage left too long in rusted bins. A row of warehouses stood in silence, their walls scarred by time, windows barred and glass warped by years of weather. But one building glowed faintly from within, its distorted panes leaking slivers of light into the night.

Parked in front were machines that didn't belong to these streets: gleaming German sedans, a Cadillac SUV polished to a mirror shine, a vintage Mustang idling like it had rolled straight out of a collector's dream. Two men in suits loitered by the entrance, cigarette smoke drifting between them. Their laughter was low, guarded, the kind men used when they wanted to look casual while watching everything at once. Each wore the same sharp tailoring, and on the backs of their jackets was stitched an emblem that caught the light when they shifted — a snarling devil's face embroidered in crimson and gold thread.

It was the mark of the Hell's Gentlemen, a gang that prided itself on blending refinement with menace. They weren't the kind to haunt alleys in sagging jeans or shout on corners for scraps. They dressed like royalty, carried themselves with the confidence of men who believed they'd already won. Even outside the warehouse, that aura was undeniable. The way the guards scanned the street, the way their hands rested near the folds of their jackets, told anyone with sense that this wasn't a place to linger.

The waterfront whispered with restless energy, a current of danger beneath the quiet. To any outsider, this was just another forgotten building in a forgotten district. But for those who knew, the glow behind barred windows marked it as something more — a lair where power shifted hands in whispers and deals were sealed with blood.

Inside, the real theater of the Hell's Gentlemen waited. Inside, the warehouse felt nothing like the crumbling exterior suggested. The first impression was light — soft, golden, spilling from chandeliers hung too low for a building meant to store cargo. Beneath them, the polished floor gleamed, dark wood shining as though freshly waxed. The air was scented faintly with cigar smoke and expensive cologne, layered with the sharper note of alcohol poured generously from the bar in the corner.

The space had been transformed into something closer to a private club than a gang's hideout. Expensive leather couches lined the floor, their deep cushions sagging under the weight of men and women who wore the same embroidered devil's grin on the backs of their suits. Jazz drifted lazily through the room, a soft trumpet climbing over the low hum of voices. It was the kind of music that smoothed edges, that turned violence into background noise.

Two women leaned against the bar, dressed in skirts and silk tops that showed just enough to make every eye stray their way. Their laughter was practiced, the kind that carried without breaking into shrillness, warming the atmosphere like smoke curling in a glass. They weren't outsiders brought in for the night — no, they were fixtures here, part of the décor, as much a part of the Gentlemen's image as the polished bottles gleaming on the mirrored shelves.

Everywhere Henry's world had been sterile, worn, or broken, here was the opposite: wealth and indulgence poured into a room meant to broadcast one message. The Hell's Gentlemen weren't just surviving in Boston's underworld. They were thriving.

And at the center of it all was Jason Farokmanesh.

Jason Farokmanesh moved through the room like a man born to it. Medium in build, his frame wasn't the largest in the warehouse, but the way he carried himself eclipsed everyone else. His suit was tailored with precision — navy wool cut sharp at the shoulders, the tie knotted neatly at his throat — yet there was nothing stiff in his movements. He flowed, unhurried, each step measured, as though time itself bent to his pace. Conversations dipped as he passed. Not in fear, but in acknowledgment, the kind reserved for a figure who needed no introduction. The Gentlemen lounging on couches tilted their heads subtly, a mark of respect without breaking their composure. Even the women at the bar straightened a touch, their smiles turning genuine at the sight of him. Jason didn't need to command the room with volume or threat; his presence was the command.

He reached the bar and gestured smoothly for a drink. The bartender — a clean-cut man who looked more Wall Street than street corner — moved quickly to pour a measure of dark liquor, setting it on the polished surface with careful precision. Jason didn't speak a word, yet the transaction had the weight of ritual.

One of the women at the bar, a brunette with kohl-dark eyes and a voice like velvet, shifted closer. Jason's smile was slight but warm, a charm that seemed practiced but not false. He inclined his head, and with a subtle gesture beckoned her to him. She came without hesitation, sliding from her stool and letting her hand brush lightly against his sleeve as though the touch alone carried privilege.

Jason accepted his glass, turning just enough to survey the room. In his eyes was a calculation hidden behind the mask of ease — he saw everything, noted every man's posture, every flicker of unease or loyalty. For him, control wasn't an act of force. It was a current he carried with him, one everyone else in the room fell into without realizing.

Jason lifted his glass, savoring the burn of the liquor as it touched his lips. The brunette leaned against him, smiling in a way that spoke of belonging, not transaction. He let her linger, an arm settling easily at her waist, when two of his men stepped forward from the cluster of couches. Their suits bore the same embroidered devil's face, but their posture was sharper, less at ease.

The first, tall and wiry with a neatly trimmed beard, cleared his throat before speaking. "Jason, the Chinatown boys came through. Coughed up enough for their first shipment." He spoke with the care of a man reporting to someone he respected, not feared — though the line between the two blurred easily here.

Jason's smile didn't falter. He swirled the liquor in his glass, watching the amber liquid catch the light. "And the Africans?" he asked, voice smooth, unhurried, as if the matter were a curiosity rather than potential conflict.

The second Gent, broader and younger, shifted his weight. "Word is their boss is still sore about the shooting. One of his boys got lit up. But..." He hesitated, then finished, "He still wants to deal."

Jason exhaled softly through his nose, almost a laugh, though it carried no humor. "Then he should send better men. Greedy lieutenants get people killed." He tilted his head, considering, then waved it off. "We'll make it right. They'll keep coming back."

The brunette pressed closer against him as he leaned down, brushing her lips with his own in a kiss that deepened quickly. The room barely stirred — no one dared watch too openly, but everyone knew the display wasn't indulgence, it was ownership. Jason broke away after a moment, setting his glass aside and nodding toward the broader Gent.

"Make sure the Chinatown drop happens clean," Jason said. "No noise, no heat. The cops are already twitchy. I don't want them sniffing around any more than they are."

The man straightened, nodding firmly. "I'll supervise it myself."

Jason returned the nod, satisfied. Then, with the same calm that marked all his movements, he turned back to the woman at his side and led her away from the bar, vanishing into a corridor at the back of the warehouse. Business handled, desire indulged, order maintained. The Gentlemen's world revolved because Jason kept it turning.

Chinatown after midnight carried a pulse all its own. The day's markets and crowded sidewalks were gone, leaving behind streets slick with drizzle and echoing with the occasional rush of a passing car. Neon signs still glowed, their colors bleeding into puddles on the pavement, dragons and kanji fractured by ripples of water. The air smelled of roasted duck fat clinging to alleyways, of incense drifting faintly from a late-night temple, of smoke from kitchens that never truly closed. But beneath the surface charm, there was tension. The usual crowds had thinned to shadows, figures moving quickly with their heads down, avoiding corners where strangers lingered too long. In these hours, Chinatown belonged not to the families finishing dinners, but to the crews who worked the streets when the city turned its head away.

At the far end of a narrow block, a dark SUV sat parked beneath a burnt-out streetlight. Its engine ticked quietly, still warm. Two men lounged inside, suits pressed sharp despite the hour, cigarettes glowing faintly between their fingers. They looked like businessmen caught between meetings, but the embroidered devils stitched across the backs of their jackets told another story. Hell's Gentlemen didn't slouch outside warehouses for nothing.

The men exhaled smoke, glancing up and down the street with the patience of predators. Their words were low, muffled by the closed windows, their eyes never fully resting. They weren't waiting for friends. They were waiting for business.

Across the block, an old homeless man pushed a rickety cart piled high with plastic bags. The wheels squeaked against the uneven pavement, a sound that carried farther than it should have in the thin night air. He passed without slowing, muttering to himself in a language no one bothered to understand. Neither of the men in the SUV gave him more than a glance. In their world, he was invisible, background noise.

What mattered was who was coming next.

The sound of footsteps carried before the figures appeared. Four of them, silhouettes at first, emerging from the glow of a neon sign shaped like a dragon coiled around a pearl. Three were men, one a woman. They walked in a loose formation, casual enough to feign confidence, tight enough to show they were together. The lead was hard to miss. His hair was dyed a brash blonde that caught every shard of light as he moved, his posture loose but sharp-edged, the strut of someone who wanted the street to know his name. Beside him, the other two men were quieter, dressed in plain jackets and jeans, their eyes darting often, cataloging everything — windows, doorways, the idling SUV. The woman trailed slightly behind, wrapped in a dress meant for a night out rather than a backstreet deal. Her heels clicked softly against the wet pavement, and her presence lent the group an air of nonchalance, though her watchfulness was no less than the others.

The two men in the SUV exchanged a glance, and the driver pushed his door open with deliberate slowness. He stepped into the streetlight, smoothing his suit jacket as though brushing away lint. His partner followed, tossing a cigarette into the gutter, both of them leaning against the building with studied ease. But their eyes locked on the approaching group with hawk-like focus.

"Evening, folks," the first Gent called, his tone light, polite in a way that didn't match the setting. He flicked the end of his unlit cigarette with a shrug. "Got a light? Seems mine went out."

The blonde smirked, tilting his head. "Don't you know smoking's bad for your health?"

The Gent chuckled, tapping his chest. "That a surgeon general fact?"

"Read it somewhere," the blonde replied, his voice casual but edged.

For a moment, the two men sized each other up, a wordless measuring of posture, confidence, intent. It wasn't loud or aggressive, but the tension slid into place, invisible and undeniable. The first Gent gave his partner a brief nod, a signal as old as street corners.

"Alright," he said, stepping back toward the SUV, hand grazing the rear handle. "You got the money?"

The blonde snapped his fingers toward the woman. Without a word, she reached into her purse and pulled free an envelope thick enough to bend under its own weight. She placed it in his hand, and he lifted it to his face, waving it casually like a fan.

"Yeah," he said, flashing his teeth in a grin that didn't reach his eyes. "We're equipped."

The Hell's Gentlemen smiled faintly at one another. On the surface, it looked like satisfaction. Beneath it, something sharper lingered — a predator's anticipation of how the night might turn.

The first Gent gave a little half-smile and motioned to his partner. The second walked with careful steps to the SUV, his polished shoes tapping against the wet asphalt, each sound sharp in the night. He pulled a key fob from his pocket, pressed a button, and the rear lights blinked red as the latch clicked open. With a deliberate slowness meant to feed anticipation, he lifted the trunk lid.

Inside, metal gleamed under the dim spill of the streetlight. The rifles were laid in rows, foam cases cut precisely to hold them steady — Heckler & Koch UMPs stacked beside long black cases that promised heavier firepower. The blonde Asian tilted his head, the reflection of steel dancing in his dyed hair. His expression shifted for the first time, the cocky grin narrowing into something sharper, more calculating.

"These aren't toys," the first Gent said, almost proud, as he reached into the trunk and lifted one free. The weight of the weapon settled into his hands with ease, practiced familiarity. He held it low but in plain sight, the matte-black finish swallowing the light, the stock pressed against his forearm. "German design. Lightweight, reliable. Thirty-round mag. Rate of fire that'll make your ears ring for days."

The blonde's companions leaned closer, their eyes catching the shape of the rifle, their breaths subtle but quickened. Even the woman in the dress, who had maintained her composure with cool detachment, let her gaze linger on the weapon a fraction longer than before. It wasn't just a gun they were buying. It was power — power in steel and polymer, power that could carve silence out of a crowded street in seconds.

The second Gent pulled a longer case from the trunk and flipped it open. Inside rested an AK-47 variant, its wood stock polished, its curved magazine unmistakable. He tapped the weapon lightly with a gloved finger. "This one's a classic. Eastern bloc lineage. Simple. Efficient. You could bury it in the ground for a year, pull it back out, and it'd still fire clean. Perfect for boys who like to make noise."

The blonde Asian's grin returned, but it was thinner now. He extended his hand, brushing fingers over the cool surface of the rifle without taking it. His eyes flicked back to his crew, then to the envelope still in his grip. He waved it again, more slowly this time. "All this hardware... and you expect me to believe the deal's clean? No surprises? Not after what you pulled on the Africans?"

The first Gent's smile froze for a second before he masked it with a chuckle. He extended the UMP, offering it to one of the blonde's companions, the gesture deliberate, almost ceremonial. "We're businessmen. Africans got greedy, wanted more than what they paid for. Sometimes... examples have to be made."

The weapon passed between hands. The metal clinked softly, heavy and final in the night air. Everyone's shoulders tightened a fraction, as if the rifles themselves shifted the balance of power on the street. The blonde gave a short laugh, more air than sound, and lowered the envelope. His eyes flicked again to the rifles laid bare in the trunk. Deadly things, sleeping dragons waiting for a spark. His fingers drummed lightly on the edge of the paper, a rhythm that carried a warning.

Then the *click* broke the air.

One of his companions had already drawn a handgun, the metallic snap of the slide loud in the empty street. Another followed, pulling a compact pistol from his jacket, muzzle leveled cleanly at the first Hell's Gent. Even the woman moved now, her clutch discarded, her hand sliding free with a chrome revolver that caught the neon light like a shard of glass.

The Gents froze, eyes hardening but hands steady. The first one still held the UMP, but the weight of three guns pointed his way slowed his movements. His partner by the trunk stiffened, his hand hovering inches from another case that cradled an AK.

"What the fuck is this?" the first Gent demanded, voice low but taut, his politeness stripped to the bone.

The blonde stepped forward, the envelope still dangling between his fingers. His pistol was steady in the other hand, his grin stretched thin but dangerous. "What this is," he said, "is insurance. We don't want what happened to the Africans happening here. Word travels, my friend. Real fast."

The second Gent bristled, jaw tightening, but he didn't move. "Don't let that spook you. The Africans? They got greedy. Wanted more than they paid for. Some of the gear had to be…" He paused, lips curling faintly, "…demonstrated."

The blonde's gaze hardened. He nodded once, and one of his crew stepped closer, eyes flicking between the rifles and the Gents. The night had shifted. What had been a business deal was now a taut wire stretched to breaking.

The first Gent moved with care, slowly lowering the UMP toward the trunk as if returning it. His smile reappeared, practiced, strained. "See? We're here for business. Nothing more."

The blonde didn't lower his pistol. His men didn't either. For a long moment, the street was silent except for the hum of the SUV's engine and the distant drip of water from a gutter.

And then a new voice cut the silence like a blade.

"That's funny," it said, deep and cold, carrying from the shadows at the edge of the street. "Because I've got some business with you too."

Every head turned. The Asians stiffened, pulling tighter together, their pistols still trained on the Gents. The two Gentlemen, caught between threats, squinted into the darkness, trying to pierce the night.

The rhythm of the city seemed to pause, waiting to see who would step forward.

Out of the darkness at the far end of the block, a figure emerged. At first only the sound of boots carried — heavy, deliberate, the kind that spoke of discipline rather than panic. Then Henry stepped into the spill of the streetlight.

He wore black fatigues tucked into military boots, his frame filling the night like a shadow given flesh. His jacket bulged slightly at the sides, the weight of gear hidden beneath its folds, but his movements were

smooth, controlled. His eyes cut across the scene —
not at the Asian crew, not at the guns drawn, but directly
at the two Hell's Gentlemen standing by their SUV. The
look was steady, cold, the stare of a man who had long
since decided what needed to be done.

The Asians were the first to move, tension flashing in
their faces. The blonde shoved the UMP back into the
chest of the second Gent with sudden disgust,
motioning to his crew. Without a word, they began
backing away, pistols still raised for a few cautious
steps before lowering. The woman slipped her revolver
back into her purse with fluid grace, heels clicking as
she turned. Within moments they had vanished into the
folds of Chinatown, swallowed by alleys and neon,
leaving only the faint echo of their retreat behind them.

Henry never shifted his gaze. He kept walking, each step
measured, his boots splashing lightly in a thin puddle.
The Gents closed the trunk quickly, the cases of rifles
sealed away in an instant. Their smiles were gone now,
replaced with watchful unease.

"Uh..." the first Gent began, voice uneven, "what can we
do for you, officer?"

Henry stopped a few feet from them, close enough to
see the nervous twitch at the corner of the man's
mouth, close enough to smell the smoke still clinging to
their suits. His face didn't move.

"I'm not a cop."

The words fell like a stone, flat, heavy, certain.

The second Gent stiffened, anger flooding where nerves had been. His hand twitched toward the SUV, eyes flashing. "What? You roll up on us like this and you ain't a cop? You're a dead man now."

Henry tilted his head slightly, his gaze unwavering. "I believe you already tried."

The silence between them thickened. The first Gent looked at his partner, then back at Henry, weighing something in the man's stance, in the way his fists hung loose but ready at his sides. This wasn't some stranger off the street. This was a man who had come looking for them specifically.

The SUV loomed behind them, its trunk sealed but still humming with menace. The street, once alive with neon and noise, felt emptied — narrowed down to this meeting, this collision.

Henry took one more step forward. He was done talking.

The first Gent smirked, trying to mask his unease, but Henry saw the twitch at his jaw, the quick dart of his eyes toward the SUV. He knew what they wanted — the guns in the trunk, the safety of steel to even the ground. Henry didn't give him the chance.

With a sudden, explosive motion, Henry's fist shot forward. His knuckles crashed against the Gent's face with a sickening crack, cartilage and bone shifting under the impact. Blood spattered across the man's lip as he staggered back, a hand flying up too late to protect himself.

The second Gent lunged instantly, anger overriding thought, his arm swinging for Henry's head. Henry pivoted, catching the man's wrist in both hands. A sharp twist followed — brutal, practiced — and a wet snap echoed into the night. The Gent screamed, knees buckling, his arm bent at an unnatural angle.

Henry didn't pause. He shoved the injured man away, sending him sprawling onto the pavement. The first Gent, clutching his face, snarled through blood and charged. He made it two steps before Henry's boot caught him square in the chest. The blow landed with crushing precision, lifting him off his feet and hurling him into the side of the SUV. The impact rang out in the empty street, metal denting beneath the force.

The second Gent tried to rally, his good arm scrabbling for Henry's jacket, but Henry closed the distance too fast. He drove his shoulder into the man's ribs, the air bursting from him in a gasp. With another twist of his grip, Henry flung him into the street, the man's body bouncing once before skidding across the wet pavement.

For a heartbeat, everything stilled. The night air carried only the ragged sound of breathing — the Gents gasping and cursing, Henry silent and steady. The SUV stood behind them like a silent accomplice, its trunk a graveyard of firepower waiting to be drawn. Both men's eyes darted toward it, the same thought etched across their faces.

Henry took a slow breath, centering himself. He could see it clearly — their desperation, their hunger for the weapons that could turn this fight in their favor. But he wasn't just fighting men tonight. He was fighting predators who sold death by the crate. That SUV was their kingdom. If they reached it, the street would be painted red.

The first Gent groaned, forcing himself upright, blood running from his broken nose. His partner rolled to his knees, cradling his shattered arm, yet still staring at the trunk like it held salvation.

"Okay, you dumb fuck," the first Gent spat, his voice ragged but alive with hate. "You really pissed me off now."

The second Gent began circling wide, trying to angle back to the vehicle. His teeth clenched, sweat gleaming on his forehead. "You think you're a badass? So did plenty of others. They're dead too."

Henry shifted his stance, ready. He knew what came next. They weren't done.

The first Gent snarled, rage twisting through the blood on his face. With a sudden burst of movement, he lunged for the SUV. His fingers stretched toward the handle of the rear door, desperation fueling his speed.

Henry was faster. He surged forward and snapped a side kick into the man's chest, the heel of his boot slamming just below the sternum. The Gent's breath exploded out of him in a hollow gasp as his body flew backward, crashing against the side mirror before tumbling to the pavement.

The second Gent didn't hesitate. Cradling his ruined arm tight to his side, he scrambled into the driver's seat, his other hand clawing at the weapons stashed inside. A magazine clattered on the floorboards before he jammed it into a rifle, pulling back the bolt with a savage motion.

Henry's eyes widened. He dove left just as the night shattered.

The muzzle flared, bright in the dark, and the roar of automatic fire ripped through the street. Bullets tore across the asphalt, punching holes in the air, shattering the SUV's passenger-side window into a rain of glass. The echo thundered between buildings, the sound carrying far beyond Chinatown's borders.

Henry rolled, shoulder grinding against the wet ground, the stink of gunpowder flooding his nostrils. He tucked low behind the rear of a parked sedan, shards of glass peppering his back as the barrage swept past. The rifle's report was deafening, every burst a reminder of just how thin the line between survival and death was tonight.

The first Gent wasn't so lucky. Still reeling from Henry's kick, he staggered upright just as his partner unleashed the volley. The bullets caught him across the torso in savage bursts, jerking his body in spasms as blood sprayed the air in a crimson mist. He collapsed in the middle of the street, twitching once before going still, his lifeless eyes staring up into the neon glow.

Henry crouched, muscles taut, lungs dragging in short, controlled breaths. He peeked around the bumper, tracking the second Gent's movements. The man shouted incoherently, fury and panic blending into a single raw sound as he swept the rifle across the street. The weapon barked again, cutting down a streetlamp in a shower of sparks.

Henry's mind ran cold calculations. The Gent was sloppy, driven by adrenaline and fear rather than control. His shots were wild, untrained — the kind that emptied a magazine without hitting the target. Henry had seen men like him in warzones, men who thought noise was power. They were dangerous, yes. But predictable.

The rifle chattered, the rounds chewing concrete into dust clouds near Henry's feet. He stayed crouched, eyes narrowing, waiting for the telltale stutter — the click of a magazine running dry.

The night was alive with violence now, Chinatown's shadows no longer quiet.

The second Gent leaned out of the SUV, teeth bared in a feral snarl, firing in long uncontrolled bursts. Each squeeze of the trigger rocked his body, the weapon jerking against his shoulder as brass shells clattered to the pavement in a golden rain. Bullets ripped across storefronts, splintering wood and glass, the echoes rolling through Chinatown like thunder.

Henry stayed low, his boots splashing through shallow puddles as he shifted position, moving with a predator's

patience. He knew better than to meet noise with noise.
He let the Gent burn through his ammunition, every
wasted shot another second closer to survival. His
breath was steady, his heart controlled — the rhythm of
a soldier who had done this dance before.

The Gent shouted curses between bursts, voice
cracking with desperation. Sweat ran down his temple,
dripping onto the stock of the rifle. His injured arm
trembled uselessly at his side, his good hand gripping
the weapon with frantic strength. He fired again, a wild
arc across the street, and the muzzle flash lit his face
like a grotesque mask — fury, fear, and arrogance all
bleeding together.

Henry slipped from cover, rolling across the pavement
to the flank. The wet asphalt chilled his palms as he
steadied himself, eyes locked on his target. He could
feel the vibration of the shots in his chest, could taste
the acrid sting of gunpowder at the back of his throat.
The rifle barked again, then stuttered. A hollow *click*
echoed in the wake of the gunfire. The Gent froze,
staring down at the weapon as though betrayed. His
hands worked frantically, fumbling with the magazine,
trying to slam another home.

Henry didn't wait. He exploded from the shadows,
boots pounding the pavement, his body a blur of
controlled violence. In three strides he was at the SUV,
one hand slamming the rifle barrel aside just as the
Gent tried to bring it back up. With his other fist he drove

a crushing blow into the man's jaw, the impact reverberating through bone and muscle.

The Gent's head snapped back, teeth clacking, blood spraying as he fell against the seat. The rifle tumbled from his grasp, clattering uselessly across the floorboard. Henry reached in, seizing the man by his lapels, yanking him bodily from the driver's seat. The man hit the ground hard, coughing, spitting crimson onto the pavement.

For a moment, the only sound was his ragged wheezing, the SUV's engine still humming faintly behind them.

Then the distant wail of sirens bled into the night, faint but growing.

Henry tightened his grip, hauling the man upright. His voice was low, calm, but carried the weight of steel.

"You sold death to the wrong city," he said.

The Gent's eyes widened, fear finally breaking through the bravado. He opened his mouth to speak, but only a wet gasp came out.

The night was his prison now.

Henry slammed the Gent against the SUV, the man's head cracking against the steel with a hollow thud. His body went limp for a second, then twitched back, hands clawing weakly at Henry's arm. The stitched devil on his jacket shimmered under the streetlight, a mockery of power that no longer belonged to him.

Henry's grip was merciless. He pressed the man tighter to the metal, his forearm digging across the Gent's throat. The man gagged, eyes bulging, the sound of his ragged choking mixing with the faint hum of the vehicle's engine. Henry leaned in close, his breath steady, his words ice.

"You think rifles and suits make you untouchable? You think you can bleed neighborhoods dry and walk away?" His voice dropped, even quieter now, the tone of a predator speaking only to prey. "Not anymore."

The Gent coughed, spit running down his chin, blood bubbling at his lip. His good hand scrabbled at Henry's sleeve, but there was no strength left. Panic swam across his eyes — not for his life, but for what he knew was coming after this night, after this failure. Jason's world was built on appearances, and men who stumbled in deals did not return unscathed.

Henry read it in him, the knowledge, the terror. He loosened the pressure just enough for the man to drag in a wet gasp of air. "Where's the next shipment going?" Henry demanded.

The Gent coughed again, voice breaking. "W– waterfront... another... another drop tomorrow night..." His words dissolved into wheezing, but Henry caught enough.

He yanked the man forward, then threw him to the ground with the force of a sledgehammer. The Gent hit the pavement, rolling onto his back, groaning, clutching his chest as though trying to hold himself together. His partner lay a few yards away, riddled with his own ally's bullets, motionless in the street. Blood pooled beneath him, spreading dark across the wet asphalt.

For a moment Henry stood above them both, breathing slow, fists clenched. The sirens were louder now, their cry weaving through the labyrinth of Chinatown, growing closer. He looked down at the Gent still alive, eyes wide, body trembling. He thought about ending it right here, a clean break, one less devil in the world. But another thought surfaced — Kalee's face, pale in the hospital bed, fragile and waiting. She needed more than rage. She needed a father who played the long game.

Henry crouched, his voice low and sharp as a knife. "Tell Jason Farokmanesh I'm coming. Tell him Boston isn't his playground anymore."

The Gent whimpered, nodding frantically.

Henry straightened, wiped the blood from his knuckles onto his jacket, and stepped back into the shadows. The sirens were close enough now that red and blue light flickered faintly against the wet pavement. By the time police flooded the street, there would be nothing left but two broken men and an SUV filled with guns. Henry was already gone, a ghost vanishing into the city he had sworn to protect.

Chapter 6

Chinatown was cordoned off like a wound still bleeding. Blue and red strobes washed over brick walls and neon signs, throwing colors across the wet pavement in sickly rhythm. Four police cruisers boxed the street, their hoods angled like barricades, lights spinning against the drizzle. Yellow tape stretched taut between lampposts, keeping back a restless crowd of gawkers craning for a better view. The sound of cameras snapping cut through the murmur of voices — news photographers and reporters pressing forward for shots of the wreckage. Two ambulances waited at the curb, their rear doors yawning open. EMTs moved briskly, one of them wheeling a stretcher loaded with a body bag, the zipper halfway closed over a bloodied face. Another medic bent over a second man strapped down with restraints, his head lolling, his suit jacket soaked dark. He was still alive, barely, his teeth chattering through muffled groans. His embroidered devil patch looked obscene under the harsh light, a red grin against ruined flesh. Uniformed cops worked the perimeter, pushing civilians back when they leaned too close. The ground was littered with broken glass and shell casings, glinting under the floodlights. The SUV stood at the center of it all — its windows shattered, the metal pocked with bullet holes. The trunk sat wide open, its secret spilled out for all to see: foam cases stacked with sleek, black rifles. The barrels caught the light like teeth.

"Jesus Christ," one rookie muttered, shaking his head as he scribbled notes. Another officer snapped photographs of the arsenal, the flash bouncing off polished steel. None of them liked standing too close. Guns in neat rows had a way of feeling alive, even without a hand on the trigger.

The scene buzzed with tension, but beneath it all was confusion. The chatter among the uniforms circled the same point: why was everything still here? Gangs didn't leave money on the table. Gangs didn't leave crates of German submachine guns untouched. Whatever had happened tonight wasn't routine.

A plain sedan rolled up slow against the tide of flashing lights. Its headlights swept the barricades before flicking off, the engine idling down. Lt. Ronald Mitchell stepped out, trench coat collar pulled high against the damp air. His face was lined with years of too many nights like this, eyes heavy but sharp. He reached into his pocket and pulled free a cigarette, cupping it against the wind as he lit it. The first drag filled his lungs, and he exhaled long, letting the smoke cut through the smell of cordite and rain.

He walked forward, hands loose at his sides. A uniform blocked his path with a firm gesture. "Hey — step back behind the tape. This is a crime scene."

Mitchell took another pull from his cigarette, then flipped open his coat and produced his badge. The gold glinted under the floodlights.

The officer squinted, unimpressed. "Oh. Go ahead, then."

Mitchell gave him a dry look, then stepped past, boots splashing in shallow puddles. His gaze swept the scene with the practiced eye of a man who didn't need notes to see the story. He paused by the SUV, its trunk a gaping wound filled with weapons. The rifles stared back at him like predators in cages.

He spotted another officer standing guard nearby, younger, nervous in his stance. Mitchell approached, holding his badge low, almost out of habit. "What do we got?"

The officer cleared his throat. "Two males. One dead. One beaten half to death. Vehicle's registered to the stiff." He pointed toward the stretcher being wheeled away, zipped tight now. "Trunk full of Heckler & Koch UMPs. Still loaded. Still here."

Mitchell took another drag, the smoke curling into the night. His eyes narrowed, drifting over the bodies, the shattered glass, the crates of rifles untouched.

The younger cop shifted, glancing toward the crowd pressing at the barricade. "Witnesses say they heard rapid gunfire. A lot of it. But when we rolled up, there was only the one dead guy and the beaten one. Guns, money — all here. Nothing taken."

Mitchell's jaw worked, his cigarette burning low between his fingers. "Nothing was taken?" He repeated it flat, as though turning the words over. He let the silence stretch, smoke rising between them. Then he said again, quieter, "Nothing was taken."

He looked back at the SUV, at the neat rows of black steel glistening under the lights. He'd worked enough gang cases to know how they operated. Violence wasn't just personal, it was transactional. Guns this clean would've vanished the moment the street ran red. The fact they were still here told him everything. This wasn't a rival crew. This wasn't some kids making a point. Whoever had done this hadn't wanted the guns. He wanted the men.

"Anything special about them?" Mitchell asked finally, nodding toward the bodies.

The officer hesitated. "They were both wearing the Hell's Gentlemen's patch. Embroidered devils, suits and all. You think this was a gang hit?"

Mitchell flicked his cigarette to the ground, grinding it under his heel. His eyes lingered on the open trunk one last time, expression unreadable. "I don't know what it is yet. But another gang would've taken the guns."

He turned without another word, the long coat swinging behind him as he walked back to his car. Sliding into the driver's seat, he sat still for a moment, eyes on the street in his rearview mirror. The scene replayed in his head — the guns, the dead man, the one still breathing, the fact that everything of value remained untouched. It didn't fit the city's usual script.

Mitchell started the engine, the hum filling the silence. As he pulled away, he kept smoking, letting the nicotine sharpen the edges of his thoughts. Something new was at work in Boston. And whatever it was, it wasn't finished.

The fluorescent lights hummed overhead, bright and sterile, washing the aisles of the home improvement store in a steady glow. It could have been any night, any errand — a man pushing a shopping cart past displays of light bulbs and tools. But Henry's presence made the scene feel heavier, sharper. His boots thudded against the polished concrete floor, his broad shoulders stretching against the dark jacket. Where the world outside bled chaos and flashing lights, here he moved with a quiet purpose.

He paused at the end of an aisle, scanning rows of heavy-duty gloves. The leather ones caught his attention, durable and thick. He slipped a pair from the hook, turning them over in his hands before dropping them into the cart. The sound was soft but final. Next came duct tape — not the thin gray strips for housework, but the industrial rolls stacked in bulk. He grabbed two, laying them flat on the growing pile. Shoppers passed him with distracted expressions, carts full of paint cans and garden soil. None looked his way twice. To them he was just another man shopping late, maybe a contractor wrapping a long day. Henry blended, but beneath the disguise of normalcy every move was sharpened by intent.

He moved deeper into the store, turning into the tool aisle. Rows of flashlights gleamed beneath plastic packaging, their beams pictured bright against cardboard. Henry picked up a pair of high-lumen models, the kind that could cut through pitch darkness or blind a man in a second. He tested the weight in his hands, then dropped them into the cart alongside the gloves and tape.

Rope was next. Thick nylon cord, coiled and stacked in neat bundles. He selected two lengths without hesitation, heavy enough to bind, strong enough to hold. He added it to the cart, his mind already working through scenarios — not with words, but with the instinctive rhythm of preparation.

As he walked, he caught his reflection in a display mirror. For an instant he studied the man staring back: tall, hard-edged, eyes hollowed by sleepless nights. A soldier without a uniform, a father without his family. He looked away quickly, pushing the cart onward. Reflection wasn't useful here. Action was.

He turned into the cleaning supplies aisle, pulling down bottles of bleach and industrial solvent. Anything that could erase traces, strip blood from pavement, dissolve what needed to be unseen. The weight of the cart grew heavier, its rattle echoing faintly in the cavernous store.

At the register, Henry paid in cash. The young cashier didn't meet his eyes, her gum snapping as she scanned each item. She bagged the gloves, the tape, the rope, the cleaners, the flashlights — her hands quick, her gaze fixed anywhere but on him. To her, he was just another late-night customer. To Henry, this was a resupply run before a war.

He loaded the bags into the trunk of his car with care, arranging them so nothing would shift. Every item had its place, every tool a purpose. He closed the trunk with a solid thump, the sound echoing in the empty parking lot.

Leaning against the car for a moment, Henry pulled in a long breath of the night air. The city seemed quieter here, but he knew it was an illusion. Violence simmered just beneath the surface, waiting. He thought of Kalee, her small hand limp in his, machines breathing for her. He thought of Dani, gone. Each breath he drew in this parking lot was stolen from them, borrowed time to settle debts.

Henry slid into the driver's seat, the engine rumbling to life. He gripped the wheel tight, his knuckles whitening. Chinatown had been a message, but it wasn't enough. The men behind the rifles weren't done. Neither was he. He pulled out of the lot and vanished back into the Boston night, the supplies rattling softly in the trunk — tools for a reckoning still to come.

The waterfront had gone quiet after midnight. The gulls that screamed during the day were gone, replaced by the low groan of ships moving out into the harbor and the whisper of water slapping against pilings. Down along the warehouses, most of the buildings stood dark, boarded windows staring blankly into the night. But one structure pulsed with life. Light leaked through its barred panes, soft jazz filtering faintly through the walls, a kind of music that pretended order where there was only vice.

This was the Hell's Gentlemen's ground — the same warehouse that earlier had glowed like a lounge hidden inside a husk of steel. Now, however, its music played over wreckage. The bar that had once been pristine, stocked and polished, was splintered. Bottles had been hurled against the wall, their contents dripping down in sticky streaks. The smell of whiskey and rum soured the air, sharp against the faint perfume that still lingered from earlier in the night.

Jason Farokmanesh stood at the center of it all. His jacket lay tossed across a chair, his shirt half-buttoned and clinging to his chest. His usual poise was cracked, replaced by a fury that broke across him in waves. He overturned a table with a single shove, the wood splintering as it crashed onto the floor. Glass crunched underfoot as he stalked back and forth, jaw clenched, eyes flashing in the low light.

On the bed in the corner sat a woman. Hours before, she had been draped across him, smiling, her laughter filling the suite while his lieutenants carried out orders. Now she sat frozen, clutching the sheets to her chest, watching with wide, fearful eyes. Jason's rage wasn't mindless — it was controlled destruction, aimed at things, never people. Still, the violence in him radiated outward like heat from a fire, and she flinched with every smash.

Jason stopped suddenly, chest rising and falling with the rhythm of his breath. His gaze cut toward her, pinning her in place. For a moment he simply stared, the room silent except for the faint crackle of broken glass under his shoes. Then his voice came, low and flat but searing all the same.

"Get the fuck out of here."

The woman didn't hesitate. She scrambled from the bed, grabbing what clothes she could, pulling them on in frantic motions. Shoes clutched in one hand, she bolted for the door, the slam echoing down the stairwell as she vanished.

Jason exhaled, closing his eyes briefly. His anger had drained into something colder, sharper. The wreckage around him wasn't random — it was ritual. A way to burn through the fury until only steel remained. He reached for his phone on the nightstand and dialed without looking at the numbers. When the line clicked, his voice was calm again, businesslike, as though none of the violence had happened.

"I want several cars ready in five minutes," he said. He paused, his eyes narrowing toward the window,

watching the reflections of harbor lights in the glass.
"We're going to visit the Africans."

The call ended, and silence returned like a held breath finally released. Jason set the phone on the nightstand with care, as if placing a scalpel back into its velvet slot. The room was a ruin, but he treated it the way a surgeon treats a bloody theatre after the patient's been wheeled out—evidence of necessary work, nothing more. He crossed to the window and pulled the curtain aside with two fingers. The harbor lights jittered on the water, bands of color breaking over the chop. Somewhere out there, ships moved like quiet fortresses, unbothered by the small wars on land.

He rolled his shoulders, felt the anger ghost over his skin, and pushed it away. Anger was a tool, not a home. He buttoned his shirt the rest of the way, smoothing the cloth over his chest, then retrieved his jacket from the back of a chair and shook glass from its lapel. The ritual of dressing calmed him. Fitted blazer. Pocket square crisp as a folded threat. Watch snug at the wrist, the second hand ticking like a metronome for the night's work.

A vibration on the nightstand—a text this time, terse as a gun report. He scanned it, eyes narrowing slightly. The summary matched what he already knew: police everywhere in Chinatown, one of his men dead, the other scooped into an ambulance, product exposed to floodlights and cameras. The line that mattered most was the last: **Nothing taken.** Whoever hit them hadn't come for steel. He'd come for a message.

Jason let the curtain fall. He paced once, twice, letting his thoughts assemble like pieces in a case. The Africans would be nervous—tonight's smoke would drift into their house by morning, and they'd start asking the wrong questions. Uncertainty is the currency of collapse. He wouldn't spend a cent of it inside his own organization.

He stopped at the mirror, meeting his reflection. Handsome, yes. Composed, yes. But what stared back wore something else beneath the polish—resolve hammered thin and cold. "Who are you?" he asked the night, not himself. The kind of man who left money and rifles untouched didn't belong to the usual chaos. Disciplined. Precise. Not a rival crew; rivals took trophies.

He stepped into the hall and moved through the private corridor of the upper floor, boots sounding muffled on thick carpet. At the stairhead he paused, listening to the warehouse below. Engines outside. Voices pitched low. The hive was awake and organized. Good. Panic, like liquor, spilled if the bottle broke. He would keep the glass whole.

He descended, each step unhurried. A runner met him at the landing and opened his mouth to speak; Jason lifted a hand and the words died there. "Three cars up front," he said. "No decals, no drama. Clean drivers, clean plates." He kept walking, and the runner peeled off to execute. Another man approached with a tablet—shipments, routes, numbers. Jason glanced, tapped two cells, and said, "Freeze those. Move the B lot to the inland cache. If anyone asks, we never had a B lot." He reached the bay door, where the night waited with its damp breath and the faint tang of the sea. He smiled once, thin as a razor. "Let's work."

The loading bay smelled of tire rubber and oil. Men in tailored jackets moved with the quick economy of stagehands breaking a set, their embroidered devils winking as they hauled cases, checked trunks, and snapped lids shut. This wasn't chaos; it was a drill they'd rehearsed until it lived in their bones. Jason's crews didn't run—they relocated.

Three cars—a midnight-black Escalade, a gray S-Class, and a low, predatory coupe—idled in a staggered row. Their headlights cut pale corridors through the misting air. The drivers stood by with hands folded, eyes forward. One of Jason's lieutenants, the wiry one with the trimmed beard, stepped close, tablet tucked under his arm. "Africans pulled their outer watch," he murmured. "Looks like they're coiling tight. Word's already crawling."

"Of course it is," Jason said. "Fear commutes faster than anything with wheels." He scanned the men, taking the temperature of his house. Their faces showed alertness, not dread—that line mattered. "We are not making apologies," he added, voice pitched to carry without lift. "We are making clarity."

Another lieutenant approached—broad-shouldered, a pale scar notched under one eye. "Chinatown?" he asked.

Jason didn't look at him. "Our man in the hospital—keep him breathing." A pause, then: "And quiet." He stepped toward the Escalade, opened the rear door, and slid inside. The interior swallowed him: leather, hush, the faint thrum of the V8 like a big cat's purr.

The wiry lieutenant took the seat beside him; the scarred one moved to the coupe. Doors thudded shut. Outside, the warehouse door rolled down on its track with a metallic sigh, sealing the hive. The convoy eased into motion.

As they pulled onto the waterfront road, Jason watched the dark panes of the city slip by—old brick factories with their ribs showing, glass towers hunched like indifferent gods, street lamps wearing halos of drizzle.

"He left the guns," he said, as if thinking aloud to the windshield.

The wiry lieutenant shifted. "Somebody making a point."

Jason's mouth quirked. "Somebody making **my** point, for me." He turned from the window. "Strength is not volume. It's precision—where it hurts, when it hurts, to whom it hurts." His eyes softened, which somehow made them more dangerous. "I want a name. Not a rumor. A name with a history that makes this make sense."

"We'll shake the trees," the lieutenant said. "Neighbors, night cops, the usual mouths."

"Not the usual," Jason corrected. "The unusual. Find me the people who notice the way doors close. The ones who keep the keys." He rested his temple against his knuckles and listened to the rain begin in earnest, a fine hiss across the windshield.

They hit the arterial and the convoy lengthened into the night, three shadows with purpose. Somewhere ahead lay the African Lords—a meeting to stitch seams before they split. Somewhere behind lay Chinatown, fluorescent-lit and crawling with cameras. Between those poles, Jason set his balance, a wire-walker carrying a city's worth of secrets on his spine.

The lieutenant checked his phone. "Boss—another headline. 'Massive Gun Cache Discovered After Chinatown Shooting.'"

Jason smiled without humor. "Good. Let them print it. Let everyone see the city's most dangerous goods sitting in the street like orphans." He closed his eyes for a beat, just long enough to feel the anger pass like a tide. "Then let them remember who takes them back."

They left the harbor and climbed into the city's midriff where blocks changed names but kept the same old bones—row houses with bad knees, corner bars with good lies, murals half-faded by winter. The convoy flowed through yellow lights, never hurrying, never dragging. A soft jazz line threaded from the Escalade's speakers, volume low enough to be a secret.

Jason's phone buzzed again. He glanced down: a pair of surveillance stills from a traffic camera—blurred figures, the shape of an SUV, the white spike of muzzle flash. Worthless to most eyes. He zoomed, studied the angle of a shoulder, the stance of a man caught between frames. There was a discipline in the blur that arrogance didn't have. He could spot it like a tailor spots a bad seam.

"Whoever he is," the lieutenant said, watching Jason watch, "he's not new."

"No," Jason answered. "He's practiced. And he thinks practice makes him invisible." He set the phone aside. "The city makes masks for men like that. Church masks, soldier masks, widower masks. Find which one he wears when the sun's up."

They passed a police cruiser tucked into a dark mouth of curb. Its driver looked up, saw nothing but tinted glass and money, and went back to his coffee. The convoy wove on, a moving room with rules Jason had written—no tailgating, no splitting lanes, no leaning into noise. They were wealth that obeyed its own speed limit.

The ride gave him time to build the conversation in his head. The Africans—sharp men, proud as river stones, their edges smoothed by necessity. One dead soldier in Chinatown meant whispers in their halls by morning. He'd bring a salve: steadiness, courtesy, the promise of clean business. He'd also bring a needle: a reminder that panic is a bad investment.

He looked past his own reflection in the window and saw a ghost of himself in other glass—the suite upstairs, the bottles exploding, the woman fleeing. He understood the narrative such scenes invited: a king with a crack in his crown. He would write another. Men didn't follow marble; they followed weather. He would be the forecast they could trust—storm when it was time, sunshine when it paid, and the long, predictable season in between.

The rain thickened into beads that raced each other down the windshield. Wipers swept. The city gave way by increments to wider streets and lower buildings. Somewhere near the edge of their territory, a lookout would already have eyes on his cars, texting thumbs busy beneath an awning. Good. Let them know he came through the front door.

He rested his wrist over his knee and let the watch tick count down the last blocks. "When we leave," he said to the lieutenant, "I want two things. Their confidence— measured, not giddy. And a whisper in their ear about a new hunter in town. It will make them hold their own dogs tighter."

"You want them afraid of him?" the lieutenant asked, surprised.

Jason's smile showed a single canine. "I want them afraid of chaos. And grateful to the man who keeps it fed and leashed."

The convoy signaled as one, turned as one, and slid into a street where shadows watched from porches like judges with no robes.

The ICU had its own weather. It snowed there in the hush of air filters and the drift of nurses' whispers, a hush that fell over everything: the blinking monitors, the shiver of pale sheets, the small rise and fall of a child's chest. Dani's mother sat in a vinyl chair pulled close to the bed, a paperback open in her lap, her finger marking a place she hadn't really been reading. The lamplight caught the silver in her hair and turned it into threads of frost.

Kalee lay still, eyelashes dark against her cheeks, skin the fragile color of new milk. The machines sang their thin, relentless song—beep, breath, beep—and the sound had become, for Dani's mother, something like a prayer. She knew when the higher whine meant nothing, when a nurse would come, when nobody would. She had learned how to sit for hours without moving too quickly, as if sudden motions could spook the body into forgetting how to stay.

She cleared her throat softly and found her place on the page. "...*and the little fox learned the river by listening to it at night, the way it gossiped over stones.*" Her voice was steady, low, a cadence children trust even when they sleep. "*So when daylight came, he already knew where the shallow path was, and he took it, and came out the other side with his tail dry and his ears pricked.*" She paused, smiled to herself, and looked up. "You hear that, baby? Ears pricked. That's you. You always listened even when your mama..." The word stopped her, a blade sliding between ribs. She swallowed, changed lanes without signaling. "Even when the world tried to be too loud."

Outside the glass, a nurse wheeled a cart past, its rubber wheels making no sound at all on the floor. The night crew spoke in that ICU way, a language of eyebrows and clipped whispers, the gospel of not waking what needs to rest. Dani's mother pressed her palm to Kalee's small hand and felt only warmth and the ghost of a squeeze she told herself was real every time. "It's late," she murmured. "I should let you sleep. But I don't like the dark sneaking up without me guarding the door." She brushed a thumb along the back of Kalee's fingers. The skin there was soft as fruit. "Your daddy came earlier. He told you he was working. He meant it." She nodded, as if agreeing with someone standing beside her. "He meant it."

She closed the book and set it on the bedside table. "I brought you the blue ribbon," she remembered suddenly, and fished in her bag—receipts, a small jar of ointment, a pen with teeth marks—and found it. She tied it carefully around the base of the bed's railing, a little banner in a room that mistrusted decoration. "There. Proof you got people who put color where the world went white."

The monitors kept their quiet score, indifferent and faithful. Dani's mother leaned back and let her eyes rest on Kalee's face until the edges of the world blurred and came back into focus. "We're here, little fox," she said.

"On both sides of the river. You take the shallow path when you're ready."

The nurse—Andre, the one with the gentlest hands—poked his head through the door. "You doing okay, Ms. King?" he asked, his voice the audible version of a warm blanket.

She nodded. "We're fine. She had a good night." The lie was harmless and necessary; 'good' meant the machines hadn't panicked and the doctors hadn't appeared with new words to learn. Andre stepped in long enough to check the lines with the deftness of a tailor sizing a hem. He smiled at Kalee the way people smile at sleeping infants, a smile that refuses to entertain the possibility of anything but waking.

"I'll be right outside," he said, and slid away, the door feathering shut behind him.

Dani's mother stood, joints complaining in crackles. She stretched her back, one hand on the small of it, and walked to the sink to rinse the dryness from her mouth. The mirror above it showed a woman who had not slept properly in days; her eyes, once quick and delighted by small jokes, had become patient instruments, reading monitors and faces with the discipline of a librarian cataloging grief.

She returned to the bed and smoothed a stubborn wrinkle in the sheet near Kalee's elbow. "You know," she said, half to the girl, half to the room, "when your mama was little, she used to steal the blue bowls from the cabinet because she said cereal tasted better from them. I told her that was nonsense. Then I tried it, and for the rest of my life I kept one blue bowl for mornings when the sky looked like rain." She laughed, a small chime. "We'll save you a blue bowl for when you get home. You can have all the cereal in the world. I'll do the dishes."

She reached for the child's hand again, the gesture now a ritual with the gravity of civic oath. There was no squeeze, only warmth. But love isn't a thermometer. It doesn't need a mechanical answer to prove itself.

Her phone buzzed in her bag; she didn't move to take it. People had learned she answered in bunches, or never, and that their words would sit on her screen like folded letters. The world could wait its turn. This room had its own clock.

"It's amazing," she said softly, "how big quiet can be." She glanced at the door as if she could see the city beyond it—the rain on the roads, the sirens, the red and blue carnival, the men in nice coats telling lies to faces. "But we brought our own weather, didn't we?" She tapped the ribbon with a fingertip, letting it tremble like a flag in a private wind.

For a long time she simply stood there, listening to the machine count beats her heart tried to match. Then she bent and kissed Kalee's temple with the practiced gentleness of someone who has been told not to disturb delicate work. "Your daddy's out there trying to change the forecast," she whispered. "You just rest. Let the river gossip to you till morning."

The hour grew thin; even the hospital's hum seemed to lower its voice in respect for whatever sleeps between three and four. Ms. King pulled the chair closer again and sat, her knees touching the bed frame, her body refusing to yield the post. She took the paperback but didn't open it. Instead, she watched the way Kalee's chest lifted, fell, the way the tiny shadow of her nose leaned toward the pillow, the way the lashes made delicate spokes on her cheeks.

She thought, involuntarily, of Dani's laugh—how it always started with breath, a soft intake, as if surprise were the cause of joy rather than its result. She let the memory come and go without clutching it. Grief was a wild animal; corner it and it clawed, let it pass and it ghosted around you with something like mercy.

Outside the window, a smudge of city light pressed against the night, the suggestion of dawn tucked somewhere behind roofs and wires. Ms. King rubbed her palms together to wake warmth and then held both hands around Kalee's smaller one, as though enclosing a candle.

"You remember the playground off Tremont?" she asked, not expecting an answer, the question a map for herself. "The slide was always too hot by noon. Your mama would lay her scarf over it so you wouldn't squeal. She said a scarf could fix anything if you tied it right." She smiled into the room, that old private joke opening a door she could still walk through. "We will tie this, too. Tight and pretty."

Andre passed again, glanced in, and offered a two-finger salute that meant *call if you need me*. She nodded back. The machines kept speaking. They were faithful, these little oracles, patient with the way humans tried to make meaning from metronomes.

She stood once more, slow as a tide; her joints had traded speed for endurance years ago. She kissed two fingers and pressed them to the ribbon on the rail. "I'm going to close my eyes right here," she told Kalee. "Don't you go anywhere showy. I'd like to be awake when you decide you're ready to call for pancakes."

She let her head tip back against the chair, mouth softening, eyes resting. Not sleep, not quite—mothers learn a way of closing their eyes without surrendering their post. She drifted in the gray between wake and dream, where memory and hope braid a rope strong enough to hold through till morning.

And in the room's soft climate, where beeps were lullabies and breath was law, the child did what children do when they are well-guarded by love: she stayed.

The neighborhood had gone to sleep the way good neighborhoods do—lights clicked out one by one, a dog complained at nothing, a television murmured behind a closed curtain. Damp air settled on hedges and mailboxes. The houses along the block were modest and watchful, porches with chipped paint and steps that remembered a hundred school mornings. Out near the end of the street, Switch's place sat back from the curb behind a sagging chain-link fence. The porch light burned a jaundiced yellow, a bare bulb under a cracked plastic shade. On the side yard, two dog cages hunched under a tarp, the animals pacing in their metal rectangles like they could feel the night looking at them. Then engines—more than one, low and smooth, threaded into the quiet like a voice you don't want to hear. Headlights slid across living-room ceilings, climbed the walls, then fell apart in rain-glossed driveways. Three, four, five cars turned onto the block and spread themselves thin, rolling slow as a procession with no priest. They were the wrong kind of cars for this street: paint wet as ink, wheels too large, windows blacker than the night around them.

Curtains lifted in careful fingers. A man in a white undershirt leaned an elbow on his windowsill and squinted, the sleep still heavy in his eyes, the old reflex that says *police?* rising and then failing when he saw the spacing of the cars, the way they owned the middle of the road. Across from him, a girl in a pink hoodie pressed her face to the glass and felt something she couldn't name run under her skin like ice-water.

The convoy didn't honk. Didn't rev. It breathed. It idled. Its patience said more than a scream would have. The dogs in the side yard went rigid, noses high, emitting a thread of sound that wasn't a bark yet, something between question and warning. The front passenger window of the first car slid down with the indifference of money. A muzzle eased through the gap, black and long, a dry snake tasting the air.

Someone on a porch whispered, "Get down," but the word carried only three yards before the night swallowed it. The cars fanned a little wider, positioning like chess pieces, angles that drew lines toward the same small house. A second window sighed open. Then a third. Metal kissed glass. The animals in the cages broke from their stillness and started up a ragged yelping, the sound too high and too fast.

It happened the way a storm breaks—without agreement from the sky. Muzzles flashed like struck matches. The first burst stitched a diagonal across Switch's clapboard, wood spitting splinters as the porch light exploded into glass dust. The dogs screamed. Mailboxes hopped on their posts as if trying to abandon the earth. Windows down the line of cars became mouths that spat fire and thunder. On the street, every blade of grass flattened under the shock of it. The hush that had held the block in its hands let go, and the night fell.

The gunfire didn't come in one long roar but in sentences—short, brutal statements separated by half-breaths. Each burst found a new target: porch posts cracked and folded, the aluminum screen door danced on a hinge, the front window coughed glass out onto the lawn and swallowed air in. The siding chewed under the rounds, pocked into a rash of pale wounds. Somewhere inside the house, a picture frame leapt from a nail and shattered on the floor, and the couch bled stuffing in a soft white cloud.

Neighbors hit the floor by instinct, the old muscle memory that outlives reason. A mother near the corner reached down without looking and swept a small boy off his feet, pinning him beneath her with both hands splayed across his back as if she were trying to hold him to the earth. In the next house, a man crawled across linoleum and grabbed the ankle of his father, who insisted on standing, and dragged him behind the counter, both of them breathing like they'd outrun something with teeth. Phones lit up—911 glowing blue in a hundred trembling palms.

The dogs in the side yard were pure noise now, metal claws scraping at bars, bodies slamming cage walls with the terror of creatures who understand that this kind of thunder chooses its own lightning. One animal went silent mid-yelp, the quiet from that cage an absence that cut through the other sounds like a wire through bread. The remaining dog kept shouting into the world, hoarse and furious and helpless.

Sparks jumped from the porch outlet where a bullet had nicked a cord. Smoke began to fail out of the torn lamp wiring in an anemic ribbon, the stink of hot plastic mingling with cordite until the air tasted like a melted appliance. A porch camera tried to hold the view steady as the lens fractured into a spiderweb, catching frames of muzzle-strobe and the stuttering blur of projectiles like comets dragging tails.

The cars didn't shout. Their doors didn't open. They sat in a calm that insulted the noise they were making, and from their black mouths they delivered the night's lesson: this is how you erase a block. Brass casings tinked onto asphalt, rolled, pinged against curbs, nested into puddles. A garden gnome's head burst into ceramic snow. The little wooden sign by the steps that said *Bless This Home* turned into a tongue full of splinters.

And then as cleanly as it had started, the first wave ended. The rifles rested for a beat, a collective inhale, gauging what was left to take. It was in that sliver of quiet that the street discovered its voice—someone screamed a name that wasn't answered, someone else shouted for the cops like a wish you make to a sky that's too busy. Sirens were distant yet, curious and uncertain somewhere in the city's maze. The silence between volleys offered a single false thought: maybe that's it.

It wasn't. The second wave arrived like punctuation— hard, deliberate, final. The house shivered under it, the porch step gave up and collapsed, and the last unbroken window shattered inward like breath sucked through teeth. When the guns were done, the block had a new shape.

The convoy held for one long, obscene heartbeat, the way a fist stays closed after it finishes. Smoke curled out of the windows, lazy as afternoon, regretless. The drivers looked straight ahead. Nobody cheered. Nobody spoke. Tires flexed, and in the same slow discipline with which they had come, the cars began to move. Rubber bit pavement, a low screech ran like a zipper down the block, and the procession slid away, one after another, turning the corner with the etiquette of thieves who believe in courtesy.

They left a weather behind them. The night didn't know how to be night anymore. House by house, lights snapped on. Doors opened on chains. People spilled out in the clothes they slept in, each face wearing the same expression the city has always trained into its people: the effort to understand what can't be understood. Voices multiplied, then overlapped, then turned into a crowd sound that didn't decide whether to be panic or anger.

On the lawn, the porch steps were a scatter of boards. The front of Switch's house looked like it had been fed through a machine that measures damage. Curtains breathed out of broken windows like lungs deciding whether to keep their job. Inside, a television continued to glow with an island of sitcom light on the wall, the canned laughter locked mute behind glass dust. Someone jumped the fence and ran to the cages. The tarp hung in ribbons. One dog lay still as a spool, wrong in its quiet. The other circled tight and fast, out of its mind, snapping at the air, then licking a stranger's hand with the shame of the saved. "Easy, boy," a man said, his voice cracking in the middle. "Easy." He tried to lift the latch with fingers that wouldn't listen until another pair of hands helped and the cage door swung and the animal exploded into the yard, then stopped and leaned its whole tremor against his leg like grief could be transferred through bone.

Casings glinted everywhere. They lay in the grass like seed. A neighbor in slippers bent and picked one up and dropped it again as if it had burned him, as if the metal carried heat from a fire the street couldn't see. The smell of gunpowder had settled into the hedges and wouldn't leave. A woman took out her phone and filmed with both hands because one hand shook too much, and her voice on the recording kept saying, "Oh my God, oh my God," as if she were trying to prove to some future listener that the past had been real.

Sirens turned from rumor to fact. Red and blue rounded the corner and painted the damage in carnival colors. Officers poured from their cars and began the choreography they knew: tape, shouts, flashlights fencing the dark into pieces. A patrolman touched the porch post with two fingers as if it might answer a question. The first paramedic through the gate looked at the house, at the people standing in the yard, at the way the air itself seemed bruised, and then called out to his partner for the big kit.

At the edge of the crowd, a kid with hair dyed an impossible blonde—wrong block, wrong night— watched for three heartbeats too long, then backed away and was gone by the time anyone thought to wonder who he'd been. Far off, the last echo of engines folded into the city's constant hum. What remained was the arithmetic of the aftermath, and the knowledge that this had not been random. It had been a message. And messages ask for answers.

The block was chaos. Porch lights burned up and down the street, their yellow glow mixing with the flashing reds and blues of cruisers now barricading both ends. Neighbors in robes and slippers crowded behind the sawhorses, whispering and pointing toward the smoking wreck that had once been Switch's pride — a black SUV riddled with holes, the driver's side window shattered inward, glass scattered across the cracked pavement. The air still smelled of gunpowder, sharp and metallic, as if the bullets were suspended in memory long after the cars had vanished.

The dogs in the yard whined and yelped from inside their chain-link cages, some limping, others silent, their fear echoing louder than the chatter of the gawkers. The grass was torn where bullets had chewed through fence posts, leaving splintered wood scattered on the lawn. Across the street, a kitchen curtain twitched, a child's face barely visible before a mother yanked it shut.

Lt. Mitchell stood just beyond the yellow tape, smoke curling from his cigarette as he took in the wreckage. His eyes swept across the house, the cages, the porch riddled with bullet scars, and finally the SUV — its rear hatch still hanging open, revealing a neat stack of hard black cases. One had slid halfway out, cracked open from the impact. Inside gleamed the matte-black silhouettes of submachine guns, magazines still wrapped in wax paper, untouched.

He gestured to the closest officer.

"First unit on scene?"

A young patrolman raised his hand nervously and pointed to the SUV. "That's how we found it, Lieutenant. Dozens of rounds fired. One victim confirmed inside, another dragged out—alive, barely. Ambulance already took him."

Mitchell flicked his cigarette into the gutter, grinding it out under his shoe as he approached the SUV. He bent low, looking at the weapon cases. Heckler & Koch. Same make as Chinatown. A fortune in firepower sitting right there, and not a single box missing. He straightened slowly, exhaling through his teeth.

"Nothing taken?" he asked.

"No, sir. Guns, cash — all here. Neighbors say the cars came through fast, emptied on the house, then peeled out. Pure spray-and-run."

Mitchell's jaw tightened. Another gang hit would've stripped the vehicle clean. These bastards weren't after profit. They were sending a message.

He turned back toward the house, eyes lingering on the cages of wounded dogs, then up to the shattered windows where Switch's family might've been sitting only minutes earlier. His shoulders sagged beneath the weight of what he already knew: Boston was about to burn hotter, and none of these idiots cared how many civilians got caught in it.

Without another word, Mitchell walked back to his sedan, lit another cigarette, and stood there in silence. He wasn't ready to leave, not yet. He needed the picture clear in his head before he drove away — because this wasn't the end of tonight's trouble. This was only the opening shot of a longer war.

The hospital at night was its own world — the corridors hushed, the hum of machines steady and relentless, the faint smell of antiseptic always just strong enough to remind everyone that nothing here was natural.

Henry moved through it like a ghost. His boots made no sound against the waxed linoleum, and yet every step seemed too loud in his own ears.

He pushed open the door to Dani's room. The soft glow of a single lamp illuminated her mother, Yvonne, seated in the chair beside the bed. Kalee lay curled up against her grandmother's side, finally asleep, her tiny fingers clutching the edge of Yvonne's blouse. Dani herself was still, her chest rising and falling faintly beneath the pale hospital sheets, a ventilator clicking softly in rhythm with her breathing.

Yvonne's eyes glistened in the lamplight. She had been staring at her daughter's face for so long that Henry wondered if she'd even noticed the tear sliding down her cheek. Only when she blinked and raised her hand to brush it away did she realize he was standing there.

"Dammit, Henry," she whispered, her voice cracking, half-embarrassed. "Don't you make a sound when you come in? You scared me."

Henry managed a tired half-smile and stepped forward, wrapping her gently in his arms. She was stiff at first, then leaned into him, the weight of her grief pressing against his chest.

"Sorry," he said quietly. "I didn't mean to. How is she?"

"The same." Yvonne pulled back, her voice resigned, eyes darting between Dani and the child tucked against her side. "Still the same." She studied Henry a moment, her brow tightening. "Where have you been?"

Henry looked down, lips pressing together. He searched for words, but what came out was evasive, shaky. "I've been... doing a little shopping. A few things."

Yvonne tilted her head. She had known Henry long enough to read the false notes in his tone. She reached out, covering his hand with hers, forcing his eyes back to hers. "Henry. What's going on? You don't seem like yourself these days."

He swallowed hard, forcing down the storm that wanted to rise. "I'm just frustrated. That's all. The police haven't found anything yet. Haven't done a damn thing." His voice grew tighter, almost bitter. "It feels like we're just sitting here, waiting for nothing."

Yvonne's hand squeezed his, gentle, steady. "She looks just like her momma did, lying there."

The words hit him in the chest. He leaned down, pressing his lips softly against Kalee's forehead before straightening. His face was sullen, his smile forced when he gave one back to Yvonne. He touched her shoulder with the same gentleness he had given the child, but his body was already shifting toward the door. "Where are you going?" Yvonne asked, her eyes narrowing, searching his face.

Henry hesitated. "I need to see Steven. There's some things I asked him to do for me. Cover for me at the job." The lie hung weakly in the air, obvious to them both.

Yvonne only nodded, giving him mercy instead of confrontation. "I'll be here as long as they'll let me." Henry looked back once more at Yvonne, then at Kalee, then walked out, carrying the weight of everything he hadn't said.

The hallway outside Dani's room was dim, hushed except for the low murmur of nurses at their station. Henry stepped out, dragging his hand down his face, forcing himself to breathe. He was trying to collect himself when the elevator doors slid open with a muted chime.

Lt. Mitchell stepped out. He wasn't in uniform tonight but wore a worn blazer that didn't quite fit his broad shoulders. In one hand, he carried a small teddy bear, its glassy black eyes reflecting the fluorescent lights. Mitchell's stride slowed when he saw Henry, surprise flickering across his tired features.

"Well," he said, shifting the bear in his grip, "Mr. Mann. Didn't expect to catch you here." His tone carried something halfway between courtesy and curiosity. "Do you have a minute?"

Henry straightened, masking the sudden tension in his chest. "Yeah. Sure. I was just... heading out for dinner." Mitchell smiled faintly, almost apologetically, and nodded toward Dani's room. "Let me drop this gift off for your daughter, then I'll walk with you. No sense you spending bus fare when I'm headed out myself."

Henry's mouth pulled into a line. "That's not necessary, Lieutenant. I haven't even decided what I'm eating yet." Mitchell chuckled, trying for warmth. "Don't worry about it. I'll eat practically anything." His eyes narrowed slightly, watching Henry's guarded posture. "It won't take a second."

Before Henry could answer, Mitchell turned and strode down the hall. Henry watched him at the nurses' desk, watched the way the bear looked out of place in his large hands.

Henry's phone buzzed in his jacket pocket. He slid it out quickly, holding it low. The screen lit his face for an instant. He pressed the phone to his ear, voice low. "Yo. I'm running late. Yeah... going to dinner with Mitchell. I'll call when I'm done."

He slipped the phone back into his jacket. As the fabric shifted, the edge of a Kevlar vest pressed against his ribs, hidden under his coat. He tugged the lapel closed, concealing it again just as Mitchell returned.

"Who was that?" Mitchell asked lightly, as if joking. "My wife? She never trusts where I am." He laughed at his own attempt, but Henry's expression stayed flat.

Henry pressed the elevator button. Mitchell, unfazed, tried again. "There was an incident in Chinatown tonight."

Henry glanced at him. "What kind of incident?"

"Looked like a gang shooting." Mitchell's voice grew low.

Henry scoffed, sharp. "You guys haven't put a lid on that kind of crap yet?"

Mitchell's smile faltered. He exhaled through his nose. "We're waging a war with people who don't respect the rules."

Henry turned to him then, his eyes cold, his jaw tight. His voice came out measured, almost trembling with restrained anger. "Rules? Rules are for honest people who mind their business, sitting at home with their families. Rules are for suckers waiting for rescue from predators. Rules..." his voice dipped, raw, "...are for victims."

The elevator chimed, breaking the silence that followed. Both men stepped inside, their reflections caught in the brushed metal walls, each locked in his own thoughts. The doors closed.

The restaurant was warm, humming with low conversation and the clatter of plates. A band played faint jazz from the corner, just loud enough to soften the buzz of chatter. Henry and Lt. Mitchell sat opposite each other in a corner booth, the detective's blazer draped on the seat beside him. Henry had kept his coat on despite the heat, his shoulders stiff, the collar turned up slightly to hide the line of the vest beneath.

The waitress approached with a bright smile, her pad in hand. "Good evening, gentlemen. Can I get either of you something to drink?"

Henry shook his head, forcing a polite smile. "No, thank you." He could feel sweat along his hairline, the jacket trapping heat he couldn't risk shedding.

"I'll stick with water," Mitchell said, taking the menu. He flashed the waitress a smile that was more habit than charm. "I'm driving."

She set down the glasses and gave Henry another look, brow creasing. "You seem a little warm, sir. Can I get you some water too?"

Henry waved it off. "I'm fine. Probably fighting a fever."

Her smile faltered, but she didn't press. "Alright then. I'll give you both a few minutes with the menu."

As she left, Mitchell's eyes lingered after her—more tired than lecherous—before he turned back to Henry. His gaze flicked to the coat Henry refused to take off. "You sure you're not hot in that jacket? You're starting to sweat through it."

Henry's tone snapped sharper than he intended. "Lieutenant, what is this? Department policy now? Cozying up to victims of violent crime?"

Mitchell didn't flinch. His hands rested on the table, fingers interlaced. His voice dropped, quiet but steady. "I want those little street bastards put away. I want the gangs off my streets. And I want to retire knowing I left this city better than I found it."

Henry leaned back, jaw tight, the weight of his silence pressing between them.

Mitchell studied him, his eyes narrowed but not hostile—measuring. "You've got reason to be angry. Nobody's questioning that. What happened to your family... it's the kind of thing that keeps me up at night too."

Henry forced a smile that didn't touch his eyes. "Well, that don't explain why you're following me around to dinner."

Mitchell didn't answer right away. He let the quiet linger, just the scrape of silverware and the muted laughter of strangers around them. Then he said, carefully: "I've been a cop a long time, Mr. Mann. Long enough to know when a man carries something heavy on him. Something heavier than grief." His eyes drifted, just for a heartbeat, toward Henry's jacket before returning. "But it's not my job to guess. It's my job to follow the truth where it leads."

The waitress returned, breaking the tension as she set down a basket of bread. Mitchell thanked her softly. Henry kept his stare fixed on the table, his hand tightening around the sweating glass of water until his knuckles whitened.

The bread basket sat untouched between them, the butter knife gleaming under the low light. Mitchell leaned back, resting his arm along the top of the booth, his posture deceptively casual. He scanned the room once—an old cop's habit—before settling his eyes back on Henry.

"You know," Mitchell began, his voice calm, almost reflective, "most people I deal with after a tragedy... they fold. They let the grief take them apart. You—" he paused, studying Henry with a faint tilt of the head, "—you carry it different. Like you're bracing against a storm that hasn't even hit yet."

Henry shifted in his seat. He forced a short laugh, brittle around the edges. "Guess everyone copes in their own way."

"Sure." Mitchell's tone carried no judgment, only the weight of observation. He sipped his water, then set the glass down carefully, as though giving Henry time to fill the silence. But Henry said nothing, his face unreadable in the dim light.

The waitress reappeared, setting plates down at the booth across the aisle. Mitchell watched her pass, then lowered his voice slightly, as though confiding something. "I've seen a lot of men try to make sense of what doesn't make sense. They work longer hours. They drink too much. Some go looking for fights they know they can't win." His eyes flicked up, steady but unassuming. "Everybody's got a tell, Mr. Mann. Everybody shows the way their hurt burns through."

Henry's jaw tightened. He reached for the menu though he hadn't glanced at it once. "You've got me pegged as what then? The drinker, the fighter, or the fool?"

Mitchell didn't smile. "I'm not here to peg you as anything. I'm here because I think you deserve more than the scraps of justice we keep handing out in this city. And maybe because I see in you the kind of man who doesn't wait on others to deliver it."

The words hung between them, heavy but deliberately neutral. He hadn't accused Henry of anything—not outright—but the undertone was there, undeniable.

Henry let out a slow breath, leaning back into the booth. "You talk like you know me."

"I talk like I've walked this beat for twenty-five years." Mitchell's eyes softened, though the sharpness beneath them never left. "And I know when a man has more inside him than he's willing to show."

The waitress returned then, menus in hand, asking if they were ready to order. Henry shook his head quickly. "Not hungry."

Mitchell handed his menu back too, polite but distracted. When the waitress left again, he spoke once more, quiet enough that only Henry could hear: "You've been through hell. I get it. But don't let that fire burn you up from the inside out."

Henry met his gaze at last, steady and unflinching. "I'll manage."

Mitchell gave the faintest nod, as if to say *we'll see*, and let the silence return.

The silence stretched long after Mitchell's last words, broken only by the murmur of other patrons and the clink of silverware against porcelain. Henry sat motionless, one hand resting on the table, the other still tucked beneath his coat, fingers brushing against the edge of the vest he had no business wearing to a dinner with a cop.

Mitchell's phone vibrated first, a soft tremor against the wood of the booth. He fished it from his pocket, eyes narrowing at the screen before he answered. "Mitchell." His tone shifted instantly—businesslike, clipped. He turned his body slightly, voice lowering though Henry could still catch fragments. "When? ... How many? ... All right, I'll be there."

The detective slid out of the booth, already reaching into his wallet. He pulled out enough bills to cover both their meals—though neither had touched a plate—and dropped them on the table without fuss. "Duty calls," he said simply, slipping the phone back into his pocket.

Henry tilted his head, playing casual. "Something serious?"

Mitchell paused, hand resting on the back of the booth. His eyes searched Henry's face for just a moment longer than necessary. "Another shooting. Could be connected to what happened to your family. Could be something else entirely." His words were careful, chosen. He didn't say *Hell's Gentlemen* outright, but Henry caught the implication in the way Mitchell's jaw tightened.

Henry feigned disinterest, though the fire was already burning in his chest. "City never quits, does it?"

"No," Mitchell agreed, his voice quiet, steady. "It doesn't." He leaned in slightly, lowering his voice so the words became private between them. "Keep your head clear, Mr. Mann. If this war gets any worse, even the strong won't walk away clean."

For a heartbeat, the two men held each other's gaze—Henry hiding his intent, Mitchell searching for it without daring to accuse. Then the detective gave a small nod, as if settling the matter for now, and straightened. "We'll talk again."

He left quickly, weaving through the tables with a grace born of long practice, a man accustomed to being called away from half-finished meals. The door chimed as it closed behind him, leaving Henry alone in the booth.

Henry sat still, staring at the cash Mitchell had left on the table. The weight of the vest pressed against his ribs, a physical reminder of the double life he was trying to balance. The detective's words echoed in his mind—warnings disguised as sympathy, suspicions wrapped in understanding.

He drew in a breath, steadying himself. Mitchell was clever, maybe clever enough to see through the lies. But sympathy wasn't enough to stop the storm Henry felt building inside. The gangs had turned his home into a battlefield. The police talked rules and procedures. None of it would bring Dani back to life or stop Kalee from growing up without her mother.

Henry reached into his pocket, thumbed the phone, and pulled up the number he needed. He hesitated only long enough to glance toward the door Mitchell had exited. Then he pressed call.

"Yeah," he said when the line clicked open, his voice low, dangerous. "I'm on my way."

He ended the call and slid from the booth, tossing a few extra bills beside Mitchell's money out of habit more than courtesy. The waitress approached and asked, "Is everything okay?" "Oh my friend was coming down with something fierce, so he left. ...and I don't want to spread any germs so I'm going as well". Henry shakes her hand and leaves. The waitress gets a panicked look on her face as she studies her own hand, then rushes for sanitizer. As he walked toward the door, Henry adjusted his coat, pulling it tighter to conceal the armor beneath.

The city outside waited, restless and violent. And Henry was ready to step back into it.

The night air slapped cold against Henry's face as he left the restaurant, a contrast to the warmth inside. The neon sign above flickered, humming faintly, while the city stretched before him in restless motion. Sirens already wailed in the distance, converging somewhere near the waterfront. He knew exactly where they were headed.

He moved quickly, slipping into the stream of pedestrians, just another man with a coat pulled tight against the wind. Every step carried him away from the glow of the restaurant, away from Mitchell's searching eyes. The detective had been close, maybe closer than Henry liked, but close didn't matter. Mitchell worked in the world of procedure; Henry lived in the world of resolve.

Across town, blue and red lights painted the narrow street where Switch's house stood riddled with bullet holes. The African Lord's dogs lay still in the yard, their bodies broken in the chaos. The front windows were shattered, curtains flapping like torn sails in the night breeze. Neighbors huddled on porches, whispering to each other, pointing at the wreckage of glass and wood. Mitchell ducked under the tape, nodding at the uniform posted by the perimeter. His face was grim as he stepped onto the porch, crunching glass beneath his shoes. Inside, the air still carried the bitter tang of gunpowder. Holes punched through drywall and furniture bore silent witness to the fusillade.

Costa was already there, notebook in hand, talking to a shaken witness—a middle-aged woman who claimed she heard the engines before she heard the shots. Mitchell listened, arms folded, his gaze sweeping the room, noting the pattern, the spread, the precision. This hadn't been reckless. It had been deliberate, practiced.

"Hell's Gentlemen?" Costa asked, his tone halfway between certainty and question.

Mitchell didn't answer right away. He crouched near a wall, running his fingers along the ragged edge of a bullet hole. "Looks like it. Too clean for amateurs." He straightened, exhaling through his nose. "Retaliation. That's what this is."

He glanced toward the street, his mind's eye painting the convoy of cars rolling through, guns flashing in coordinated rhythm. He knew what war looked like, and Boston was teetering on the edge of it.

Meanwhile, Henry moved in silence through a different neighborhood. He kept his pace measured, not hurried, not slow—just another man in the crowd. But beneath the surface his heart thudded with steady purpose. The call he had made wasn't casual. It was a summons. A reminder to his allies that he was still in motion, still pushing.

As he turned down a side street, the sounds of the city shifted: less laughter, more silence, the kind of block where eyes peered from behind curtains but doors stayed closed. He knew these streets, knew their rhythms, and tonight every rhythm told him the same thing—pressure was building.

Behind him, the city reeled from another eruption of violence. Ahead of him, another choice waited.

And in the middle, Henry carried his secret war, walking straight into it with no hesitation.

Henry walked alone, his steps carrying him through the city as if the streets themselves expected him. Every corner of Boston whispered a memory now—some tied to Dani, others to Kalee. Dani's voice had been silenced forever, her absence a hollow space he could never fill. But Kalee—his little girl—still breathed, though trapped in that cruel stillness of machines and quiet monitors. A father wasn't meant to watch his child live like that.

The grief weighed heavy, but it had hardened into something sharper. He couldn't simply sit in the hospital, staring at his daughter while the people responsible prowled the streets freely. He needed leverage, tools, a way forward. And for that, he needed Steven.

Steven had been there since the beginning, long before the gangs had names, before the city rotted in plain sight. They'd shared shifts, shared fights, shared the kind of loyalty you didn't question. If Henry was going to move from rage to action, Steven was the one man he trusted to stand beside him.

He pulled his phone from his pocket, thumb hovering over the screen. For a moment, he thought of Dani's mother back at the hospital, her tearful eyes fixed on Kalee. Henry hadn't told her the truth—couldn't. He'd lied about where he was going, called it "shopping" and "covering shifts," as if errands could explain the storm building inside him. Better she didn't know. Better she believed he was simply lost in grief.

The phone buzzed to life, its screen glowing against the dark. Henry scrolled through until he found Steven's name. His hand tightened, a flicker of hesitation passing over him. Calling Steven meant making the choice real. It meant stepping off the edge.

He pressed the button. The line rang once, twice, then a voice answered.

"Henry?" Steven's tone was cautious, low.

"Yeah." Henry's own voice carried the gravel of sleepless nights. "I need you."

There was no surprise on the other end. No demand for explanation. Steven only asked, "Where?"

"Your place in Half an hour," Henry said.

"I'll be here," Steven replied, and the line went dead.

Henry pocketed the phone and leaned against the cold brick wall of the alley where he'd stopped. The city around him hummed with its usual chaos—sirens in the distance, muffled voices from open windows, the clatter of a bottle kicked by some stranger. But inside, Henry felt only silence.

He thought again of Dani's smile, of the life stolen from her. The promise of a good future stolen from him. He thought of Kalee's small hand in his, limp beneath the hospital's fluorescent light. The gangs had torn his world apart. Denied him sanctity. Denied him his love. They tore his world apart...

Now, with Steven's help, he would begin tearing theirs down.

Chapter 7

The night air hung heavy over the suburban street, the kind of damp quiet that made every distant sound stand out sharper than it should. Henry moved with deliberate calm, his boots striking the pavement in a steady rhythm as he approached the cluster of low apartment buildings. The lights of Boston's skyline burned faintly in the distance, but here, the neighborhood felt detached, a pocket of stillness hiding beneath the greater storm. He stopped before a modest brick building and scanned the row of exterior doors, his gaze sharp but not anxious. He wasn't nervous—he had left nerves behind long ago. What he felt now was more akin to curiosity, a soldier's instinct to take measure of the ground he was stepping onto. His large hand reached for the iron railing of the short stairwell, and then he climbed to the landing. A porch light flickered on as he knocked once, its pale glow spilling across his shoulders.

The door opened with a creak, and Henry, without hesitation, placed his palm against the knob and pushed his way inside.

Steven Fitzgerald's apartment was the opposite of Henry's brownstone—smaller, neater, and humming with an energy that came from screens instead of family. Hardwood floors caught the faint glow of a television left running in the background. The walls bore no photographs, no signs of permanence, only the impersonal imprint of a bachelor who lived more in his mind than in the room around him.

Dominating the corner was Steven's true sanctuary: a fortress of monitors, speakers, and towers of humming electronics. It looked less like a living room and more like the control hub of some clandestine operation. A couch and coffee table were pushed to the side as though they were afterthoughts, pieces of furniture meant to fill space rather than invite comfort.

Steven himself was dressed like the room—casual, functional, unconcerned. A baggy t-shirt hung loose from his frame, jeans sagged against his hips, sandals slapping against the hardwood as he moved. His sharp eyes lit when Henry entered, though his words carried more unease than his posture betrayed.

"Man, you had me sweatin' bullets," Steven said, running a hand over his scalp. "How'd you get away from that cop?"

Henry's deep voice rumbled low, carrying fatigue. "Got lucky. He was called to another shooting."

Steven's brows rose. "Heard about that on the police band. Retaliation, they're saying. All tied to that mess in Chinatown."

The mention brought Henry's head down, his gaze drifting to the floor. Escalation had never been his goal. He wanted justice for his daughter, vengeance for his wife. The thought that his war might be fueling theirs was a bitter weight pressing against his chest.

Steven's tone softened. "It's not on you, man. You're just trying to set things right—for your family, for yourself."

Henry slid off his jacket, the weight of Kevlar hidden beneath it pressing a mark across his shoulders. He unstrapped the vest, set it aside, then lowered himself onto the couch. His frame filled the seat as he leaned back, eyes closing for a moment as though sleep might sneak up on him.

Steven leaned against the back of his chair, watching his friend's massive frame sag into the cushions. There was something almost childlike in the way Henry let his head fall back, as though the weight of battle had finally caught up with him in this quiet room. The television murmured faintly, voices from a sitcom no one was listening to, the laugh track jarring against the silence between them.

"You know," Steven began, his voice measured, "I only agreed to help with this craziness because I know the cops won't get you what you need. They can't. The gangs are too bold now. Too many of them, too much money flowing. The city doesn't stand a chance."

Henry opened his eyes, staring at the ceiling. His voice came low, tinged with a reluctant honesty. "I didn't want to add fuel to the fire. Thought maybe if I kept it quiet, kept it sharp, I could strike at the right places. But if I told the police... what then? What would happen if I came clean?"

Steven's laugh was short, bitter. "You'd get charged with some made-up crime, dragged through the mud in the media, stripped of your daughter, and locked in a cell. And after all that, the gangs would still run the streets like nothing happened."

Henry turned his head, eyes narrowing. "You think this through a lot?"

Steven met his gaze with a shrug. "When you first came to me—at the cemetery—I thought you were just venting. Angry words. But when you started doing things? Making moves? I had to start thinking about where it could go."

Henry's lips curved in something that wasn't quite a smile. "So you think I'm crazy?"

The pause was heavy. Steven shook his head. "I think you're still hurting."

Henry rubbed his temples with both hands, the pressure of his fingertips barely containing the storm brewing behind his eyes. His lids fluttered shut, and for a moment he seemed less the soldier, less the avenger, and more the grieving husband who had lost the anchor of his world.

Steven's voice softened further. "If this is what you have to do to get through that pain... then I'm with you."

Henry opened his eyes again, his gaze clearer now, almost vulnerable. "Thanks, man. I'm going through something, and this feels like the only way forward."

Steven nodded once, decisive. He swiveled toward the glow of his monitors, his demeanor sharpening like a commander preparing a mission briefing. His fingers danced across the keyboard, and lines of data sprang to life on the screens.

"Okay," Steven said, gesturing toward the display. "This is what I've got."

Henry pushed himself from the couch, the leather groaning beneath him as he leaned over Steven's shoulder. The screens flickered with maps, reports, fragments of digital chatter gathered from places most men couldn't reach.

"This is a map of the address from tonight's shooting," Steven explained. "Cops found the place torn apart. Empty of people—but full of dogs. And…" He hesitated, his tone dipping lower. "And what they think was half a man's body. They're not telling the media that."

Henry's jaw tightened, the muscles ticking beneath his skin.

Henry's brow furrowed as his eyes roamed the screens, the glow of shifting data reflecting off the hard lines of his face. The idea of a mutilated body, gnawed by dogs, was grotesque even to him, a man who had seen more than his share of war's brutality. This wasn't combat—it was savagery.

"You ever think the cops'll trace this back to you?" Henry asked finally, his voice carrying both concern and skepticism. "All this digging in their systems, pulling information no one else sees—it's dangerous. You don't worry they'll catch you?"

Steven almost laughed, his confidence palpable. He raised his hands in mock surrender, as though the question itself was an insult. "Are you kidding? My system re-routes IP addresses every twenty minutes, automatically. I bounce around the globe—Hong Kong, Berlin, Nairobi—before looping back stateside. No one's tracing me, Henry. Not unless I want them to."

Henry shook his head, half in disbelief, half in resignation. He'd trusted Steven this far, trusted the way his friend's mind could reach into places beyond the touch of a soldier's hands. Still, he couldn't quite wrap his head around a war fought on screens instead of streets.

Steven smirked, leaning back in his chair, arms folded as though the conversation was settled. "You stick to the muscle. I'll stick to the tech. That's why this works." Henry's eyes drifted again to the digital map, red pins marking places in the city where the gangs had left scars. "So what can you tell me about the African Lords?"

The question pulled Steven's focus back to the monitors. His fingers flew across the keys, summoning files from databases that should have been locked behind layers of clearance. A string of mugshots, reports, and blurred surveillance images filled the screen.

"According to the law enforcement database," Steven said, tapping one of the images, "the African Lords are spreading into the States faster than anyone thought possible. Started in Nigeria. Real bad news, Henry. These aren't your average street punks. They roll deep, organized, with resources most gangs only dream of." He let out a dry laugh. "And they've got hyenas. Hyenas and baboons. Pet ones. Can you believe that? Who the hell brings hyenas into Boston?"

Henry leaned closer, his face unreadable. "Lieutenant thinks they were the ones there the night Dani and Kalee were shot. Says they're the reason bullets flew."

Steven turned sharply in his chair, eyes wide. "Damn. And the lieutenant just hands you that kind of intel? Feels like he tells you everything but when he takes a shit."

Henry shook his head slowly, his voice heavy with uncertainty. "I can't figure him out. It's like he knows I'm up to something, but he won't say it outright. Feeds me pieces, then tries to hold me back at the same time. Like he's torn between stopping me and helping me."

Steven leaned forward, resting his elbows on his knees, gaze hard. "It's a serious game you're in, brother. You can't trust anyone. Not me, not him, not the streets. You watch your ass with everybody."

Henry's eyes softened just enough to reveal a sliver of gratitude. "I know. But I'm glad I've got you."

The two men clasped fists, knuckles striking together in the dim glow of the monitors. It was a soldier's gesture, an unspoken oath.

Steven exhaled slowly and turned back to the monitors, scrolling deeper into the reports until a name appeared across the screen. He tapped the keyboard, enlarging a grainy profile photo. "Now, I don't have much yet, but here's what I dug up on their chief here in the States. Mykelti N'tumbe." Steven's voice hardened. "This guy… he's not right in the head. I don't mean street crazy—I mean off balance, real psychological breaks. Dangerous in ways you can't measure."

Henry straightened, his arms crossing as he studied the face. The man in the photo was lean, sharp-eyed, carrying a predatory sort of confidence even through the low-quality image. "So how the hell did he end up here? Shit, when I go near an airport TSA is up my ass. So how did they let a psycho in?"

Steven clicked another window open, pulling up a report stamped with official insignia. "Looks like he came over on an athletic scholarship. Northeastern University, track and field. Promising runner, strong prospects. But something snapped. He assaulted people—badly. Got himself hospitalized for a stretch. They tried to deport him, but somewhere along the way they lost track of him. Slipped into the cracks and resurfaced with a gang at his back." Steven leaned back in his chair, watching Henry for a reaction.

Henry stared at the screen a long moment before shaking his head. "That's funny. We're always teaching lessons to the same type of men who want to kill us. Schoolin' them, caging them, deportin' them. And somehow, they keep coming back sharper, meaner. I.C.E. is always messin' with the wrong people."

His voice carried no humor, only a quiet disgust. He turned away from the glow of the monitors, his gaze drifting to the bare walls as though they might offer an answer. After a moment he looked back to Steven, his tone edged with caution. "Listen. The deeper I get, the worse this'll get. It's gonna get heavy. If you want out, I'll understand."

Steven raised an eyebrow, half serious, half teasing. "Out? Man, I'm here for the duration. We're like Batman and Robin." A faint smirk tugged at his lips. "Only I'm more the 'stay in the cave Robin.' You're the one out there swinging at the bad guys."

For the first time that night, Henry let a chuckle slip free, low and brief. The sound didn't erase the weight pressing against him, but it softened it for a moment. "Guess that makes me the one wearing the cape."

Steven grinned, tapping a pen against the desk. "Long as you don't expect me to start wearing tights, we're good."

The air between them eased, the heaviness of strategy giving way to something almost resembling normal friendship. Henry broke the moment by moving toward the kitchen, his deep voice calling back over his shoulder. "You got anything to drink?"

Steven didn't look away from the monitors. "Whatever's in there is all yours."

Henry's voice drifted from the other room, half amused, half exasperated. "You got nothin'. Don't you ever shop?"

Steven snorted, muttering under his breath. "How do you go from Death Wish to Martha Stewart in the same night? Maybe you do got somethin' wrong with you." Henry's laughter carried faintly from the kitchen, a rare, human sound in the middle of their war.

The city pressed down hard on its servants, and in the fluorescent glare of downtown Boston's government buildings, Assistant District Attorney Collier carried that pressure on his shoulders. From behind the glass walls of a conference room, his expression was taut, jaw clenched as he endured the fire of an animated superior. Voices carried muffled through the pane, one man shouting, hands carving through the air, others scribbling furiously in their notepads. The meeting ended with a dismissive wave, the officials scattering like soldiers leaving a battlefield.

Collier emerged first, his face a map of agitation. He strode quickly down the hall, suit jacket tugging at his shoulders, and entered his office with a hard swing of the door. Dropping into his chair, he loosened his tie, exhaling a breath he hadn't realized he was holding. His hand drifted to the desk drawer, rummaging until he pulled free a folder. The papers inside whispered of cases, unfinished threads, and too many unanswered questions.

He was scanning the lines when a voice at the door startled him.

"Hey, you wanted to see me?"

Collier jerked upright, his eyes flashing before softening with recognition. "Jeez, you startled me. Come in. Have a seat."

Lieutenant Mitchell entered with the casual weight of a man who had seen too much in his years of service. He settled into the chair across from Collier, leaning back, preparing himself for the tirade he knew was coming. Collier, however, forced himself into civility, even warmth. "Water?" he offered.

Mitchell shook his head. "No... thank you."

Collier folded his hands, the mask of cordiality sitting uncomfortably on his face. "I just got out of a meeting—no, an ass whipping—from the Mayor and the Attorney General. They're furious we don't have anyone—anyone at all—to parade in front of the media. They want a name, a face, a neat package to tie all these shootings up with."

Mitchell arched an eyebrow, voice dripping with sarcasm. "I must have missed that memo."

Collier's lips twitched. "Don't worry. You'll get the unabridged version directly from the Mayor soon enough." He leaned forward. "So tell me, what have you got?"

Mitchell spread his hands. "I don't *got* anything. Two very public shootings and the only lead I have is one punk beaten so badly he can't even speak. No weapon, no witnesses who will talk. Just silence and fear."

Collier's brows knit together. "Somebody beat him. Who?"

Mitchell's shrug was weary, his tone laced with frustration. "Damned if I know. But I've got my suspicions."

Collier leaned in. "Mind sharing?"

The lieutenant paused, eyes drifting to the floor. He weighed the thought carefully, then met Collier's anxious gaze with a long breath. "I think it's Henry Mann."

Collier blinked, unfamiliar with the name. "Who's that?"

"The guy from the gang shooting last month. The bystander. Lost his wife that night. Kid's still in a coma."

Recognition flickered across Collier's features. "Oh. Why him? Why now?"

Mitchell shook his head. "Not entirely sure. But he's got motive."

Collier tilted his head, skeptical. "And that would be?"

Mitchell's voice was flat, almost cold. "One of the oldest motives of man—revenge."

Collier scoffed, exasperated. "Haven't we evolved beyond that cowboy crap by now?"

Mitchell's gaze hardened. "I'm just saying, if someone had offed my wife and I wasn't a cop..."

He let the unfinished sentence hang, heavy in the quiet office.

Mitchell let the words trail off, but Collier could hear the truth beneath them. The lieutenant's tone carried no theatrics—just the raw honesty of a man who had lived long enough to understand what grief could sculpt out of another human being.

"If I wasn't a cop," Mitchell continued quietly, "I'd probably be looking for my own justice too. Mann's no hardened criminal, but pain... pain will make you pick up a weapon faster than any gang initiation."

Collier leaned back, running a hand across his jaw. "So you think this guy, this grieving husband, is suddenly out there waging a one-man war?"

Mitchell shrugged. "Not suddenly. More like slowly. Desperation builds like water behind a dam. At first it just seeps through the cracks—small things, questions he shouldn't be asking, places he shouldn't be. But when it breaks, it floods everything."

Collier tapped a pen against his desk, eyes narrowing. "What evidence do you have? Anything that could stand up in court?"

Mitchell gave a hollow laugh. "Evidence? I don't even have a decent hunch that would hold up with my own detectives. The kid who was beaten? Won't be talking for a long while. Witnesses? They see nothing, hear nothing. The gangs? They've gone quiet, which is louder than any confession. And through it all, Mann's name keeps circling in my head."

Collier pressed, irritation creeping into his tone. "Circling in your head doesn't mean a damn thing to the Mayor or the Attorney General. They want someone *in handcuffs.*"

"I know," Mitchell said, his voice low, steady. "But what do you want, Collier? A headline to keep City Hall off your back? Or the truth?"

The ADA froze, caught between political obligation and a gnawing sense of conscience. His lips parted, then closed again. Finally, he exhaled. "I want both. And I want it soon."

Mitchell leaned forward, elbows on his knees. "Then you'd better understand what you're asking. If I move on Mann without hard proof, I ruin a man who's already lost everything. And if I don't, the gangs keep bleeding this city until the streets are unrecognizable."

Collier frowned. "You're saying he's dangerous, but you don't want to stop him?"

Mitchell's gaze was sharp now, cutting. "I'm saying I don't know if he's the danger... or the answer."

The words hung in the air, weighty and dangerous.

Collier shifted in his seat, his patience thinning. "Look, the Mayor doesn't care about answers. He cares about optics. He wants this wrapped up yesterday. If Mann is your suspect, find a way to make it stick."

Mitchell rose slowly, towering over the desk, his face carved with resolve and weariness both. "I'll keep watching him. I'll keep digging. But understand this, Collier—if Henry Mann *is* behind these retaliations, he's not some thug making noise in the streets. He's a man on a mission. And that makes him the most unpredictable kind of threat."

Collier's fingers drummed nervously on the folder in front of him. He looked up at Mitchell, his voice almost a whisper. "Then pray you figure out which side of the line he's on before the city burns."

The fluorescent lights of the intensive care unit cast a sterile glow down the narrow corridor. The hum of machines, the low murmur of nurses, the muted shuffle of shoes against linoleum—all of it blended into a rhythm that should have felt safe, almost sacred. But when Assistant District Attorney Collier appeared, flanked by two uniformed policemen, the air shifted. He carried tension with him like a storm cloud, and the nurses at their station instinctively quieted as he passed.

Collier's stride was purposeful, his face tight with impatience as he cut through the hall. He turned the final corner and pushed into the room where Kalee Mann lay in her fragile sleep. The sight that greeted him was far from adversarial—an elderly woman sitting in a worn chair, her grief etched into her every feature.

Dani's mother looked up, startled, as though the walls themselves had betrayed her by letting this man in.

"Where is he?" Collier's voice was clipped, almost cold. There was no sympathy in it, no softness for the child tethered to machines just feet away.

The woman's back straightened, her eyes sharp with defiance. "Who are you?"

Collier dipped a hand into his jacket and produced his badge, flashing it with the mechanical precision of someone who no longer cared whether the gesture comforted or threatened. "Collier. District Attorney's office. I'm looking for Henry Mann. Where is he?"

Her grief boiled quickly into rage. "Well, he's not here. And I don't appreciate you barging in here like this. Why do you want him?"

Collier ignored her, scanning the room instead. His gaze lingered on the pale child in the bed, then on the walls, as though Henry might somehow materialize out of them. His hand pressed briefly to his temple, a sign of weariness—or calculation. Then, decision hardened across his face.

"You," he barked, pointing to one of the officers. "Wait for him here. If he shows up, I want him arrested and brought in."

The officer nodded once, moving to stand at rigid attention by the door. The assignment was clear.

Dani's mother said nothing more, but her eyes spoke enough. They burned with a fury that only a mother could wield—the silent accusation that Collier's intrusion had crossed every line of decency. But Collier met her look with empty eyes, offering neither apology nor explanation, before he turned and strode out.

In the hall, the remaining officer fell in behind him, the echo of their steps fading toward the elevators. The one left behind shifted his stance at the doorway, settling in for a long vigil.

What none of them noticed was the shadow in the adjoining corridor.

Henry Mann stood partially concealed behind the edge of a supply door, his shoulders taut, his breath measured. He had heard every word, had seen Collier's callous intrusion into the room where his daughter clung to life. The sight of the badge flashing, the cold command to have him dragged off in cuffs—it ignited something dark inside him.

His lips curled into a sneer. This wasn't justice. This was theater—politics.

As the officer outside Kalee's room adjusted his stance, Henry slid back into the dim corridor, his movements practiced and silent. He retreated into the deeper shadows of the hospital, disappearing into the maze of sterile hallways. His eyes, though, burned with new resolve. If Collier wanted a criminal, Henry thought bitterly, then maybe he was ready to show him one.

Henry moved swiftly through the hospital's back corridors, each step fueled by a growing storm inside him. The smell of antiseptic clung to the air, sharp and sterile, but it did little to cleanse the bitter taste in his mouth. His daughter lay hooked up to machines, fighting for breath she could not take on her own, and instead of offering solace, the system was hunting him. Not for what he had done, but for daring to want justice in a city too broken to deliver it.

He found the emergency exit at the far end of the wing and pushed through, the heavy door closing behind him with a muffled slam. Outside, the night had settled deep and cool, the suburban glow of Boston filtering faintly against the horizon. He drew in the air, steadying himself, but the weight pressing against his chest did not ease. Collier's words echoed: *If he shows up, arrest him.*

They weren't looking to understand. They weren't looking to heal. They wanted a scapegoat—his face in front of the cameras, his name on the headlines, his life destroyed in the process. It was easier that way. The gangs would keep spilling blood, the neighborhoods would keep burying their children, but the mayor would have his man, and Collier would look strong.

Henry clenched his fists until his knuckles whitened. They had no idea what it felt like to hold your wife's lifeless body, to hear your child's laughter cut short by gunfire. They didn't understand that every day since, he had been walking through a storm of silence and rage.

He started down the narrow side street away from the hospital. His jacket collar was pulled up high against the cold, his eyes scanning instinctively for tails, for watchers, for anyone who might connect him to the building he had just left. Every step was measured. He had learned to live with caution pressed against his skin like a second layer.

The city around him was alive with its own nocturnal sounds—distant sirens, the growl of engines, the occasional burst of laughter from a bar too close to the hospital district. It all sounded foreign to Henry, like he was walking through a world he no longer belonged to.

He needed a plan. Collier wasn't just sniffing around anymore; he was setting traps. If they could plant an officer outside Kalee's room tonight, tomorrow it would be his home, the streets he walked, the people he trusted.

A shadow of doubt brushed across his mind. Maybe Mitchell had been feeding him information to keep him on a leash, maybe even to smoke him out. The thought made his pulse quicken. If Mitchell had sold him out, if Collier had convinced him Henry was just another vigilante to reel in, then there was no one left on the inside. He was truly alone.

Henry's jaw tightened. *So be it.*

He turned another corner, slipping into a patch of darkness between streetlamps, his breath ghosting out before him. For now, he would vanish into the city's underbelly, out of reach from Collier's eager grasp. But one thing had crystallized in his mind as sharp as glass: they were coming for him, and he wasn't going to wait to be taken.

If they wanted a fight, he would bring it to them.

The Hell's Gentlemen's warehouse still reeked of sweat, liquor, and cigarette smoke when Jason and his crew stepped inside. They had been laughing, loud and unguarded, riding the adrenaline of the night—until the laughter died in their throats.

Across the room stood Mykelti, the towering presence of the African Lords' leader, a heavy chain looped through his hand. At the end of it, his pet hyena sat in eerie stillness, its guttural laugh echoing faintly through the cavernous space. Around him, half a dozen African

Lords raised Heckler & Koch submachine guns, black steel glinting under the warehouse lights.

Jason's men froze, shoulders tightening as their eyes darted toward him for guidance. For a moment, Jason's jaw clenched. Then his features shifted, softening into calculation. Without a word, he broke formation, walking toward the bar that ran along the far wall. The sudden movement had two rifles snap upward, muzzles trained directly on his chest. Jason stopped, lifted his hand slowly, and plucked a bottle from the counter. He turned it outward like an offering.

Mykelti's expression didn't waver, but he gave the smallest nod. Jason poured himself a glass, his movements deliberate, calm. Then, with a sly grin, he filled a second and carried it toward Mykelti, careful to stop just short of the hyena's range. The beast strained, lips pulled back over sharp teeth, but Mykelti reached out, his large hand engulfing the delicate glass. The two men locked eyes as they drank, an unspoken duel simmering between them.

Jason was the first to break. "Well, it seems as though you have us at a disadvantage."

Mykelti smiled thinly, showing no humor. "No. I have you beat."

The air in the warehouse grew heavier. Jason motioned for his men to stand down, their hands slowly easing away from their weapons. "Then tell me," he said smoothly. "What can I do to rectify this... situation?"

Mykelti tilted his head, studying Jason as if he were examining a flawed diamond. "You sound like a salesman. Even in the face of defeat, still trying to close a deal."

Jason bowed slightly. "It's how I survive."

But Mykelti's gaze had sharpened. "There was an accident at one of my houses. I lost some... very dear pets. Police now breathe down my neighborhood's neck. So I thought to myself—where can I go to watch the game in peace? And then I remembered. The Hell's Gentlemen invited me once, did they not? After all, why would they shoot up my house?"

Jason's mask cracked, his voice rising with anger. "We only retaliated because of your guy in Chinatown."

The words seemed to strike Mykelti like a slap. His face contorted with fury. In an instant, he dropped the hyena's chain and lunged, his hand clamping around Jason's throat. The Hell's Gentlemen reached for their weapons, but the chilling chorus of clicks from African Lords' rifles froze them in place.

Mykelti's voice was raw, almost feral. "No. You lie. You think me weak, you think me stupid. Now I take your guns, your place, and your life!"

The tension was a live wire ready to snap when a cell phone's shrill ringing cut through the silence. The sound was absurdly mundane against the backdrop of death. Mykelti raised his weapon, finger tightening on the trigger, but the call persisted until one of his men answered.

"Boss, stop!" the man stammered, eyes wide. "It's Switch. He's at the hospital—he says he knows who's been stirring all this."

The words made Mykelti pause. Slowly, reluctantly, he lowered the gun and snatched the phone. His face changed as he listened. Then he turned back to Jason, an ugly smile breaking across his features.

"It seems we have both been duped," he said.

Jason's eyes narrowed. "What the hell are you talking about?"

Mykelti's grin widened. "A common problem. Some man trying to be a rough neck."

The phrase hung in the air, strange and dangerous.

Jason bristled, snapping back. "What the hell's a rough neck? And get those guns out of my face."

Mykelti let the silence stretch before waving his men to lower their weapons. "Come. Sit. Let's have a drink. I'll tell you everything you want to know." He leaned in, voice lowering to a conspiratorial growl. "We have a jackal to catch."

The warehouse atmosphere shifted once the guns were lowered, but the tension didn't vanish—it merely settled deeper, like smoke that refused to clear. Jason sat at the bar across from Mykelti, his posture deceptively casual, though every line of his body suggested restraint, calculation. Mykelti, towering and broad, leaned forward with predatory ease, his hyena crouched at his feet like some grotesque herald of death.

Jason poured himself another drink, sliding the bottle toward Mykelti. "So. This ghost you speak of—the one spooking both of us. Tell me why I shouldn't put a bullet in your head right now and blame him for it."

Mykelti chuckled low, the sound jagged, unsettling. "Because then you'd never know what you're up against. And let me tell you, brother—you're not facing some kid with a stolen pistol. This one... he's different."

Jason swirled the amber liquid in his glass. "Different how?"

Mykelti's eyes hardened, memories of Chinatown flickering behind them. "You remember how your deal got interrupted? My men tell me it wasn't the cops. Wasn't some rival gang either. One man walked in, like he belonged there. Not with a crew, not with backup. Just one man—and he tore through the place like a soldier at war."

Jason stiffened, hiding the ripple of unease that ran down his spine. "One man doesn't make that kind of mess unless he's trained."

"Trained?" Mykelti leaned closer, his grin twisted. "Disciplined. Focused. Deadly. Switch says this man has a personal stake in all of this. He ain't fighting for turf, not fighting for money. He's fighting for something else—something that makes him dangerous."

Jason raised a brow. "And what exactly does Switch know? He's half-dead last I heard."

"He's alive enough to talk," Mykelti shot back. "Said the name Henry Mann. Said this Mann has blood on his hands already. You see it now? We've both been played. All this smoke between us, and the fire's coming from somewhere else."

Jason sat back, the name rolling in his mind like a loose bullet in a chamber. He remembered whispers from his street guys—an ex-soldier, someone with a dead wife and a daughter clinging to life in the hospital. He hadn't believed it at first. Too neat, too much like the start of a tragic folk tale. But now, hearing it from Mykelti's lips, it gained weight.

"Revenge," Jason muttered. "That old poison."

Mykelti nodded slowly, stroking the chain around his hyena's neck. "And poison spreads. You and me, we've been shooting at shadows while this man turns us against each other. That stops now. We find him. We end him. Then we go back to business."

Jason's lips curled in something between a smirk and a snarl. "You think I'm just going to trust you? After you barged into my house, pointed guns at my men?"

Mykelti raised his glass. "Not trust. Necessity. There's a difference."

The two men clinked glasses, the sound sharp in the cavernous room. For the first time that night, the warehouse was quiet—save for the low, uncanny laugh of the hyena, as if it knew the city's blood was about to run hotter than ever.

Henry paced the length of Steven Fitzgerald's cramped apartment, his boots striking the scuffed linoleum in restless, angry rhythm. The place smelled faintly of burnt coffee and stale pizza, wires snaking everywhere from Steven's cluster of monitors that bathed the room in a ghostly blue glow. Steven, hunched at his desk, looked up from his keyboard just long enough to shake his head.

"You're gonna wear down the poly on the floor, man," Steven muttered. "My landlord barely fixes the plumbing, forget about patching new grooves in his flooring."

Henry ignored the jab. His hands raked over his bald head, his mind racing faster than his body. "I can't believe the police are watching me now. They've even got a cop outside Kalee's room. I thought... I don't know, I thought I had more time." His voice cracked against the name of his daughter.

Steven's fingers clattered over his keys, his attention fixed on a changing waveform that shimmered across the monitors. "More time? You kicked up hell in Chinatown. Put a guy through a wall. Threatened to toss another off the Pru like it was training day back in Kandahar. You think the cops wouldn't notice? Please."

Henry stopped pacing, jaw tight. "I figured Mitchell... maybe he'd keep it quiet for a while." He let out a bitter laugh. "What the hell was I thinking?"

Steven's expression changed suddenly, his eyes narrowing at the shifting patterns on-screen. "Hold up. Something's coming through the band." He keyed commands into his rig, and the central monitor split into two—a wall of binary on one side, a pulse of waves on the other.

Henry leaned over his shoulder, scowling. "What the hell am I even looking at?"

"This is me listening in," Steven said quickly. "The police don't transmit over wires anymore, not like old days with taps and clicks. It's all binary through satellites now. You can't hear a tap—you gotta see it. And what I'm seeing? Somebody else is listening too."

Henry stared at the code, the lines of numbers crawling like ants, meaningless to him. "So? What does it mean?"

"It means if I can follow the chatter, so can someone else. And if I had to bet?" Steven's voice dropped. "It's the gangs. They're tracking the same frequencies. They know what the cops know."

Henry's stomach turned. He pressed a hand to his face, a cold sweat breaking across his brow. "Oh my God." His voice was almost a whisper. "Kalee."

The room went heavy and silent except for the television muttering in the corner. Steven didn't need to answer. Both of them knew what it meant if those men realized Henry's daughter was their way in.

"I need a plan," Henry said finally, voice steadier now. His pacing resumed, but there was purpose in it. "Something smart. Something that takes both crews down before they figure out how to use her against me. Can you find out where the Hell's Gentlemen are holed up?"

Steven shook his head, his shoulders sagging. "Man, this is surveillance, not GPS. I got nothing to go by." Henry stopped again, rubbing at his temples, then straightened as a new idea flared. "What if I make myself visible? Force them out. You piggyback the police band, report a sighting, they'll all come to me." Steven swiveled around in his chair, staring at him like he'd lost his mind. "You want to make yourself bait? Boy, are you crazy?"

"No," Henry shot back. "It's controlled. I move first, they follow. I keep them away from Kalee."

Steven leaned back, sighing. "Controlled or not, cutting into the cops' system isn't just illegal, it's federal. That's prison time, my guy."

Henry's eyes hardened. "Prison's better than burying my daughter."

Henry stood frozen in the glow of Steven's monitors. His friend's warning about federal prison barely registered; it was drowned beneath the roar in his ears. For the first time since the night his world split apart, he let himself stop moving.

The silence pressed in on him. Not just the silence of Steven's cluttered apartment, but the silence of his own choices laid bare. He'd been chasing ghosts of control since the shower tiles turned red, since Dani's eyes dimmed and Kalee's small frame lay still under the paramedics' hands. He thought he could claw his way back by fighting the city itself—fists against gangs, anger against despair. And now, here he was: a wanted man.

Henry lowered himself onto the edge of Steven's old couch, head in his hands. His breath came shallow, uneven. The smell of solder and dust in the apartment mixed with phantom scents—Dani's perfume, Kalee's shampoo. For a second he swore he could hear his daughter's laugh echoing from the kitchen where she used to sit coloring. The weight crushed him deeper. What the hell had he done?

He saw Chinatown again—the blur of faces, the panic when the guns went off, the sick thud of his fist against bone. He remembered the rooftop, Switch dangling over the city like some grim executioner's toy. In those moments, rage had driven him, sharpened him into something unstoppable. But stripped of the adrenaline, the echoes were different. He wasn't a soldier anymore. He wasn't a protector. He was becoming the very monster he swore he'd fight.

Henry dragged a hand over his face. His fingers trembled when they reached his mouth, and he bit down to stop the shaking. It didn't work. His chest felt hollow, like someone had carved him out and left only a shell running on fury.

The cops weren't wrong to look for him. Mitchell's eyes in that hospital had been careful, guarded, like a man already weighing whether to hand him over. And the gangs—God, the gangs—were circling tighter with every move he made. If what Steven said was true, they were already listening, waiting for the chance to rip apart what little he had left.

His stomach knotted. Dani was gone. Kalee was clinging to life, her world held together by machines and strangers in white coats. And him? He was standing in a friend's dim apartment, talking about hacking police signals and baiting two armies like it was some war game.

Henry leaned back, staring at the cracked ceiling. A laugh pushed out of him, dry and bitter. He'd always thought of himself as a man of discipline, a man who knew the line between soldier and savage. But the line was gone now, blurred into nothing. Each step forward just dragged him deeper into a place he couldn't recognize.

He whispered, barely audible: "What if I can't come back from this?"

Steven glanced over, hearing it but not answering. The question hung in the air, raw and unanswered, as Henry sat in the glow of screens, every memory pressing against him like ghosts at his back.

Steven finally pushed his chair back, breaking the weight of Henry's silence. "Alright," he said, rifling through a stack of papers and boxes against the wall, "enough staring holes in the carpet. I think I've got something that'll keep you a step ahead."

Henry dragged his eyes away from the ceiling. The room still felt heavy, but Steven's voice was the kind of ordinary distraction he needed—sharp, impatient, real.

From the other room came the sound of drawers slamming, a string of curses, then the shuffle of cardboard boxes hitting the floor.

"Ah-hah! Here it is."

Steven emerged holding a small box bristling with wires, two slim earpieces dangling from his fingers. He crossed the room with the zeal of a man unveiling a new invention, not a jury-rigged device cobbled together in a cramped apartment.

"Here, take this." He tossed one of the earpieces into Henry's palm.

Henry turned it over skeptically. "You're gonna have to give me an explanation before I stick random junk in my ear."

"Relax," Steven said, crouching at his desk to hook up the wires. "This is our lifeline."

The box hummed to life with a sharp crackle that filled the room. Henry winced, holding the earpiece away as the noise climbed to a piercing whine.

Steven winced too but kept working, fingers dancing over the mess of wires like a mechanic coaxing life out of an engine. "I got this, don't worry." He adjusted a switch on the back, then typed something rapid into his keyboard. The shriek dulled, then cut off, leaving behind only the murmur of the TV and the soft pulse of the monitors.

Henry rubbed his temple. "Besides almost making us deaf, what the hell did you just do?"

Steven leaned back, grinning like a man proud of his own genius. "I just created our own private two-way Bluetooth. No phones, no towers, no records. You talk, I hear. I talk, you hear. As long as it's in your ear, I'm your second pair of eyes and ears."

Henry studied the piece again, weighing it. "So I can talk to you directly without pulling out a phone."

"Exactly," Steven said. "And better—you'll be listening in on the bands at the same time. If your cop buddy calls you in, you'll know immediately. If he doesn't, you'll know that too. And trust me, if the gangs are listening, they'll come running. It's a win-win."

Henry slid the earpiece in, still wary but unwilling to dismiss the tool. The quiet connection buzzed faintly, a ghost of sound pressed against his ear canal. For a moment, he felt tethered—anchored to something other than his own dark thoughts.

Steven leaned forward, his grin softening. "Look, man. You've been playing this solo since day one. You can't keep fighting blind. This way, you've got backup. Not a gun, not fists, but information. And in this city, information's the only thing keeping you alive."

Henry gave a small nod. He didn't say thank you, but the weight in his chest loosened, just enough for him to breathe again.

Boston Police Headquarters. The station buzzed with its usual rhythm—phones ringing in quick bursts, officers carrying stacks of reports under one arm, the faint scent of burnt coffee drifting through the air. The chatter mixed with the sudden bark of a printer jam, the grumble of someone cursing their computer, and the occasional call of "Coffee?" offered across the room. It was routine chaos, a steady tide of noise and motion. Lieutenant Ronald Mitchell moved through it slowly, carefully balancing a paper cup of coffee in one hand. His eyes were rimmed with fatigue, the lines across his face carved a little deeper from another night of too little rest. He nodded once at a pair of officers escorting a cuffed suspect past the front desk before weaving through the maze of tables and chairs toward his own. When he lowered himself into his chair, his body gave him away. A quiet groan pushed out of him, unbidden, betraying his age. He set the coffee down, rubbed the bridge of his nose, and then opened the bottom drawer. Out came a thick manila folder, its edges worn soft. From his jacket pocket he fished out his glasses and perched them on his nose before flipping open the first page.

The phone rang before he made it through a single line. He let it ring twice, took a sip of coffee, then picked it up.

"Mitchell here."

The voice on the other end was unmistakable. Gravel edged with urgency, heavy with something deeper than fear.

"Lieutenant," Henry Mann said. "I hear there's folks looking for me."

Mitchell's back straightened, his hand fumbling for a pen. He yanked a notepad toward him, but his voice remained steady. "There's a lot of questionable acts going on, Henry. Higher ups are pressing for answers. Where are you? I can come get you, clear this up real fast."

Silence bled through the line before Henry answered. His words were quiet, deliberate, almost weary. "All I wanted was some justice. I wasn't trying to do the law's work. But the law—" his voice faltered, then steadied, "—the law isn't about justice, is it? I just want to make sure my daughter has a chance. That she's safe. That's all I've been trying to do. Not too much to ask from a father."

Mitchell froze, eyes drifting toward the framed picture on his desk. A boy and a woman smiled back at him— his son, back when life was simpler, and the wife he'd buried too soon. His throat tightened. For a moment his vision blurred, glassy with unshed tears. He set the picture down gently and shook himself free, forcing the weight off his chest, forcing duty back into the space Henry's words had occupied.

"Okay, Lieutenant," Henry's voice returned, firmer now. "I'll be at the waterfront. Near the Garden. Ten-thirty tonight. I'll surrender then."

Mitchell scribbled something down on the notepad, though his hand moved slower than it should have.

"For what it's worth," he said finally, his tone flat, deliberate, "I think you got a bum deal out of all this."

There was a pause. The kind that carried more truth than words.

"I know," Henry said. Then the line clicked dead.

Mitchell sat there, the dial tone fading in his ear. He set the phone back in its cradle, his eyes settling on the words scrawled on the pad. But what he'd really written wasn't for his superiors. It was for himself. A choice, not an order.

He leaned back, staring at the paper until the noise of the precinct dissolved into nothing.

Mitchell stayed in his chair long after the call ended, the murmur of the station dimming to a low drone in the background. His hand rested on the notepad, fingers brushing over the words he had written—just the time, the place, and Henry's name—but they felt heavier than any report he had ever filed. It wasn't evidence. It wasn't procedure. It was a man's trust, laid at his feet like a fragile offering.

He let out a long breath, leaning back until the chair creaked beneath his weight. His eyes drifted upward to the ceiling, unfocused. Henry Mann was no saint—that much was clear. The Chinatown mess, the Pru incident, the trail of bruised and broken men left behind. Mitchell could see the headlines already, the political fodder being chewed in city hall. "Vigilante Veteran Disrupts Gang War." The kind of chaos that made careers for prosecutors, but ruined lives for everyone else.

By the book, his next step was obvious: notify Collier at the D.A.'s office, have a task force on the waterfront before sundown, make the arrest, write the report. Clean and simple. Duty done.

But nothing about it felt clean.

He picked up the picture again—the one of his wife and son. His thumb traced the edge of the frame as if the movement alone could bring them back. He remembered the long nights when his wife would tell him he was giving too much of himself to a system that gave nothing back. "You're burning yourself hollow, Ron," she had whispered once, when she thought he was asleep. "And for what?"

For justice, he had told himself. For order. For a city that devoured its own and still demanded protection. But Henry's voice over the phone—low, raw, and undeniably human—echoed in the corners of his mind.

All I wanted was some justice... I just want to keep my daughter safe.

Mitchell's stomach knotted. He knew the truth of it. The law was not always about justice. Sometimes it was about politics, appearances, headlines. Sometimes it swallowed men like Henry whole and spat out what was left without a second thought.

And yet—Henry was breaking the law. That was fact. No amount of sympathy changed the danger he posed, the instability he brought with him. Mitchell had seen good men justify worse in the name of family, or vengeance, or pride. He'd seen where that road ended.

He rubbed his temples, glasses sliding down the bridge of his nose. *Do I give him over to Collier? Or do I give him a chance?* The thought itself was dangerous. A man in his position couldn't afford to blur those lines. But what if those lines had already blurred?

The precinct's noise swelled for a moment as an officer burst into laughter across the room. Mitchell blinked, grounding himself in the hum of duty that pressed in on him from all sides. He closed the picture frame, set it face down on the desk, and pulled the folder back toward him.

Still, his pen didn't move. His mind stayed at the waterfront, at 10:30 tonight, replaying Henry's words like a weight pressing deeper into his chest.

For the first time in years, Lieutenant Ronald Mitchell wasn't sure if following the law meant doing the right thing.

Mitchell drummed his fingers against the edge of the folder, listening to the rhythm as though it could drown out his thoughts. The station bustled around him—phones ringing, shoes squeaking against linoleum, typewriter keys clacking—but he felt detached from it all, as if a pane of glass separated him from the rest of the room.

He thought of Collier. Sharp suit, sharper tongue, the kind of prosecutor who lived for press conferences. The man thrived on quick wins and political theater, not the messy reality of streets soaked in fear and blood. Mitchell could already hear the speech Collier would deliver: *"Tonight, thanks to the diligent efforts of this office and the Boston Police Department, a dangerous vigilante was taken off our streets…"*

The words turned Mitchell's stomach.

Because Henry wasn't just a headline. He was a father, a soldier, a man trying—however recklessly—to push back against a tide of rot that the courts themselves had failed to stem. Mitchell had worked too many cases where men like Mykelti or Farokmanesh walked free on technicalities, smirking as they slipped into waiting cars. And every time, Collier's office had shrugged, muttered about "burdens of proof," and moved on to the next spectacle.

Mitchell had stayed silent through it all. That was the job: keep your head down, file your reports, keep the machine running. But now the machine wanted Henry Mann ground up in its gears, and something in Mitchell resisted.

He sipped his coffee, now gone lukewarm, and studied the notes he'd jotted. Waterfront. 10:30. That was it. He had deliberately written nothing else, not even Henry's words, though they echoed with more permanence than ink ever could. He tapped his pen once against the paper, then flipped the notepad shut and slid it into his drawer—not on the pile marked "to be filed," but deep enough that no one rifling through his desk would stumble upon it.

A small act of rebellion, but an act nonetheless.

Leaning back, Mitchell cast his eyes across the bullpen. He saw Costa arguing with a desk sergeant over a stack of paperwork, saw uniformed rookies laughing too loudly at some crude joke. The day moved forward, unbothered by moral questions. For them, orders were orders. For Collier, ambition was enough. But Mitchell... Mitchell still had ghosts.

He turned the photo frame face-up again, this time not to comfort himself, but as a reminder. His wife would have told him not to trust Collier. She had seen right through men like that, men who spoke about justice but meant only power.

His jaw tightened. Maybe he didn't have the authority to rewrite the law, but he had discretion. He could decide what he reported, when, and how. He could decide how much Collier knew before tonight.

And maybe, just maybe, he could decide whether Henry walked into a trap or a fair chance to tell his side.

The thought hardened inside him like wet cement setting fast. Mitchell reached for his phone again, but not to dial the D.A.'s office. Instead, he pulled his Rolodex closer, flipping through numbers with deliberate slowness. People he trusted. People who didn't answer to Collier. If tonight was going to spiral— as Mitchell suspected it would—he wanted eyes on it that weren't looking for headlines.

For now, he would say nothing to the D.A. The less Collier knew, the better.

Mitchell exhaled, steadying himself. He was still a cop, bound by oath and badge. But he was no longer sure that following orders meant serving justice. Tonight would test which side of that line he truly stood on.

Henry moved through the press of bodies downtown with his hood up, earbuds snug against his ears, though the blue-tooth wasn't playing music. It was Steven's voice he heard, calm and certain, grounding him. The city was loud—snatches of laughter, car horns, the shuffle of feet—but Henry felt strangely apart, a single thread running counter to the weave of the crowd. Women's glances caught on him here and there, some curious, some cautious, yet none lingered. His mind was already elsewhere.

"I called him," Henry said lowly, his breath misting in the chill. "Set my surrender for ten-thirty. Waterfront. Did you pick up anything on that digital thing of yours?"

"Actually, yeah," Steven replied in his ear. "They bit the bait, sloppy as hell. Left me an IP address. From that, I got an actual street address. Real solid. Now—" his tone sharpened, brotherly but firm, "—you sure you've got everything you need?"

Henry's stride never faltered. "I'm set. Give me the address. It's time to bring this to a head."

He slipped into the current of commuters pouring from a transit station, swallowed by the moving tide of strangers. To them he was nobody, another face under the hoods and haloes of neon. But inside, he burned with grim purpose.

Above the crush of heads and shoulders, the camera of imagination tilted skyward, tracing the night until the faint ghost of the moon looked down, pale and cold.

Boston's nightlife pulsed to its own chaotic rhythm. Sleek cars idled outside velvet-rope clubs, bass notes thumping from within. Homeless men were passed like shadows by perfumed couples in tailored coats. A street musician bent over his guitar, fingers bleeding chords that carried farther than any shout. Student artists clustered near lamp posts, canvases propped against iron poles, hawking sketches under halogen light. The city was alive, every corner beating to a different drum.

But across town, in a cavernous warehouse claimed by the Hell's Gentlemen, the beat was darker.

Jason lounged in an open shirt and half-undone belt, the smell of sweat and cologne heavy in the air. His laughter was shallow, masking unease, as he kept one eye on Mykelti. The warlord's presence unbalanced him—too raw, too uncontained. Shirtless, dressed in fatigues and boots, Mykelti seized women by their wrists and throats with the same careless strength he might use to lift a weapon. Jason made a weak attempt at humor, trying to rein him in.

"Hey, hey," he said, forcing a smile. "We can't abuse the ladies, my man. Break 'em and they're not so easy to replace."

Mykelti's lip curled. "Meat," he said flatly. "Only meat."

He clamped a woman's face in his palm until she whimpered. Then, almost reverently, he drew a machete from his side pocket. The room stiffened. The woman's tears shone in the dim light, streaks of terror.

Mykelti's eyes glazed, his voice dropping into a chilling monotone. "When I was sixteen, I took part in the massacre at Nyarubuye. Either you hacked, or you were hacked. So I hacked."

As he spoke, he slid the blade across his cheek like a lover's caress, eyes closing in remembered ecstasy.

"They screamed, begged. I wanted silence. I chopped until there was nothing left to beg me for. I was baptized in their blood. I became the lion."

The blade lowered. The woman scurried back to her companions. Jason stared, shaken, but silent.

A gang member burst in, breathless. "Jason, we got a lead on that guy you were looking for."

Jason straightened. "What'd you hear?"

"Name's Henry Mann. One of the victims from that deal—the one the cops are stirred up about."

Jason's gaze flicked to Mykelti. "The African Lords' sale?"

The man nodded.

Mykelti pulled on his shirt with sudden focus. "Who else was listed as a victim?"

"Why's that matter?" Jason asked.

"When you strike a hornet's nest," Mykelti said coldly, "they don't come for safety. They come for their queen."

Mykelti moved through it like a predator, each step measured, deliberate, a man accustomed to owning every inch of ground he set foot upon. His machete gleamed faintly under the overhead bulbs, catching reflections that seemed more like memories than light. Jason shifted uncomfortably, but Mykelti's attention was elsewhere. His eyes—dark, unreadable pools—fixed on nothing, as though he were staring through the walls, through the city, back into the depths of his past. He pressed the flat of the blade against his cheek again, this time not in rapture but in judgment, as though testing the edge against himself. "Do you know what happens to the soul when it's forced to choose between killing and dying?" His voice was low, dangerous, the question not really meant for anyone in the room. "It breaks. It hardens. It becomes something unrecognizable, even to the man himself."

The women huddled closer together, sensing his words were less a story and more a confession. One whimpered softly, and Mykelti's head snapped toward the sound with an animal sharpness. He let out a laugh that held no mirth.

"Meat," he repeated, savoring the word. "The world is filled with it. Dressed in fine clothes, walking the streets, making deals, pretending at power. But strip it down—" he slapped the machete against his palm, the crack echoing through the warehouse, "—and it's all the same. Flesh. Weakness. Fear."

Jason tried to inject a note of control, though his voice wavered. "That's not how business works, brother. You scare off the meat, and you've got nothing left to eat." Mykelti's gaze swung toward him, slow and heavy. "You think I am here for business?" He smiled, broad and unsettling. "I am here because this city is a new jungle. And jungles... belong to lions."

He prowled a few steps closer to the huddled women, not touching them this time, only circling, letting the silence weigh. "Back home, when the fire started, when the blood filled the ditches, the world looked away. The world does not care about the meat. It only fears the lion. And so, I became the lion."

Jason swallowed hard, unsure whether to nod or push back. He settled for silence, eyes fixed on the floor. Mykelti chuckled, catching the fear in that choice. "Even you," he said, pointing the machete loosely in Jason's direction, "even with your polished shoes and silver tongue—you are only another scavenger. You don't want to rule. You want to feed." He dragged the blade across the air as if drawing a line between them. "But I... I want the kill. I want the silence after the screaming stops."

The words hung in the air, heavy, rancid. Mykelti's breathing steadied, almost meditative, as though speaking his truth brought him peace. The women dared not move. Jason sat rigid, held fast by the gravity of the man beside him.

It was in this hush, this suffocating pocket of stillness, that the warehouse door creaked open and the gang member entered, shattering the fragile calm with hurried footsteps.

The rooftop was slick with dew, but Henry moved across it as if it were his natural ground. He kept low, crouched into the shadows of rusted air ducts, his black fatigues blending into the night. A bulky duffel bag bounced lightly against his shoulder with each silent step. It looked heavy, though the way he carried it suggested discipline, control—like the weight had already been measured, accepted, and folded into his body's rhythm. He wore no body armor. The absence of that bulk beneath his sweatshirt was telling. Protection would have slowed him, and in this kind of war—his war— speed was survival. His hands and mind would have to be his only shield.

From his vantage, he paused and let his eyes scan the street below. Two cars sat idling, parked half in shadow against the curb outside the Hell's Gentlemen's warehouse. Their chrome caught the spill of a streetlight like blades catching moonlight. Even from above, Henry recognized them as belonging to the crew—low-slung bodies, dark tinted glass, the kind of vehicles that existed to announce possession. The men inside were ghosts for now, hidden behind the smoked glass, but he knew they were there. Watching. Waiting.

Beyond the first roofline, an adjacent warehouse stretched out like the twin of the one he stalked. The two buildings pressed against each other, a single wall dividing them, brick laid decades earlier when the neighborhood's bones were first poured. Henry studied that wall carefully, mapping the seams and imagining the thickness. He didn't need to breach the gang's front door—alarms, guards, cameras would be waiting. No, the side walls were simpler. Old, unreinforced. Brick upon brick. Get inside one, and you could bleed into the other.

He scurried across the rooftop, slipping into the darkness cast by a larger ventilation unit. With practiced ease he climbed down the rear of the structure, boots finding narrow ledges and forgotten footholds, his fingers gripping rusted piping without hesitation. When his feet touched the ground, the alley behind the building was hushed and empty.

Crouching low, Henry slid the duffel bag from his shoulder and laid it on the cracked pavement. His breath came steady, controlled. He pulled the zipper and began setting out the tools of his intent: drill, bits, wrapped cloths to muffle sound.

A faint crackle broke the stillness. Henry froze, head tilting, then reached into his pocket. He pulled out the small earpiece Steven had given him and pressed it into place.

The voice that hissed through it was sharp, laced with irritation. "Hey man, what are you trying to pull? You trying to leave me out of the loop?"

Henry closed his eyes for a beat, exhaling through his nose before answering in a whisper. "Sorry, dude. I'm at the location you gave me. I think it's the Hell's Gentlemen's crib."

The night air carried the smell of oil and mildew, and Henry's voice felt small against it, swallowed by the emptiness of the alley. The connection goes dead as Henry sizes up the key mechanism in the exterior door and inserts the drill in it and starts. The grinding whine of steel against steel filled the alley, muffled beneath Henry's gloved hands as the drill bit gnawed through the lock's cylinder. Sparks spat briefly in the dark like tiny flares before vanishing into the dirt. He leaned his weight into the tool, eyes narrowed against the heat, until at last the cylinder gave way with a dull clink and dropped into his palm. Henry exhaled through his teeth. Clean. Efficient.

He pushed the heavy steel door open with just enough space to slip through, then pulled it closed behind him. The darkness swallowed him whole. He dragged the bolt into place with a low scrape, bracing it so nothing outside could interrupt what he had planned.

The warehouse greeted him like a tomb. Dust filmed the floor in thick layers, undisturbed for years. The air smelled of rust and rot, a stale mixture of old wood, mildew, and something chemical that lingered in the brick. Shafts of moonlight cut through gaps in the boarded windows, revealing emptiness—no crates, no pallets, only wide space and the exposed brick walls that had been sweating and decaying for decades.

Henry slung the duffel bag onto his shoulder again and padded across the hollow space. His boots pressed soft prints into the dust. He reached the far wall and crouched low, setting the bag down. From it he retrieved a flat, palm-sized device with a coiled cord dangling like an insect's antenna. He pressed the listening device against the wall and tilted his head close, one eye shut as though tuning his whole body into the vibrations.

Muffled sounds—voices, distant footsteps, or perhaps only the humming of electrical units—breathed faintly through the wall. Enough to tell him what he needed: the Hell's Gentlemen weren't far. They were on the other side.

Henry dug deeper into the duffel, pulled out a drill, and affixed a bit longer than his hand. He slid on clear goggles, the plastic fogging for a moment with the heat of his breath before settling into place. With practiced movements, he braced the drill against the old brick and pressed the trigger.

The bit screamed into stone, sending shudders through the entire wall. The sound reverberated across the empty chamber, bouncing off steel beams and echoing through the rafters like a swarm of angry hornets. Henry gritted his teeth and kept steady, grinding forward until the resistance broke and the tool punched through. Dust trickled out like sand, coating his gloves and the knees of his fatigues.

When the drill bit emerged on the far side, Henry released the trigger. Silence rushed in. He disassembled the drill quickly, sliding it into its foam-lined pocket inside the bag. No wasted motion. No second chances.

Next came a steel chisel. He jammed it into the hole, widened the breach, and pulled free several stubborn chips of brick. Then, hefting a short-handled sledge, he swung with controlled precision. The wall groaned, cracked, and surrendered one brick after another. Henry worked in a rhythm, careful to muffle each strike. By the time he was finished, the jagged hole opened into a darkened room beyond. The Hell's Gentlemen treated the warehouse like their private kingdom. The main bar room was a haze of smoke and sweat, neon light bleeding across sagging couches and dented tables. Eight of them lounged and swaggered in the glow of a big screen, trash-talking over a video game while bottles clinked and ashtrays overflowed. Music thundered from battered speakers, bass rattling the walls and floor until it was hard to hear anything but the rhythm.

It was a party, the kind they believed no one could touch. A world where no law could reach them, no rival could breach their sanctuary. Laughter carried over the noise, joined by the thud of boots and the muffled moans of a girl pinned against the wall by one of the men.

Then—without warning—the music died.

The silence fell sharp as glass breaking. The men froze, half-drunk smiles fading. Someone cursed at the sudden cut, another shoved a friend, convinced it was just a loose cord. But then the sound came—deep, concussive, hollow—BOOM. The walls quivered. Dust sifted down from the rafters. Then again. BOOM. A third time, BOOM, each strike louder, closer, like the earth itself was cracking open.

The party disintegrated into chaos. Guns were snatched from tabletops, safeties clicked off in unison. Bottles rolled across the floor, spilling liquor in nervous trails as the men rushed toward the source of the noise. Adrenaline drowned out the alcohol.

They stormed through a doorway into one of the far rooms—only to stop short.

The room ahead was black, darker than night. No music, no glow of electronics, no ambient city light seeping through cracks. Just silence and the echo of their own boots on concrete. A faint metallic groan underfoot broke the stillness as one of them shifted his weight.

Something about the sound made their skin crawl.

Their eyes darted, adjusting, scanning for movement. For a shadow. For a trap. Then—blinding.

A sudden burst of white light cut across the room, forcing them to recoil, hands shielding their faces. In the glare, shapes blurred, and then they heard it: the slow, measured rhythm of footsteps approaching.

Boots.

From the ground's perspective, the boots grew larger, clearer. Black, dust-streaked, moving with unhurried precision. The outline of a man materialized behind them.

The gang members squinted through the fading haze of blindness, weapons rising shakily.

A low voice, steady, controlled, froze them in place.

"I wouldn't do that if I were you."

The voice cut through the room like steel drawn across stone. Every man stiffened, guns wobbling as the figure advanced from the light.

One of them, blinking furiously, managed to rasp out, "Who the fuck are you?" His words held more fear than defiance.

Henry stepped closer, his face still obscured by the harsh lamp he carried, his silhouette stark against the glow. His free hand held something small, innocuous-looking—a black box with a single switch. He lifted it just enough for them all to see.

"I'm the man holding the trigger," he said evenly, almost casual, "to all that C4 surrounding you. So, I wouldn't shoot. I wouldn't run either."

The words sank in slowly. One by one, the gang members looked down, around, above—scanning the room with frantic eyes. Their vision adjusted, the glare giving way to reality. The room was lined with packages, neatly set along the walls like silent sentries. Wires spiderwebbed out from them, all converging toward the very place where the men now stood.

The platform beneath their boots groaned again. They looked down, realizing it wasn't concrete but a thick steel door, propped just so. Wires ran from its edges, taut and deliberate, connected into the mess of explosives ringing the chamber.

The panic was instant. One of them jerked forward, instinct screaming to leap clear, but another caught him by the arm, holding him back with wide eyes.

Henry tilted his head, his tone almost mocking. "Oh... you've seen this before, have you?"

The man said nothing, his chest heaving.

Henry's voice dropped lower, deliberate, every syllable pressed like weight against their lungs. "For those of you who don't know the science lesson here—I'll spell it out. That platform you're standing on? It's pressure-rigged. As long as the weight stays steady, nothing happens. You move wrong, jump, even shift too much— well..." He gestured vaguely at the wired walls. "You won't have to worry about your hangovers tomorrow."

The men shifted uneasily, fear chewing through their bravado. Slowly, reluctantly, they lowered their guns. Metal clicked against the floor as each weapon was discarded, the sound sharp in the silence.

Henry gave a small, humorless smile. "See? Today's youth can be taught—with the right motivation."

He paced in front of them, his voice calm, almost instructional. "Now here's what's going to happen. You're going to stay right where you are. You're going to wait for the police, and they'll help you off that platform without decorating the walls with your insides. Understand?"

Murmurs rippled, curses half-swallowed.

One of them barked out, voice cracking, "You just gonna leave us here?"

Another shouted, desperate, "What the fuck, man?"

Henry stopped in the doorway, looking back at them with a shrug that carried no sympathy. It was the gesture of a man already gone in his mind, the judgment passed.

Then, without another word, he turned and walked out, his boots echoing until they were swallowed by silence.

Henry stepped out into the night air, lungs pulling in the faint scent of oil and rain-damp asphalt. The warehouse door closed behind him like a chapter sealing shut. He dug into his pocket, thumb finding the Bluetooth piece, and slipped it into his ear.

"—What's up, man?" Steven's voice cracked through, rough with static and tension. "I thought you might've been toast."

Henry allowed himself a short exhale, something close to a laugh. "Naw. Went easier than I thought it would."

"So," Steven pressed, curiosity piqued, "what did you do to them?"

Henry's mouth tugged into a hard smile, pride carried in his low tone. "Sold them on the idea they're surrounded by hotwired C4."

Back at his cluttered apartment, Steven sat hunched in nothing but boxer shorts, the glow of his monitors painting his tired face blue. He leaned toward the mic, eyes narrowing. "How'd you pull that off?"

"Three-liter soda bottles. Candy. A little imagination."

Steven blinked, and then the realization sank in. His jaw dropped before a crooked grin spread across his face. He chuckled, shaking his head at the audacity. "So wait—you mean... are they actually rigged?"

Henry's voice came back with an edge of amusement. "Not really. Modeling clay."

Steven's laugh filled the earpiece—then a thunderclap cracked the night. A gunshot. The bullet smacked against brick, spitting shards across Henry's arm. He ducked hard, rolled into the shadow of a doorway, and pressed flat against the stone.

"Henry?" Steven's voice sharpened, all laughter gone. "Hey—did I hear gunfire? Talk to me!"

Henry squinted toward the street, breath heavy, pulse racing. He muttered low into the mic. "Think I'm in some shit now. How fast can you get police here?"

"I'm on it. Just hang tough. Don't get yourself killed."

The words were hardly finished before the low growl of an engine rose. From the corner, headlights burst into view, cutting across his hiding place. Jason leaned out of the passenger window, eyes wild and blown, jaw clenched in fury. His pistol barked fire in Henry's direction as the car screeched past.

Henry ducked low, heart hammering as shards of brick chipped around him. Another gang member leaned from the back window, firing blind into the night, while the driver wrestled the wheel into a sharp turn, preparing for another pass.

Henry's thoughts cut sharp, cold. *One of the platform rats called for backup. Should've seen it coming.* He darted across the open street, dodging gunfire that cracked like whip strikes at his heels. His eyes scoured the pavement, frantic for anything—pipe, bottle, trash can lid—but the street was swept clean, stripped bare as if mocking him.

"What a time," he hissed through clenched teeth, "for the damn street to be clean."

Tires screamed. The car swung around, bearing down on him like a predator circling prey. Jason leaned out again, glee twisted in his bruised face as he leveled the pistol, steady now despite the blood dripping from his forehead.

Henry braced against the doorway, breath catching, mind whispering that this might be the end—another bullet, another wound he wouldn't walk away from.

But fate interrupted.

Another car roared from the cross street, slamming broadside into the gang's vehicle. The impact was brutal, steel twisting, glass exploding into the night. Both cars spun, screeching against the asphalt until they lay in a heap of smoke and shattered silence. Airbags detonated, muffling the cries of the men inside.

Henry blinked, stunned, but instinct surged before doubt. He bolted toward the wreck, ripped the driver's door open, and hauled the dazed man forward by his hair. Bone and metal collided as Henry slammed his skull against the steering wheel again and again until the man sagged unconscious.

Jason spilled from the wreck, crawling, still gripping his gun. He staggered upright, but Henry was faster—rolling across the hood, lashing out with a kick that slammed the car door into Jason's chest and dropped him hard onto the pavement.

Jason coughed blood, face cut open, but his hatred flared alive. He spat crimson toward Henry. "You fuck! You're the one doing all this? I'll put more holes in you than you'll ever count."

He fired. Missed. Fired again—off balance, bleeding too much.

Henry lunged, ripped the weapon from his hand, and drove him down with a savage force. Jason hit the ground with a bone-deep thud. Henry tossed the gun into the gutter and planted his boot on Jason's throat, pressing until the man gagged, clawing at the air.

Henry leaned close, his whisper colder than any shout. "How's it feel? Knowing you're losing everything you live for? That the things you love won't ever be yours again?"

The weight crushed Jason's breath until his lips purpled—then Henry pulled away, chest heaving, restraint cutting deeper than violence.

Sirens wailed now, climbing closer. Henry glanced toward the flashing lights, then back at Jason, who wheezed and sneered through blood.

"You ain't got the balls to kill me," Jason rasped. "But that African—he'll find you. He'll kill you. And everyone you care about."

The words cut deep, sharper than the bullets had. Henry froze, the realization crashing like cold water. He hadn't thought it all through—not everyone, not every possibility.

"Oh my God," he muttered aloud, eyes wide, voice breaking. "Kalee..."

He ran. Past the wreckage, past the warehouse now glowing red and blue, past the shriek of sirens and scattering shadows. Down the center of the dark street he sprinted, a lone figure chased by both his choices and the night.

Above him, the city lights flickered weakly, unable to burn away the secrets twisting in the dark.

Chapter 8

The hospital ward slept in hushed tones, its air heavy with antiseptic and fatigue. In Kalee's room the machines kept their steady rhythm—slow, patient beeps echoing like a metronome of fragile life. The child lay in her induced sleep, face pale but serene, untouched by the storm raging outside her walls.

In the corner, Dani's mother sat with a paperback folded in her hands. Her eyes lingered on the words, though her mind wandered. Every few minutes she glanced toward her granddaughter, gaze soft, weighted with both hope and worry. The book closed in her lap as she rose, easing stiffly to the doorway.

Beyond, the officer stationed outside shifted his weight. Middle-aged, with a spread creeping around his midsection, he turned at her movement and caught her eyes. He gave her a quick, friendly smile.

She answered with a roll of her eyes and the faintest sigh, then shut herself back into the chair. The officer shrugged, amusement tugging his lips as he pulled over another chair, settling in with the patient air of a man resigned to the long haul.

The hall stretched quiet, broken only by the murmur of televisions spilling from other rooms. Nurses' shoes clicked faintly against the linoleum, and an orderly hummed as he wheeled a cart down the far corridor.

A petite nurse's aide approached, barely older than a student. She leaned toward the officer with a half-shy smile.
"Coffee? You want some?"

He pushed himself up, stretching with a groan. "Coffee would be great."

She gestured to the station at the end of the hall, where the pot steamed beneath fluorescent lights. Together they crossed, her voice light with routine chatter.
"Long night ahead of you?"

"Long enough." He tore open sugar packets with practiced ease, pouring far too many into the steaming cup. "All I know is, I've gotta stay awake for it." He chuckled, sipping noisily.

She laughed politely, then slipped back to her duties, leaving him to amble toward his post.

Passing Kalee's open doorway, he slowed, leaning slightly in. Dani's mother hadn't noticed him until he spoke, voice softened now.
"Ma'am, want me to have the nurse's aide get you something?" He raised the cup as an example, his tone warm, almost apologetic.

This time her expression softened. "No... no thank you."
A faint smile tugged her lips, weary but genuine.

He returned the smile, nodded once, and sat down. Silence reclaimed the corridor. The only sound was the steady tick of his watch, marking time with the same inevitability as the machines that kept the girl alive.

The second hand ticked. The officer's eyes followed it without thinking, lulled by monotony. The sweep landed on the six—and then the world cracked apart.

The gunshot split the silence with brutal suddenness. The impact threw him against the wall. His coffee cup spun free, its dark contents scattering through the air like blood in slow motion.

Instinct took over. He rolled to the side, gasping at the pain in his ribs as he yanked his weapon free.

Through his blurred vision he saw them: two hooded figures advancing down the corridor, pistols out, their strides carrying the cocky rhythm of boys who thought they were men. Baggy pants hung loose over sneakers. Their faces were hidden, but their intent screamed loud.

He fired once. The report thundered in the corridor. The pair scattered, one diving into a doorway, the other slipping into the stairwell.

A burning ache spread across his chest. For a moment he thought the bullet had torn through him—until his hand pressed to the hole in his shirt and felt the hard plate beneath. The vest had saved him. He swallowed hard, forcing his trembling hand to his radio.
"Officer needs assistance! Two African-American

males, twenties—shots fired at the hospital!" His voice shook, but the words carried.

Doors slammed up and down the hall. Nurses herded patients inside with whispered urgency. Orderlies ducked behind counters. A mother clutched her child's hand tighter as the echo of violence rolled through the ward.

Glass rained down as another shot shattered an overhead light. Darkness claimed half the corridor, long shadows stretching across the polished floor. The officer squinted into it, trying to find shapes in the black.

Movement—a muzzle flash—and he jerked back as a bullet cracked past his shoulder. Then the two fled into the stairwell, sneakers slapping metal.

The officer forced himself upright, breath ragged, weapon extended. He pushed the stairwell door open with the barrel, eyes sweeping.

The stairwell yawned before him, sterile and lit too brightly, mocking the chaos outside. He pressed his back to the wall, weapon raised, climbing steps in careful increments. His radio hissed faintly against his shoulder until he reached up and dialed the volume down, leaving only his breathing to fill the silence.

A noise below. Not footsteps above—below. His stomach dropped. He spun, aiming downward, edging toward the sound. Each step echoed like thunder. The stairwell swallowed him as he descended, his silhouette shrinking until it vanished into the lower levels.

Silence.

Then—boots. Heavy, deliberate, not sneakers but military tread. They descended with patient rhythm, each step filled with certainty.

From the shadows emerged Mykelti. His face cold, eyes burning with the quiet flame of purpose, he stared downward into the stairwell where the officer had gone. For a moment he stood motionless, a hunter scenting prey. Then he turned, striding to the door that opened onto the intensive care floor.

The hinges groaned as light spilled across the shattered corridor. His boots crushed fragments of glass as he walked, surveying the room numbers like a man reading names from a list.

Nurses peeked from behind counters. An orderly rose cautiously, stepping forward.
"Excuse me, can I help you?"

Mykelti spun. The kick came so fast the orderly never even raised his hands. His body hit the floor hard, air rushing out of him in a grunt. Mykelti followed, raining fists down until the man's face slackened into unconsciousness.

Breath coming fast, eyes alive with adrenaline, Mykelti straightened. His steps quickened toward Kalee's room. He tried the handle. Jammed. He pulled harder—the door held.

He yanked again, and the door groaned, wedging tighter, as though the room itself resisted him.

Inside Kalee's room, Dani's mother could only stare in horror, her body shaking as the pounding of Mykelti's boots rattled the door. She fumbled with the phone, her trembling fingers stabbing 9-1-1. The line clicked, but Mykelti's next kick reverberated through the frame, drowning the dispatcher's greeting.

Her eyes darted around the room. No weapons, no protection. Only her purse. She tore it open with frantic desperation, lipstick tubes and receipts spilling across the linoleum until her hand closed around a pen. She gripped it like a knife, every ounce of her maternal instinct crystallizing into that single, ridiculous weapon.

The door cracked. Wood splintered. Hinges screamed. Mykelti burst through, a shadow backlit by the corridor's chaos. She lunged. The pen flashed, her hand striking out with more courage than strength. They collided in a flurry of limbs, her attack wild, desperate. For a heartbeat it surprised him. But then his sheer weight bore her down.

One violent shove and she struck the floor, her head hitting tile with a sickening thud. She lay still, hair spilling across her face.

Mykelti's breath came in short bursts as he reached for his pocket. His fingers curled around the hilt of the machete. He drew it slow, savoring the scrape of metal leaving leather, eyes igniting with fire. He looked first at the unconscious woman, then at the child hooked to tubes and monitors.

For a moment, something flickered behind his gaze — a memory. Blood and cries, smoke rising over bodies, machetes cleaving through flesh. Rwanda. The Tutsi massacres. His lips quivered, but not with regret. With hunger. He raised the blade high.

The machete descended—

CLANG!

Steel struck steel. Sparks leapt in the darkness. The strike halted mid-air, caught on a wheelchair pole. Henry stood there, face carved with fury, his arms braced as he shoved the pole upward with all his strength.

Mykelti's head snapped toward him, eyes narrowing. He swung backhand with the machete, a brutal counter meant to cleave flesh. Henry ducked low, the blade screeching as it buried into the plaster wall.

Mykelti blinked—curiosity mixing with insanity.
"Who are you?"

Henry didn't flinch. His voice was cold, deliberate.
"You know who I am, asshole."

For the first time, Mykelti smiled — lips stretching in contentment, as if he'd been waiting for this moment. His gaze shifted, flicking briefly to Kalee.

Henry felt his stomach tighten. He couldn't let the fight stay in here. One swing of that machete and Kalee's fragile body wouldn't stand a chance. He studied Mykelti in a single sweep — massive frame, fast reflexes, the kind of man who feared nothing because he had nothing left to lose.

So Henry made a choice. He'd draw the fire onto himself.

"So you're an African Lord," Henry said, voice dripping contempt. "Things are tough all over."

The taunt hit. Mykelti's jaw hardened, his body angling forward. Henry backed away in measured steps, pulling him toward the doorway.

"What kind of man are you?" Henry pressed, words sharp, deliberate. "Predator of the weak and small? Ever fought a man your own size?"

The machete twitched. Muscles rippled. Mykelti lunged, blade carving the air. Henry sidestepped and countered with a left cross, his fist smashing into Mykelti's jaw. The bigger man staggered—then grinned, wiping a trickle of blood with his thumb.

Henry stepped back further, his heart pounding. He could see Dani's mother stirring on the floor. He prayed she stayed quiet, gave him time.

"I'm surprised you don't have a glass jaw," Henry said, keeping his voice steady. "Does that compensate for the lack of spine?"

Mykelti's teeth glinted in the flickering light.
"You joke, but I know you fear me. I am a lion. You? You're just a bastard child of America."

Henry feigned a smirk. "So you're from Africa? That explains the smell."

The words worked. Mykelti's eyes burned hotter. His slow prowl turned into a stalk, each step carrying the weight of ritual.

Henry kept edging back, crossing the threshold into the hallway. Nurses huddled in corners, faces pale, watching with wide eyes. They seemed to understand his intent — to drag the monster out, to keep the child safe.

Henry caught their stares, nodded slightly. They'd know when to act.

He turned back to Mykelti. "I heard about you. Missing some meds, huh? Good thing you're at a hospital."

The machete gleamed. Mykelti lunged, this time fast as lightning. Henry pivoted—but the blade kissed his side. Pain detonated through his ribs. He clenched his teeth, refusing to scream, even as hot blood spilled down his shirt.

Mykelti's grin widened. "Yes...a good thing indeed."

Henry staggered, pressing a hand to the wound, his blood slick against his palm. His vision blurred, but he forced a smirk. "Yeah, yeah. And a click-click, lock-click to you too."

The thrust came again—Henry dodged—but Mykelti's fist hammered his skull. Stars burst across his vision. He slipped, shoes skidding in his own blood. A side kick to the chest hurled him back.

He slammed against the stairwell door, gasping, the hallway spinning. The world narrowed to pain, sweat, and blood.

But he still had breath. Still had fight.

He grabbed the door handle and yanked it open, forcing his voice through a shredded throat. "Hey stinky...let's go outside. Where I can breathe."

The machete came again, missing his ear by an inch. Steel screeched into the metal doorframe, buried deep. Henry rolled through the doorway, tumbling into the stairwell as Mykelti fought to rip the blade free.

Henry dragged himself upward, one concrete step at a time, the stairwell spinning around him like a tightening noose. His left hand pressed hard against his bleeding side, sticky warmth seeping between his fingers. Every rise of his boot felt heavier than the last, his lungs refusing to draw in enough air. His breath rasped in the shaft, the echo bouncing back at him as if mocking his struggle. Still, he forced himself on. He could not collapse here—not while Kalee lay helpless only a few floors away.

Behind him came the sound of another set of feet. Not hurried. Not clumsy. Each step landed with a deliberate rhythm, steady as a drumbeat in a death march. Mykelti was following. Leisurely. Patient. The man knew the wounded soldier above him could not last forever.

Then came his voice, smooth as polished stone, carrying upward through the stairwell.

"So… you are Henry Mann." The words rolled off Mykelti's tongue like a judge's verdict. "I read about you this evening. You lost your wife in a gunfire. How… sad."

Henry clenched his jaw. He wanted to block out the words, to fix his focus only on climbing, but his mind betrayed him. Dani's face flashed before his eyes, her smile bright, her laugh soft against his ear. The memory weakened him more than blood loss. He pressed harder into his side, shoving forward another step.

"And that child in the room," Mykelti's voice echoed again, closer now, carried with the confidence of a predator who already knows his prey has nowhere left to run. "She is yours, yes? Sleeping. Peaceful."

Henry bit down against the ache of his wound. He refused to answer, refused to give the monster the satisfaction.

"In a way," Mykelti continued, "it is good she does not wake. Better to sleep than to watch her father run." He let the word ring. "Coward."

The scrape of steel shrieked through the shaft, jarring and ugly. Sparks hissed against the wall as Mykelti dragged his machete along the railing, sharpening it on the concrete as he climbed. The sound cut into Henry's ears, digging at his focus.

"And when she does wake," Mykelti said, his tone rising into a sermon, "I will be there. She will watch what I do… before I take her head."

Henry stopped. He could not help himself. His chest heaved, rage forcing air through blood-filled lungs. That single thought—the image of his little girl's small head lifted toward the machete—burned through his exhaustion.

Below, Mykelti reached the next landing, the door open to the cool night air. He paused, noting the smear of blood on the concrete, following the trail with a hunter's satisfaction.

Then he noticed it ended.

He tilted his gaze upward.

A shadow surged. Henry hurled himself down from the upper landing with a guttural roar, slamming into Mykelti's broad shoulders. The two of them crashed together through the open doorway, tumbling out into the night.

Henry staggered back, his hand braced against the rough concrete half-wall of the parking deck. Below him, the city stretched wide and indifferent, its lights glimmering like distant stars. He searched the streets desperately for a flash of blue and red, for the sweep of headlights from a squad car, anything that might mean help was finally coming. Nothing. Just the silent sprawl of Boston, unaware that death was circling on the eighth floor of its hospital.

Behind him, Mykelti was already on the move. The African Lord had shaken off Henry's last kick and was prowling toward the weapon that lay discarded on the concrete. His face gleamed with sweat, his chest rising and falling with controlled fury. Henry lunged forward, summoning what strength remained, and slammed into him with a shoulder block straight out of a football drill. The impact hurled Mykelti into the hood of one of the few cars left in the lot.

The alarm screamed to life, wailing across the garage in mechanical terror. Its shriek ricocheted off the walls, echoing into the night, a warning that this battle was no longer hidden. Mykelti rolled off the hood, grimacing, the wear of the fight finally tugging at his movements. Still, when his eyes locked on Henry, there was nothing but feral hunger in them. He snarled like an animal cornered but not yet beaten.

Henry's chest heaved as he braced himself, a flicker of second wind pushing through the exhaustion. He knew he couldn't let Mykelti reclaim the blade, but the man was fast—too fast. In one sudden surge, Mykelti dove, his long arms snapping around the machete's hilt. He rose with a savage glint in his eye, spinning on his heel with brutal efficiency.

The blade hissed downward and slashed across Henry's thigh. Pain ripped through him like fire, searing bone and muscle. He cried out, stumbling as hot blood streamed freely down his leg, adding to the crimson already spilling from his side.

Another swing. Sparks shot from the ground as the machete kissed the concrete, missing Henry by inches. He spun, fighting past the haze of pain, and swung a back fist that cracked hard into Mykelti's cheek. The blow opened skin, blood pouring across Mykelti's eye and clouding his vision.

Henry seized the moment. He unleashed a flurry of punches, kicks, wild strikes born of desperation more than technique. Each landed, each stole a piece of

Mykelti's balance, but every hit also drained Henry further. His strength was gone, spent in the flurry, and he finally dropped to his knees, his body trembling.

Mykelti laughed—a dark, throaty chuckle that echoed under the siren of the car alarm. "Is that all you got, boy?" he jeered, his teeth flashing red in the emergency light. "I can take whatever you dish out."

He lifted the machete high, the steel glinting above his head. He rushed forward, gathering all his speed into one murderous swing meant to sever Henry in two.

At the last second, Henry rolled aside. The machete cut only air. He surged upward, fueled by instinct alone, and heaved Mykelti off his feet. With a roar, Henry lifted the man high above his head and flung him over the parking deck's edge.

Mykelti plummeted silently. His eyes widened in disbelief, but no scream escaped him. He struck the asphalt below with a sickening thud, his body crumpling, blood spreading outward in a dark halo.

Henry collapsed against the wall, his vision swimming. Too much blood, too much pain. The city lights blurred into nothing, and darkness swallowed him whole.

The world came back in fragments.

Flashes of light, of uniforms moving quickly through blurred corridors. Red strobes, then blue, then sterile white overhead. The squeal of wheels on polished linoleum. Voices tangled together—police radios squawking clipped reports, doctors barking orders, nurses murmuring reassurance. Somewhere close, the flat thump of another stretcher passing by, a body shrouded under a sheet.

Then, silence.

Darkness pressed in like a curtain drawn tight. For a long stretch there was nothing, not even the sensation of his own breath.

When the void finally broke, it was with the faint beeping of a monitor and the low hum of machines. The world leaked back in, slow and jarring. A door clicked. A shoe scuffed against tile. The smells of antiseptic and plastic tubing settled around him like an unwelcome fog.

Henry's eyes fluttered open. His vision burned with brightness at first, the ceiling light blurring into a white star. Gradually it sharpened, shapes emerging, two figures coalescing into clarity. Lieutenant Mitchell and A.D.A. Collier stood over him, their shadows leaning across his bed.

Henry tried to rub at his face, only to realize his arms wouldn't move. Cold steel bit into his wrists. He was cuffed to the rails, both sides secured. A bitter laugh rattled in his throat.

"I should've known," he muttered, voice rasped and cracked.

Mitchell's voice came back measured, almost careful. "Mr. Mann—Henry—you've been busy these past few days."

Henry tilted his head, grimacing at the pull in his side where the bandages clung tight. "Well, you know," he said, tone dripping with sarcasm, "idle hands are the devil's playground."

His eyes drifted to Collier, standing with his jaw tight and his face carved into stone. Outside the door, a police radio squawked and crackled, a reminder that the law stood just beyond the walls, waiting.

"Should I have a lawyer present?" Henry asked.

Collier stepped forward. The man's expression was calm, but there was a current beneath it—anger straining against the dam of control. "That depends, Mr. Mann. You've left us in a very precarious situation."

Henry's eyebrows lifted, curiosity dulling the pain for a moment. "How's that?"

"You've broken numerous laws over the last few days," Collier said, his voice low, deliberate, "but none severe enough that we can prosecute without public backlash. To the citizens of this city..." He exhaled sharply, disgust flickering across his features. "You're some kind of hero."

Mitchell's tone lightened almost despite himself. "The media's having a field day. You took down two of the city's worst gangs with little to no collateral damage. Only casualty outside the gangs was a bruised warehouse driver—who'll probably sue." He gave his head a small shake, the trace of a grin tugging at his mouth before he caught himself.

Collier's voice cut back in, cold as steel. "You're a vigilante, Mr. Mann. You operated outside the law for your own gain. If I had my way, you'd be rotting in jail. But the mayor and the governor are willing to overlook your... indiscretions—provided you leave the state of Massachusetts. If you don't, you'll be brought up on every charge we can find and prosecuted to the fullest extent of the law."

Henry's voice dropped into a grave whisper. "And my daughter?" He forced a swallow. "What happens with her?"

"She'll be transferred to the nearest facility at your new location," Collier said. "Or remanded to the state, if you stay."

The words settled like a weight on Henry's chest. He turned his head, searching for air, and then froze.

At the doorway, his mother-in-law stepped into view, her eyes wide and full of grief. Her entrance shattered the tension like sunlight breaking into a storm.
Henry blinked, his chest rising in a slow, heavy breath as he took her in. A bandage wrapped around her head, clean and white against her graying hair, but otherwise

she stood steady—stronger than he'd imagined she could be after all they had endured. She smiled at him, warm and unwavering, and for a moment Henry thought he might weep.

"Henry," Dani's mother said softly, her voice carrying both promise and command, "you know anywhere you and Kalee go, I'll be there with you."

Henry's throat tightened. The handcuffs weighed on him again, heavy metal reminders of how close he was to losing everything. He forced a smile, glanced down at the cuffs, then back up at her. "Okay," he said, voice hoarse but sure. "You got yourself a deal."

Across from him, Collier gave the faintest nod, lips pressed tight, as if finalizing a contract he despised but couldn't void. His eyes flicked to Mitchell, who reached into his pocket, produced a key, and with a metallic click freed Henry's wrists. The relief was immediate— skin stung where the cuffs had chafed, and Henry rubbed the marks absently, savoring the fragile taste of freedom.

"You're not to speak to the press," Collier said crisply. "We'll cover the cost of transporting your child. You'll receive paperwork covering all we've discussed, along with a copy of a warrant that will be issued if you return. Consider this your one chance."

Without waiting for an answer, Collier turned on his heel and strode from the room, leaving the faint scent of legal authority in his wake.

Mitchell lingered. He scratched the back of his neck, exhaled through his nose, then muttered, "For the record, that was a dumb-ass thing to do." His eyes softened, the hard lines of duty giving way to something closer to admiration. "Off the record, every cop in the city sings your praises." His gaze drifted to the door Collier had exited through. "He's just made of a different cloth."

Henry let out something between a chuckle and a sigh. Relief washed through him—not the kind that promised joy, but the kind that carried finality. Mitchell extended a hand, firm and steady. Henry clasped it, their grip strong, sealing an understanding neither could ever put in a report.

"Good luck to you, Henry," Mitchell said. A smile flickered, brief and genuine. He turned toward the door, but before stepping out he stopped, glanced back, and added, "You should take your friend Steven Fitzgerald with you when you move."

The corner of Henry's mouth lifted. A faint smile, touched with gratitude and recognition. *He knew.*

Several weeks blurred by in a haze of paperwork, arrangements, and sleepless nights. Then, at last, the road opened before them.

A moving truck rumbled down the highway, followed by an ambulance that carried Kalee with her machines and monitors. Green signs rose overhead: *Now Leaving Massachusetts.* Mile markers ticked past. Bridges, toll booths, and open fields replaced the city skyline. Henry drove behind, every landmark passed shedding one life while hinting at another.

Freedom, exile, and family—all bound together in the uncertain road ahead.

The house looked small from the street, but sunlight poured over it, washing the paint and the porch railings in gold. A moving truck sat in the driveway, its back yawning open, and Henry stood with a box balanced against his side as Dani's mother directed Steven on where to place things. The day was almost offensively bright—sky a perfect blue, the kind of backdrop painters once used to convince a weary nation that peace could be captured in oils.

Henry glanced up and down the block. It was tidy, almost unreal. A row of maple trees bent into the street, dappling the sidewalks with shade. Across the way, a park stretched green and inviting, its swings swaying lightly in the summer breeze. A grocery store stood within easy sight, no more than two blocks away. Children's bicycles leaned against chain-link fences. To anyone else, it was Norman Rockwell's America, stubbornly preserved in this quiet corner.

But Henry's face betrayed nothing. He carried the box inside, shoulders tight, eyes cold.

Dani's mother came out onto the porch, wiping her hands on her jeans, the bandage on her head now a faint reminder of darker nights. She had color in her cheeks again, and hope—something Henry hadn't seen in her since Dani's funeral. "Henry, are you alright?" she asked, her voice tinged with both concern and optimism.

"Yeah," Henry said, the word flat, almost mechanical.

Her smile didn't falter. "Well, then I'll start lunch. I know you must be hungry." She patted the railing with satisfaction, as if grounding herself in the solidity of this new place. "After that, we can go visit Kalee in the hospital."

"Uh-huh. That'll be fine," Henry muttered, eyes already drifting past her, past the house, to the horizon beyond.

She turned and slipped back inside, humming faintly, the sound of a woman determined to root her family in new soil.

Henry stayed on the porch. A car had rolled into the park across the street, moving slow, deliberate. His body stiffened. A young man hopped out of the passenger side with a spray can and, with casual arrogance, scrawled bold letters across the park's brick wall: **PIT DOGZ RULZ.** The hiss of paint reached Henry even at this distance, each stroke of vandalism a violation against the postcard-perfect scene.

The young man jumped back into the car, laughing, and it pulls out of the park, drifting lazily toward Henry's street. He stood perfectly still, eyes fixed, his jaw set. The vehicle crept past, its windows down, several faces inside half-shadowed but unmistakably marked by the swagger of gang life.

One of them leaned out, catching Henry's stare. "What the fuck you looking at?"

The car erupted in laughter, ugly and sharp, before screeching away, tires screaming against the asphalt.

Henry didn't move. He watched them until the car rounded the corner and disappeared. His chest rose, slow and steady, though his body hummed with something coiled and dangerous.

The street grew quiet again. Only the sound of a bird somewhere in the trees.

The camera of fate circled him, drawing closer until his face filled the frame.

Henry smiled.

Character Notes

Henry Clarence Mann-Main character. African American male. Ex-Delta Force sergeant. Age 31. Husband to Dani and father to Kalee. Works construction and lives in a brown-stone house off Boston's Massachusetts Avenue. Stands 6' 5" tall. Weigh 283 pounds of muscle.

Danielle (Dani) Mann-wife to Henry (5 yrs) and mother to Kalee Mann (5 yrs). Smart and sensitive. Henry's anchor.

Kalee Mann- the 5-year-old daughter of Henry and Dani. Cute and carefree. Feels safe around her parents.

Yvonne Barros-Dani's mother. a woman of 62 yrs. Still very attractive and shapely. Fiercely protective of her family.

Steven Fitzgerald-Good friend to Henry. Helps him in many ways. Average build. Age 33. Self-described Computer nerd. African American male. 5' 10" tall weighs 175 pounds.

Lt. Mitchell- white male, age 54, gray hair. Boston police detective. Wiser than he seems. Long term police man. Typically knows more than he lets on.

Mykelti N'tumbe-African immigrant. Leader of the African Lords gang. 6' 1". Age 44. Hostile and controlling. Athletic build. Operates primarily in the South End and Roxbury. He's ruthless and often barbaric, A survivor of genocide in his country.

Jason Farokmanesh-Leader of the Hell's Gentlemen gang. Anglo-American. Wants to be old time gangster. Deals illegal guns and firearms and runs numbers. Operates primarily in South Boston and Bay area.

Piranha Gang Leader (Real name unknown)-6' 6" tall. Weighs 325 pounds of muscle. Purposely (rumor has it) had his lips cut off and his teeth replaced with steel razor tips so that his mouth resembles that of a piranha fish. Often described as a sociopath. Operates primarily in the South Shore part of Massachusetts.

Other supporting characters-

Switch-a member of African Lords.

Various relatives of Dani-uncles, cousins

Gold-Dragons (gang in Chinatown)-Buyers of firearms from Hell's Gentlemen

A.D.A. Collier -Prosecutor who wants to stop the gang violence.

Locations- Greater Boston, Massachusetts area:
Massachusetts General Hospital
Prudential Center
Copley Place

Premise-After returning home from work, a former Army Delta-Force Sergeant and his family become innocent victims of a battle between two gangs, where stray gunfire penetrates their home striking the entire family. The former soldier survives but his wife does not, and his daughter lay in a coma. Enraged by the violence on the streets the soldier takes it upon himself to avenge his family shooting bringing the major gangs and the entire city of Boston into a battle for the streets. Aided by his best friend and pursued by police, he wages war on the gangs in the city leading to a climatic battle with one of the leaders of one of the gangs involved in the shooting.

Resources on Gangs & Intervention

"While Rough Neck is a work of fiction, the issues of gangs and community violence are very real. For readers seeking information, education, or help, here are some official resources you can reference."

-Megaverse City

U.S. Federal & National Resources

- **National Gang Center (NGC)**
  https://nationalgangcenter.ojp.gov/
- Provides research, prevention strategies, and information on intervention programs.

Office of Juvenile Justice and Delinquency Prevention (OJJDP)

https://ojjdp.ojp.gov/

Offers guides on youth violence prevention, mentoring, and gang intervention.

National Institute of Justice (NIJ) – Gang Research

https://nij.ojp.gov/topics/crime/gangs

Federal research on gang dynamics, community impacts, and exit strategies.

Community & Intervention Programs

- **Cure Violence Global**
  https://cvg.org/

Treats violence as a public health issue, using community-based "violence interrupters."

G.R.E.A.T. Program (Gang Resistance Education and Training)

https://www.great-online.org/

School-based program designed to prevent youth involvement in gangs.

National Gang Crime Research Center (NGCRC)

http://www.ngcrc.com/

Offers data and publications on gang activity and intervention.

Hotlines & Support (U.S.)

- **National Runaway Safeline**: 1-800-RUNAWAY (1-800-786-2929)
  Support for youth at risk of gang involvement, homelessness, or violence.

- **Local Crisis & Community Centers**: Many cities (like Boston, Chicago, L.A.) have neighborhood-specific "gang intervention units" — you could suggest readers look up *local resources in their community*.

About the Author

E.S. Bennett is the creator of Megaverse City L.L.C. and the author of multiple works including *The Rings of King Solomon*, *Marshal L.A.W.*, and *Tidal-Man*. With a focus on myth, grit, and human struggle, Mr. Bennett continues to build worlds that challenge and inspire.

E.S. Bennett currently resides in North Carolina, USA among family and friend.

Other Books From Megaverse City

For Children

Megaverse City's Edward Bear & Friends-A New Anthology

The Rings of Kings Solomon: Kong's Perspective

Megaverse City's The Little Mermaid

Megaverse City's Aladdin

Amok and Myre-Daze on the Farm

Oliver and Audrey Adventure Series

For Mature Readers

Laila Aurora Wright: The L.A.W.

The Rings of King Solomon

Marshal L.A.W: Court of L.A.W.

Gene Lemmings' Tidal-Man

Angry Andie-Spoils of Vengeance

Marshal L.A.W.-The Ogre Directive

Rough Neck-The Gang Buster

Megaverse City L.L.C.

'The Pulse of Entertainment!'